CURSE OF KINGS

ALEX BARCLAY

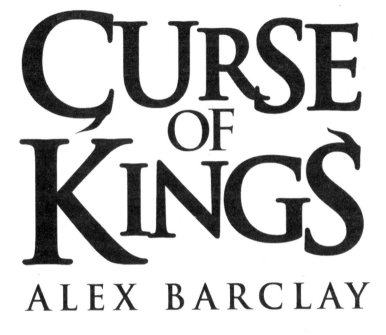

CURSE OF KINGS

ALEX BARCLAY

HarperCollins *Children's Books*

First published in Great Britain by HarperCollins *Children's Books* in 2013
HarperCollins *Children's Books* is a division of HarperCollins*Publishers* Ltd,
77-85 Fulham Palace Road, Hammersmith, London, W6 8JB.

The HarperCollins website address is: www.harpercollins.co.uk

1

ISBN 978-0-00-733575-6

Alex Barclay asserts the moral right to be identified as the author of this work.

Printed and bound in England by Clays Ltd, St Ives plc

To the loveliest loves in all the land:
Lily, Abigail, Sophie, Emily, Michael and Lucy

CONTENTS

THE ARCHIVIST'S OATH

I am Archivist Tristan Ault.
I vow to tell the untold tales, and my master is the truth.

PROLOGUE

FOURTEEN YEARS AGO...

Wind rushed in from the cold night and quenched all but three of the torches that lit the great hall of Castle Derrington. King Micah, weakened by illness, lay slumped on his throne, his breathing dry and shallow. A towering band of men on horseback surrounded him, flames dancing in their eyes, their cheeks streaked with blood.

Outside, against the beating rain, the king's most loyal counsel, Villius Ren, rode his white horse across the burning drawbridge and charged through the deserted barbican, through the courtyard and into the great hall.

"Your Highness," he said, drawing his sword from its scabbard.

King Micah looked up from the shadows, and saw that his trusted servant bore the same blood markings as the pale warriors before him. He bowed his head.

"It is not your betrayal that saddens me, Villius. It is the world and how it has turned to darkness to find its way. And how can we be guided without light?"

The wind whipped around the last of the torches and the room went black.

"You have succumbed, Villius, as the weak and the ignorant do," said King Micah. "Since you were a child, happiness held no value for you. I was foolish to think that you could change. You have defeated a man on his deathbed. Your courage is commendable."

The filthy white horse reared up on its hind legs. Villius Ren wrenched the reins, the hot breath from his laughter misting the cold air around him. He said just one word: "Release."

"Farewell," said King Micah, "but know that this is not the end."

When all the arrows had arced from their bows, Villius Ren jumped down from his horse and went to where King Micah lay bleeding. One by one, Villius twisted the arrows in his master's wounds, and tore them free. King Micah's eyes shot open. He reached out and gripped Villius Ren's arm. The two men locked eyes. Villius felt as if his flesh had been sucked towards the bone and released, as if he had been drained, then replenished. A feeling of sickness and loss swept over him. He staggered away from the king, whose eyes had closed, whose chest had ceased to rise.

Villius Ren and his warriors had laid claim to the Kingdom of Decresian, but only by defeating a dying man. Henceforth, to all but each other, they would be known as The Craven Lodge.

The Curse of Kings was cast.

Somewhere in the castle, a baby cried.

1

UNSETTLED SOULS

ENVAR WAS A LAND OF TWELVE TERRITORIES AND ITS northeasterly was Decresian. In the time of King Micah and Queen Cossima, the people were looked after, employed and respected. Ever since The Craven Lodge took over, only a desperate few sought work at the castle, hired and fired at the whim of Villius Ren.

Mostly, the people of Decresian were poor, angry and sleep-deprived, for, in a walled garden in the grounds of Castle Derrington, nine hundred and ninety-nine corpses were buried and every night, when the clock struck twelve, their unsettled souls screamed for mercy until daybreak.

It was said they were the remains of the botched experiments of the Evolent brothers, Doctors Malcolm and Benjamin, one-time allies of Villius Ren. For decades, while the people of Decresian slept, the Evolents crossbred humans and animals and they failed – nine hundred and ninety-nine times. The bodies were thrown one on top of the other, often before they had the chance to draw their last breath. It was a final, grotesque indignity in a kingdom of honour and tradition, where the bodies of the dead were held sacred.

Some said it was fitting that the sound of a ruined kingdom was the sound of pain, and that, in their bleakest moments, the people of Decresian found comfort in it. If there were other souls out there screaming in the darkness, unable to rest at night, they knew that they were not alone.

Even The Craven Lodge couldn't bear to stay at the castle during the kingdom's darkest hours. Instead, they found courage in the bottles of wine and the tankards of beer they drank; a vicious, concocted courage that sent them rampaging on horseback through Decresian and beyond, lawless and wild. The only person to be found in the castle from midnight was their servant from birth – a young man of fourteen. His name was Oland Born.

It was close to dawn as Oland rushed around the great hall, behind in his nightly task of cleaning up after The Craven Lodge's banquet. Bones and gristle and potato skins littered the flagstone floor. The air was rank with sweat and liquor and grease. The gaping carcass of a pig still lay on the vast gold-edged dining table. Rings of red wine marked its surface and candle wax had melted into the narrow cracks. As Oland bent to pick up a fallen goblet, he heard the gruff voices and heavy footsteps of his masters. He rolled under the table and lay on his back, arms by his side, rigid.

"What a shambles!" roared Villius as he strode into the room. "A shambles! Where is that runt, Oland Born—"

"Who wants to be bothered with him?"

Oland recognised Wickham's voice. At twenty-nine, Wickham was the youngest of The Craven Lodge, a short, mercurial man, favoured by Villius Ren as a storyteller. Of all of The Craven Lodge, Oland found Wickham the most tolerable, perhaps because he had never quite reached the violent extremes of the others, perhaps because it was Wickham who had taught him to read. For the first time, Oland realised that anyone who had taught him anything in life was likely a thief, a brute, a killer and most definitely a coward.

"To the Peak with young Born!" said another of the men, this time Hazenby, whose quarters had been so filthy, its scrubbing and airing was the cause of Oland's delay. Hazenby was seldom to be found when baths were being filled or garments washed. He was speaking of Curfew Peak, the island prison for young criminals, where they remained until their twenty-first year.

Curfew Peak was black and forbidding and, according to myth, crawling with beasts.

Not unlike Castle Derrington, thought Oland.

2

WICKHAM'S TALE

WICKHAM STRUCK HIS GOBLET WITH A KNIFE, AND called for silence. "While we await our morning revivals," he said, "let us sit, light the candles, share one more glass. Allow me to entertain you with a dark tale of comings and goings."

The Craven Lodge cheered. Oland, alarmed, glanced left and right as they began to pull back their chairs and sit down, their mud-caked soles inches from him.

As Wickham strode the length of the table, Oland could hear the scrape of the stone he had embedded in the sole of the storyteller's boot. He had added something different to the boots or garments of all ten of The Craven Lodge, so he would always know which monster approached.

Wickham began: "In the depths of Castle Derrington on the

night a king was to be overthrown, a boy was born as his father lay dying beside him…"

It was a story Oland had first heard when he was eight years old. It had pained him then, and would pain him always, but he was forced to listen once more.

Wickham continued: "This man, this father of the newborn, had committed many bad deeds, and for this he was bound to be punished. As his wife brought their child into the world, a man in robes of black entered the room and stabbed the child's father through the heart. Then he turned, dagger in hand, to the young mother lying weeping on the floor, clutching the delivered infant to her breast.

"As she looked up at this insidious intruder, she was possessed by a fierce love for her child, a child brought into a world of instant cruelty. She reached back and grabbed a poker from beside the fire, striking it hard against the man's face, opening up a bony, bloodied chasm—"

A tankard fell on to the floor, spilling white wine across the flagstones as it rolled towards Oland's hand. He uncurled his little finger and sent it rolling back out. Wickham, candlestick in hand, bent down to retrieve it.

Oland's heart started to pound. He was struck with a sensation that enveloped him like a shroud. A fleet of images flashed through his mind, and ended in a vivid scene of dripping blood that quickly fled as Wickham stood up and carried on with his tale:

"The terrified mother crawled past the felled man to the door, and through the deserted hallways of Castle Derrington she ran. Door after door was locked. On she ran. Eventually, she stumbled into the kitchen, and there she found a small recess in a brick wall and a teetering tower of crates. She pulled off the topmost, then the next, then the next and, in the crate beneath that, she laid her silent baby. She scrawled his name on a piece of paper, and pinned it to his chest. That boy's name was—"

"Oland Born!" roared Villius, reaching under the table, grabbing Oland by the ankle and wrenching him out. He pulled him up to standing. Oland's eyes were level with Villius' chin, and he dared not raise them higher. Being so close to Villius' face, and breath, and spite, repelled him. He was so close now, he could make out the tiny raised scars that marked his jaw like the slashes of a tiny blade.

"What are you doing, you eerie little runt?" roared Villius. "Is your bed not comfortable enough, that you prefer to lie on the floor? Or is spying what interests you? Look at me! Is there someone you have taken to spying for?"

A treacherous man will forever see treachery in the eyes of others, Oland had once read.

"N… n… no," said Oland. "I… I…"

"I… I… what?" roared Villius. "If you are not here to spy, what is it? What have you been doing all night?"

Despite himself, Oland's eyes flicked towards the stinking Hazenby, reminding him his earlier work had, ultimately, been in vain.

"Why are you looking at him?" said Villius, grabbing Oland's face, and squeezing it.

"N… no… no reason," said Oland.

"This room is in no fit state for our morning revivals!" said Villius. "The Villian Games take place today! The event of the decade! And you're lying on the floor like a dog!"

"Like the dog he is!" shouted Hazenby.

The Craven Lodge all kicked back their chairs, and staggered up, gathering around Oland, bearing down on him, drunk and roiling.

In the midst of these murky thugs, Oland Born was like a light in the dark. His hair was fair, his eyes pale green, his skin sallow and unravaged by careless living. He had pale, angular lips. As the cheekbones and jawbones of The Craven Lodge had been vanishing under layers of fat, Oland's were emerging. And though there were slight flaws in the symmetry of his features, his was a face that drew the eye of many, twice over. His body was long and lean, but hidden by loose tunics and trousers. In contrast, The Craven Lodge wore garments that highlighted their spreading girth. Villius Ren was the fittest of his pack and, even as he aged, his shoulders appeared to broaden, and his chest and torso thickened. He had the build of a warrior, and the vanity to retain a private tailor to proclaim it.

Without warning, Villius' hand shot out and he grabbed Oland by the back of the head, pushing him towards a candle at the centre of the table. Oland gripped the edge of the table to try to stop him.

"Worried your girl-hair might go up in flames?" said Villius, shoving his face closer to the heat.

Oland cried out. He could hear his hair crackle. The smell filled his nostrils. Panicked, he released his grip on the table and grabbed at his head.

The Craven Lodge laughed loudly.

Villius pulled Oland up again. "Shall we cut off his long blond locks, then? A head of short hair won't ignite… quite so quickly."

Croft, a dull-eyed sycophant, stepped forward and handed Villius a knife. Oland again kicked out, catching Villius hard on the wrist. The knife spun through the air towards them. Villius flinched, and released him. Oland fell, half twisting, striking his cheek hard on the table, but quickly finding his feet. The Craven Lodge swayed in front of him, then descended, their faces warped with anger.

Oland ran.

3

THE HOLDINGS

OLAND TOOK GIANT STRIDES ACROSS THE HALL AND out into the courtyard. He knew how Wickham's story ended: the mother fled the castle, never to be seen or heard from again. But she had vowed to the last person she had seen that night, a terrified young maid, that she would return one day to reclaim her son. *To reclaim me,* thought Oland.

The story would always end with Wickham's dramatic, low-pitched judgement: "To deprive a son of his father is unpardonable." And Oland agreed.

As Oland ran, he heard footsteps behind him and guessed, from the damp, rasping breath and the clank of his loosened belt buckle, that it was Viande, a true savage, the crudest of The Craven Lodge. He liked to hack and spit, scratch and belch. He grabbed and sneered at the women who visited the castle, calling them sweetlings, never caring for their names.

Oland glanced back and saw a doubled-over Viande try to point at him and speak. He kept running. At the end of the hallway, he took a sharp right into the games room, continuing on through the portrait room. Only one portrait had replaced the hundreds that The Craven Lodge had destroyed. Anyone passing could now admire the broad, leather-shouldered expanse of Villius Ren. His elaborate black chest plate was adorned with an entwined V and R in garnet-coloured leather that matched the flaming corners of his eyes. His stare was defiant, the squirrel-brown of his irises like the unvarnished gates to an elaborate hell.

Oland ran into the hallway. The last room he passed was the throne room. Oland had never been inside it, never even seen the door opened a crack. Its only keyholder was Villius Ren. All Oland knew of it were its two unremarkable doors. But instinct told him that, like the eyes in Villius' head, what lay behind them was best left unexplored.

Oland ran into the outer ward and came to an eventual stop at the deserted northeast tower. He made his way up the winding staircase that led to the vast library. Here, always, he would be safe, for behind the tall mahogany bookshelves was a hidden room, filled with the rescued culture of the castle: books, plays, portraits and paintings, musical instruments and costumes from the king's theatre. Oland did not know who had gathered the relics and kept them so wisely from The Craven Lodge.

He had found the room six years earlier, yet in all that time, had explored only a fraction of its treasures. He had added to it his own creations: drawings and ships, and tiny tin soldiers arranged in mock battles. But more valuable than the room's contents was the sanctuary it offered. Instead of his damp and miserable bedroom, instead of the rattling cavern of the great hall, or the disarray of his masters' quarters, Oland could hide away here, by the warmth of a log fire that burned, unseen.

He called his room The Holdings... where everything was held dear. Its only keyholder was Oland Born.

Oland closed the door of The Holdings gently behind him. He went to the small table by the fire and picked up one of his recent finds: a book called *The Ancient Myths of Envar* that had almost toppled off the shelf as he had been looking for another. He opened the chapter on 'The Drogues of Curfew Peak' and read:

One mythic beast was four engulfed: vulture, bull, bear and wolf.
Oland read on:

It was said that hundreds of years ago, as the last fracture opened up on the southernmost tip of Envar, the only creatures that remained were a vulture, a bull, a bear and a wolf. As the ground they stood upon began to crumble into the sea, these four beasts vaulted the huge chasm and landed on the black shores of Curfew Peak. And, alone for years on this island-mountain, miles from the mainland, they were transformed, by breeding, into the Drogues of Curfew Peak.

Drogues were seven feet tall, black as coal, their bull-like torsos tapering into thick hind legs that carried their weight like loaded springs. They had rapid-clenching jaws and sword-like fangs that tore quickly through their victims. Each knotted vertebra of a drogue's spine was visible, even though the flesh that covered it was thick and unyielding, the surface coated with coarse black hair. As a victim lay dying at the hooves of a drogue, his final indignity was to be drenched in vile secretions vomited from the pit of the beast's insides; secretions that would quickly dissolve its prey, bones and all, without trace.

Oland wondered whether, simply by living among The Craven Lodge, he too was slowly being dissolved.

4

THE LUNATIC PRINCE

COME MORNING, THE CRAVEN LODGE WERE STILL sleeping, most of them having made it no further than the dining chairs of the great hall. The inner ward of Castle Derrington was exclusively their domain, the ten men and their one servant, Oland Born. A guarded barbican connected the inner ward to the outer ward, where a staff of forty worked, led in and out strictly at the times they were required to carry out their duties.

One hundred of Villius Ren's soldiers stood on watch in the outer ward every day, filing in from their garrisons by the ten towers he had commissioned when he took power. He had cobbled together a ragged army of one thousand from all across Envar and the precision of their numbers was because of Villius' strict belief in the Fortune of Tens.

Good fortune was said to come in tens in Decresian. Ten hills bounded the village, forty silver birch trees bordered its square, ten houses lined each of its fifty cobbled streets. Twenty market stalls crowded Merchants' Alley, all opening at ten o'clock in the morning and closing at ten o'clock at night. But more important than the superstitious grouping of objects was what someone achieved by their tenth birthday and by every decade thereafter. That was the true meaning of the Fortune of Tens.

King Micah had been born at the turn of a century in the tenth minute of the tenth hour of the tenth day of the tenth month – an unsurmountable Fortune of Tens. In contrast, Villius Ren grabbed wildly at tens, taking them in whatever form he could: his soldiers were all in the last year of their teens, twenties, thirties or forties, men fearful of reaching another decade without having achieved their Fortune of Tens. Villius Ren had been haunted by a similar fear until he overthrew King Micah in his twenty-ninth year.

The ranks that clung to the craven of Castle Derrington stank of ill will, desperation and bitter contest.

Oland walked down the spiral staircase from the library, and across the courtyard into the kitchen. As he reached out for the handle of the back door, he heard a rough choking sound behind him. He jumped. When he turned, he saw Viande curled in the corner, snoring and twitching. Someone had tucked him inside one of the dogs' blankets. Oland quietly put on his boots then slung his bag over his head, securing the strap across his body. Viande stirred and opened one eye.

"Running from Villius Ren... roxworthy," he said.

Oland flinched at the insult. Prince Roxleigh was King Micah's lunatic uncle, sent for his ramblings to an asylum on the eve of his twenty-first birthday. Prince Roxleigh was a tall, skinny man with a long face, a slender neck and light brown hair that sat on his head like tumbleweed. In the sunlight, it shone like a halo. Roxleigh had been a popular prince, happiest in the company of the Derrington villagers, brightening their spirits with his jaunty walk and cheery smile, calling out to them with a sweeping wave of his skinny arm.

Roxleigh's very best friend was a Derrington man called Rowe, who was as tall as Roxleigh, but moved, as he would himself admit, "with more ballast". His canted walk was no match for Roxleigh's loping stride, and he would bound behind him like a giant puppy. Rowe spoke from his warm heart and shining mind, his head swooping down, then up with a flourish at the end of each burst of inspiration. And he had many, as did Roxleigh. Both fiercely intelligent, they were part of a small group of great thinkers who met every month in The Derrington Inn to discuss matters of importance in the Kingdom of Decresian, always with the intention of enhancing the life of its people.

But in the year before he was carried, wailing and flailing, from the castle, something had changed in Prince Roxleigh. Rowe, from whom he had been inseparable, had vanished from Derrington quite suddenly. Roxleigh had begun to pace the dungeon hallways of the arena at night, talking of beasts and monsters, of dark creatures with secret chambers, scribbling his notions on reams of paper that he stacked to the ceiling in the musty cells.

From then until now, if you were called 'roxley' or 'roxling' or if your actions were deemed 'roxworthy', the message was clear: you were as mad as the mad prince that was locked away in the madhouse. Years later, when Roxleigh's younger brother, Prince Stanislas – King Micah's father – became King of Decresian, a messenger arrived at the castle to say that Prince Roxleigh did not mind one bit. But everyone agreed: Roxleigh had no mind with which to mind.

Oland left Viande and the sleeping beasts of The Craven

Lodge behind. As he walked, he pondered the story of Prince Roxleigh. The year leading up to his descent into madness had been a bleak one for the kingdom, when a bermid-ant plague struck the northern coast. The small black ants moved south, ravaging the land, turning the rich vegetation from vibrant green to barren bronze. No one had ever seen such a beautiful trail of destruction. The bermids poisoned crops and the animals that fed on them. The people of Envar died from eating the produce of the land, the meat of diseased livestock, or they died from eating neither.

Prince Roxleigh's father, King Seward, a kind, strong leader, vowed to the surrounding territories that he would do everything he could to contain the plague within Decresian's borders. Yet, despite the best efforts of this honourable king, it was not to be, and the plague spread.

Almost one hundred years had passed since Roxleigh and Rowe had last walked the plague-ravaged ground to the village market, ground that had eventually been restored, only to be ravaged again by neglect. It was as if, from the parapets of Castle Derrington, The Craven Lodge had thrown a grey veil over the whole of Decresian.

Oland had one stall to visit in Merchants' Alley – that of the butcher, Malachy Graham. It was Oland's fourth visit that week and it was not just for meat for The Craven Lodge.

"Your leg of lamb," said Malachy, but, as he reached under the stall, he stopped when a voice rose over the bustle of the market.

"The Great Rains are nigh! The Great Rains are nigh!"

The crowd parted and allowed the shouting man through. He looked to be in his sixties, his hair grey and his face battered by the elements, lined by suffering, sunken by hunger. His pale, doleful eyes were sparking with panic. Between cries, his lips were pursed and trembling. He was dressed in a long, faded blue robe. The ties at the neck hung loose, exposing his bony chest and a scattering of wispy hair. Over his robe, he wore a beautiful, pristine sheepskin. Oland had seen the man before and heard his wild preachings about the impending return of The Great Rains.

"He's roxley!" laughed the butcher's young son, sticking his head up from behind the stall.

Malachy laid his hand on the boy's shoulder. "Daniel, I don't ever want to hear you say that again," he said. "Great tragedy lies behind that man's ramblings, and it is no surprise that his mind broke under the weight of it."

"But Father! The Great Rains are over!" said Daniel. "Everyone knows that."

"The Great Rains are nigh!" shouted the rambling man again as he disappeared into the crowd ahead.

Daniel laughed.

Malachy leaned down to him. "Son, some people's minds travel back to the past and are forever trapped there. We need to care for them, not mock them." He was wrapping slices of ham as he spoke. He handed the package to his son. "Go after the man, and give him this. His name is Magnus Miller. Call him by his name."

Daniel was open-mouthed.

"He won't bite," said Malachy. He smiled as he turned back to Oland. Then his face darkened. "I wish I could threaten him with no trip to The Games tonight, but who am I to overrule the decrees of The Craven Lodge?"

Oland nodded. He had no desire to go to The Games either, but, as The Craven Lodge's servant, he had no choice. "I should get back to the castle," he said.

Malachy lowered his voice. "Before you go, you need to know that there are already whisperings around the village about the final round, Oland. One of the soldiers has been talking…"

Oland raised his eyebrows. "What has he said?"

"Well, what you told me: that instead of King Micah's final

round, Acuity, a test of sharpness of mind, Villius' final round is to be called Agility and that it's more about the sharpness of a blade."

Oland took in a breath. "Has he said any more than that?"

Malachy shook his head. "No, but no one needs a fool soldier to tell them that the final round will be a bloody one. It's Villius Ren – it will be designed not just to bring a contender the dishonour of defeat, but to bring him the dishonour of a savage and public demise."

He reached under the stall. "The lamb," he said. He slid another thick package underneath it as he handed it over. "And the rest…"

"Thank you," said Oland. He turned to leave, then glanced back. "Do you know anyone competing?"

"Two of my nephews were taken by The Lodge from their homes last night," said Malachy. "'To make up numbers' they were told. A neighbour's son is competing willingly, believing the promises of land and glory that we both know will never come… no matter how many medals hang from his neck."

"I wish them well," said Oland.

Oland hurried back to Castle Derrington, first to the kitchen, then to the dungeons beneath the arena and the same dark hallways the troubled Prince Roxleigh had paced. As Oland passed the cramped cells, lions, tigers and leopards moved towards him, swiping at the bars that had imprisoned them for weeks. Oland's task was to starve them ahead of the Agility round, when they were to be unleashed for a man-versus-beast battle to satisfy Villius' bloodlust.

He unwrapped the second package Malachy Graham had given him, revealing the bloody steaks that would quiet the animals' hunger and tame their angry spirits.

Oland sat in the corner as the animals ate. He was reading a play called *The Banon Servant*, about a servant boy who bravely faced his master's taunts. Oland wished he had his courage and was eager to read what became of him. The light in the dungeon suddenly dimmed. Oland pushed the play back into his bag. In the entrance ahead, Villius Ren stood blocking out the sun.

"Get over here," he roared. As Villius walked down the steps, the light again streamed in. Barely breaking his stride, he slapped Oland across the face.

"You will never run from me again," said Villius.

Oland nodded.

"Speak!" said Villius. "Find your tongue! There's nothing

more pathetic than a cowering mute." But he didn't even wait to hear Oland. "Now, show me the starving monsters you have made me…"

Oland's heart pounded. Barely half an hour had passed since the animals had eaten their largest meal of the week. They were curled up and resting in the back of their cells. Oland's hands were still stained with the blood of the meat he had fed them.

Villius Ren walked past the cells, studying each animal. He rattled some of the bars, and got little response.

"They are weak with hunger," said Oland.

"They should react," spat Villius.

"There are bars between you," said Oland. "They know that it's pointless to attack."

In a flash, Villius grabbed Oland by the wrists and held up his palms.

"Weak with hunger…" said Villius. As he spoke, each word was lengthened, its delivery darkly mocking. "Yes. That explains why a ravenous beast wouldn't rush to feast on the blood-stained hands of a foolhardy boy."

He flung Oland's hands from his grip. "I'll have Viande slaughter these worthless beasts… and you will help him." He raised his eyebrows. "Have you nothing to say?"

"I... I'm sorry," said Oland.

"I... I... I..." spat Villius, pushing his face closer and closer to Oland's. "Ha! Look at you – you're paler than Wickham." If Villius could insult more than one person at a time, it gave him great pleasure.

He spun around and walked away, leaving Oland staring after him, deeply ashamed of the single trickle of cold sweat that ran down his side.

5

STARVELING

ESPITE THE MISERY OF HELPING TO SLAUGHTER THE
animals he had so carefully tended, Oland found
relief in avoiding the cruel spectacle of Villius'
version of The Games. But, when the ninth round ended, he was
summoned to the arena. The sky had darkened and the sun was
beginning to set. Oland stood where he was ordered to, in the
shadow of the royal box.

The voice of Villius Ren boomed from above.

"Guards, for our final round, remove the females from the arena."

The crowd was silenced by his feigned chivalry: Villius
Ren excusing women from watching violent scenes of his own
making, and standing in front of the Decresian people whose
lives he had destroyed, to offer them entertainment of the kind
only a twisted few sought.

Oland always knew enough of The Craven Lodge's plans to fulfil his role as servant, but never enough that he could not be surprised by new ones hatched in his absence. Without the slaughtered beasts, Oland no longer knew what Villius Ren would do for the final round.

Around the arena, The Craven Lodge began to light torches as lines of women and girls were guided roughly along their rows.

"Oland Born!" whispered Villius, leaning over the edge of the box, stretching a hooked, gloved finger towards him.

Oland turned and looked up at him. "Yes, master?"

"I thought perhaps you might clean up after our next event. I'll be watching, of course, because it appears that working unsupervised is something of which you are incapable."

Oland had no plans to reply, until Villius' eyes continued to bore into him. "Yes, master," he said.

"You don't have much ambition, do you?" said Villius. "There is not much point to you. But you do have a moderate talent for cleaning up. At the very least, I can remind you of that."

He stood up straight, and gripped the edge of the royal box.

"Gentlemen!" he roared. "It is time for a test of... Agility! Time for a champion to step forward! For a true leader, one who can be declared the champion of all champions, and forever be seen as the ultimate power in Envar, someone the Kingdom of Decresian can look to with pride!"

It was clear to everyone that Villius Ren was setting himself up to garner this impressive string of accolades, because he would never bestow such praise on another man. Whatever he had planned, he was confident that he would be victorious.

Oland looked around and realised how easy that would be – there appeared to be no remaining contenders. Not one man had made it through the earlier rounds.

"I promised you a spectacle," roared Villius, "and a spectacle I will deliver!"

To Oland's left, at the entrance to the dungeons, a chained panther slowly made his way into the arena, dragging two guards behind him. As he struggled wildly against them, a shaft of torchlight struck the protruding contours of his ribs. Without warning, a thickset man was thrown into the arena from the gates at the opposite side. He was clearly no athlete. He appeared to be a simple villager, a hairy, stocky man, with a huge belly and small wide feet that turned inward. He was holding a sword as if for the first time.

As he came closer, Oland was struck by a sickening recognition. It was the butcher, Malachy Graham.

"Tonight," roared Villius, thrilled by the rippling fear before him, "our panther will confront his opponent, a gentleman you may recognise as one who is used to slaughtering animals. Shall we see the panther's fine haunches on his market stall by morning?" He laughed, joined only by The Craven Lodge, then gestured for the animal's release.

The guards struggled again with the panther's chains, fighting to keep their balance. When he was finally set free, he stood, blinking in the fading light, casting a long shadow across the dusty earth. Then, snarling and grunting, his belly close to the ground, he moved, painfully slowly, towards his prey.

Malachy Graham trembled before him, smelling, as he always did, of blood.

6

SPECTATOR

OLAND BORN LOST ALL SENSE OF HIS STATION. HE started to run along the barrier towards Malachy, who was now stumbling wildly around the arena. As Oland reached him, Malachy turned his way with the terror of a thousand men in his eyes. The panther drew back on his hind legs. Oland watched as the butcher went limp and dropped to the ground, his arms over his head, his body curled into a ball, his eyes shut.

Oland was possessed by something that he had no time to comprehend. Before he realised what he was doing, he had jumped up on to the barrier, and was roaring. The panther spun towards him, whipping up a cloud of dust. The crowd gasped. A man who was clutching his young son to his chest reached out with his other hand to pull Oland back. But Oland broke free and he jumped into the arena. The panther pounced, but, as he moved through the air, Oland rolled underneath him, and was quickly on his feet. He reached down for the butcher's sword.

The panther pounced again, his jaws gaping. Oland vaulted into the air, wielding the sword above his head, swinging it swiftly downward, slicing through the animal's flesh. The panther howled. Oland stared, horrified at the depth of the wound; he had almost halved him. The panther slumped to the ground where he writhed briefly, whimpered, then died.

Oland could not speak. The first sound he heard was that of the sword hitting the ground as it slid through his sweat-soaked palm. The second was the thanks that coughed out of the fallen butcher. The third sound – the loudest – came from the cheering crowd. But it was short-lived; they quickly fell silent as the dungeon gates were opened and two more panthers were released.

As if possessed, Oland picked up his sword in one hand and, with the other, grabbed Malachy Graham and dragged him to the barriers, where people rushed to haul him over to the other side.

Oland ran towards the centre of the arena, drawing the panthers away from the crowd. He turned and roared as he ran towards them, swiftly engaging them in a converging fight. The battle between them was a blur of sword and blood. First one fell, then the other. And, in minutes, it was over.

The three panthers lay dead in the arena and, beside them, stood Oland Born, rigid in the smoking torchlight. The crowd was as silent as six in the morning. Oland felt as if he were among them, a spectator watching a boy he did not know. Slowly, their cheers filled the night sky. Oland's eyes were fixed on his own bare feet, mesmerised by the dark blood spattered across them. It led to a rich crimson pool that spread from beneath the animals. A violent image of a ferocious, towering beast flashed into Oland's mind, and his chest started to heave.

Cries broke out across the arena and, when Oland looked up, a boy no older than him was being wrestled from the crowd by a guard. He had short, choppy black hair and fierce, dark eyes that were almost black. He fought hard, struggling against the guard's bulging arm around his waist. Oland wondered what the boy had done. He watched as the guard carried him up to the last step. The boy struggled one last time. He raised his arm, tensed it, tightened his hand into a fist, then sent a sharp elbow backward into the stomach of the guard. The man's face contorted and he dropped him. A smile broke out across the boy's face and it was transformed. Oland's eyes shot wide. He knew then why the boy was being kicked out. For he was not a boy at all. He was a girl. A very pretty girl, in fact. And then she was gone.

A loud bell tolled over the uproar, until the still-cheering crowd was quietened. Villius Ren gestured for Oland to approach the royal box. Oland didn't move. Villius beckoned him again. Oland moved slowly towards him.

"People of Decresian," roared Villius, "are we witnessing the historical first meeting of slavery and bravery?" He laughed loud.

The crowd was utterly silent as Oland walked up the steps to the royal box and stood beside Villius. Oland's heart pounded. He looked out at the people of Decresian. He knew that they had been cheering not because he had taken lives, but because he had saved one.

A rumbling noise grew from the crowd.

Ignoring it, Villius laid his hands on Oland's shoulders and turned him slowly towards him. He leaned down and whispered into his ear: "I will enjoy seeing if you can clean up the mess that will be the rest of your life."

Oland thought about his mother and father, their goodness and badness, the terrible circumstances in which he was born: a night of violence and betrayal, of murder and flames and loss. Could any good come of a child born amid such devastation?

Would misfortune forever shadow him?

A man's voice echoed from across the arena: "Champion!"

Another voice joined it. "Oland Born! Champion!"

And another. "Champion! Champion!"

"Enough!" roared Villius, raising his head, his eyes wild. "Enough! Enough! Enough!"

He was still gripping Oland's shoulders. His fingertips were white. As he pulled away, he locked eyes with his young servant.

In that moment, Oland could have sworn he saw, in the eyes of Villius Ren, a spark of fear.

7

TEAL AND GOLD

THAT NIGHT, AT CASTLE DERRINGTON, THE BANQUET had the grim air of a celebration that had persisted in the face of tragedy. The Craven Lodge shifted in their seats as Oland served them, nudging against plates and tankards, making no secret of the fact that they were inviting a transgression. Oland had hoped his earlier strength would stay with him, but the truth was that, amid the hostility, he felt nothing but weakness. He had saved a life, drawn more attention to himself than he could bear, and the only place he wanted to be was alone in The Holdings.

Villius Ren was turned towards Wickham as Oland passed.

Wickham was speaking. "Yes, Villius," he was saying, "for how long?"

"No more than a week," said Villius. "I suppose you could call it a commission. I am anticipating the arrival of many dignitaries to Decresian. They will expect after-dinner tales that reflect a more… Envarly view. Settings that go beyond small tales of Decresian."

Oland could see Wickham's jaw clench and unclench rapidly.

"We must show these dignitaries that we understand their culture…" said Villius.

Wickham leaned to the side to allow Oland to fill his goblet. "Perhaps, Villius, as an alternative," he said, "I could speak with the countless soldiers you have taken from all these dignitaries' homelands… and have them enlighten the dark recesses of my tiny mind."

Oland's arm froze between Wickham's shoulder and Viande's on the other side. He had never heard Wickham so bold. He glanced at Villius Ren to see his reaction.

At first, Villius was silent. "You may leave immediately," he said, after a moment. He stood up and walked away. This came as no surprise to Oland. Villius Ren delivered orders, never expecting them to be questioned, so he often left without registering a response. It was, in fact, Wickham's reaction that surprised Oland: he was sitting motionless, with an expression of utter panic on his face.

As Oland moved on to Viande, Wickham jumped up and fled. Viande had pushed back his chair and positioned himself with one leg bent to the side, the other one straight out in front as if he were poised to trip someone up. He had been throwing Brussels sprouts into the air and catching them in his mouth, and he was now gnawing on a bone, drooling, snorting through his cavernous nostrils. He came to a piece of gristle and he growled, spitting it out with such force that it shot forward, striking Oland's face, where it hung briefly from his jaw, then fell. Oland's stomach turned. He rushed from the room, ignoring the familiar discord of The Craven Lodge's laughter.

Oland scrubbed his face at the kitchen sink and, while he was there, took two plates of leftovers to eat in The Holdings – the second to keep for later that night. The Craven Lodge would not miss him for half an hour, and, certainly, he would not miss them. He took out his tinderbox and lit a small fire. He sat on a stool beside it with a plate on one knee and *The Banon Servant* open on the other. As he turned to the page where he had left off, something slipped from the play and fell to the floor. He glanced down. It was a teal-coloured envelope, sealed in gold wax stamped with the intricate royal D of Decresian. Teal and gold were the colours of King Micah's reign. Oland set his plate and the play on the floor, wiped his hand on his napkin and picked up the envelope. He turned it over. He froze. There was a name written across it. And the name was Oland Born.

8

BY NIGHTFALL, BE GONE

OLAND LOOKED AROUND THE ROOM AS IF HE WOULD find something or someone to explain how his name could be written on anything, how anything at all could be meant for him. With trembling hands, he opened the envelope and began to read the first letter he had ever been sent.

You live in the ruins of a once-proud kingdom destroyed by greed and misguided ambition. But fear not — Decresian shall be restored. And it falls to you, Oland Born, to do so. On such young shoulders, it will prove astonishing how light this burden will be.

Your quest is to find the Crest of Sabian before The Great Rains fall, lest the mind's toil of a rightful king

be washed away.
In life, a father's folly may be his son's reward.

In case this letter were to fall into the wrong hands, to
guide you, know this:
Depth and height
From blue to white
What's left behind
Is yours to find.

Be wise in your choice of companion and, by nightfall, be
gone.

In fondness and faith,
King Micah of Decresian

The letter was dated the night King Micah died. Oland reread his name on the envelope. He reread it in the letter. He was utterly bewildered. How could King Micah have ever known the name of a boy who was born after his death? Oland read the king's words several times more and, each time, new questions arose. Where was Sabian? Why was its crest important to Decresian?

Why was he chosen to find it? Oland thought of the homeless man in the village, how only a crazy man believed that The Great Rains would return. A crazy man and a dead king. Whose 'mind's toil' was King Micah speaking of? Who was the rightful king? King Micah and Queen Cossima had had no children; Oland knew that to be the absolute truth. What father, what son was King Micah talking about? Why was he to leave before nightfall? How could King Micah have even known what night he would discover the letter? How could Oland possibly just leave everything to go on a quest?

But what was 'everything'? thought Oland. For years, he had been praying for release from Castle Derrington, but had always thought it would be linked to his mother. Instead, a dead king had responded to his prayer.

Now, his choice was to trade a world he knew but hated for a world he did not know and feared.

But, thought Oland, *is there any place on earth worse than Castle Derrington?*

And from that simple question came the simple answer, *No.* There could be nothing in the wider world that could eclipse the fear he felt, festering, as he was, in the black walls of Castle Derrington. Outside, surely, there could only ever be more light.

Oland folded up the letter and put it back inside the play, sliding it between two other plays on the shelf. Villius would be looking for him in the great hall. Before he could go anywhere, he would have to show his face. But, as he made his way down the spiral staircase, his first surge of excitement was replaced with thoughts of his mother returning to find that no son had awaited her, even though, for fourteen years, he had.

Oland quickened his pace and darted across the courtyard. Most of The Craven Lodge had left the great hall, though it was still an hour to midnight. On the table, he saw the toppled candlesticks, and the rivulets of wax that had bled from them, now hardened. Oland patted his pocket for his knife then remembered he had left it in The Holdings when he had changed clothes after The Games. He grabbed a candlestick from the table, lit it and moved as quickly as he could along the hallway.

As he passed the throne room, he was startled to see a figure clothed in black emerging. He must have been six-and-a-half-feet tall. Only his eyes were exposed; the rest of his face and neck was swathed in layers of fine black gauze that did little to conceal the strange contours of his bones. Oland and he froze, inches from each other.

In a flash, the man reached out and pinched the wick of

the candle to quench the flame. In the windowless hallway, the darkness was absolute.

"Oland Born..." whispered the man. When he spoke, the air was filled with the scent of cinderberry. Oland noticed that the gauze was glistening. It must have been soaked in cinderberry salve. This man, whoever he was, had been wounded.

"Who are you?" said Oland. "What do you want?"

"You," said the man.

They heard footsteps behind them, and, shockingly close, the voice of Villius Ren calling for Wickham.

Before Oland could react, the man in black had dragged him into the throne room and closed the door. Oland thought his heart would explode from his chest. He was in the forbidden room, with an intruder, and Villius Ren was only seconds away.

The room stank of stale breath and rotting meat. Oland had often seen Villius Ren walking towards the throne room with a plate of food, and he wondered if what he was smelling now were his rotting leftovers. After all, even those who cleaned the castle were forbidden to enter the throne room.

"What do you want?" said Oland.

"Shh," said the man. His left hand was clenching the back of Oland's neck, pressing his cheek against the cold stone wall.

Outside, Villius Ren's footsteps were drawing closer. By the jangle of chains, Oland knew that Viande was by his side. The relief was overwhelming; Villius would not be coming in unless he was alone. Oland could feel the intruder's grip slacken a little, as if he too knew about the sanctity of the room. Oland took the chance to push back hard, breaking the man's hold. He could feel the same overwhelming sensations he had felt in the arena, a surge of strength and focus. The man grunted, and stumbled backward.

"No!" he hissed. "No!" He reached out to grab Oland, but Oland used his forearm to block his advance. In one motion, he turned, raised his knee to his chest and slammed his boot down on the intruder's knee, with enough force to drop him to the ground.

Oland pulled open the door, slipped into the dark hallway and ran. He heard the man come out after him; he heard him lock the throne room door. He wondered who he was, and how he could have stolen the key from Villius Ren.

The advice in King Micah's letter came back to Oland: 'by nightfall, be gone'.

9

THE BEAST HE WOULD SLAY

I N THE HOLDINGS, OLAND GRABBED HIS BAG, AND IN IT HE quickly threw his book, his play, his knife, a tinderbox and a change of clothes. He wrapped up the second plate of food and added that. He read the king's letter one more time, then put it in his breast pocket. He had hoped it would fill him with belief, or courage, or inspiration, but all he felt was sorrow and uncertainty. He looked down at his tin soldiers. His latest addition, bought from a stall in the market, stood holding an arquebus to his shoulder. Oland had never seen a real arquebus before; he doubted that anyone in Decresian had. He admired this new, magical weapon that fired balls of lead, and meant a soldier could be more than a sword's swipe away.

Oland took the soldier and put it in his pocket for good luck.

He left his room, locked the door and put the key in his bag. He was ready. Villius would be about to leave and The Craven Lodge wouldn't be far behind him. At that moment, the nine hundred and ninety-nine screaming souls began their wailing, as if reassuring Oland it was the right time to go. He thought of his mother coming back for him, but he shook the thought away.

Then, rising over the screaming souls, Oland heard a tormented, wolf-like howl. He ran to the tiny window and looked down. He could see nothing or no one to explain it. He ran down the spiral staircase and along the hallway to the great hall. A chill overcame him, and he went to button his tunic at the neck. The button was gone. It must have broken off the previous night when Villius had pushed him towards the flame of the candle in the great hall.

As he was about to turn the corner, he heard the voices of Wickham and Viande. He stopped to watch their distorted reflections in a shield that was mounted on the wall. He had placed and polished shields on almost every busy corner of the castle, so he could see – and perhaps avoid – what lay ahead.

"I am telling you, he has gone insane," said Viande, tapping his chubby fingers against the side of his head. "Those were the howls of a man gone roxley! This place is possessed! And I am telling you he said to me not to let the boy live one more night."

"What?" said Wickham.

"I'm telling you Villius insisted 'not one more night'!" said Viande. "I'm not going near him. You saw what he did in that arena! How am I to—"

"I'm sorry, but I don't understand this," said Wickham. There was panic in his voice. "I thought Villius wanted Oland bound in slavery to this castle for life. Why else would he have me invent a ridiculous tale to keep him here: oh, his tragic birth, and how one day his mother would return to claim him…?"

A fierce pain swelled in Oland's chest. Everything he had believed about his birth was the product of a storyteller's imagination. All the ideas Oland had ever had about who his parents might be were now worthless: anyone could be his father; anyone could be his mother. They could be living or dead, they could be looking for him, or they could have abandoned him with no further intentions. For six years, he had built hopes on these words, he had built a future on them. And now he could feel something deep in the pit of his stomach replace them: a dull and powerful aching anger.

It was at this moment that Oland knew he would never again

spend a night in Castle Derrington. But one day he would return. And on that day the beast he would slay would be a man named Villius Ren.

Wickham had trailed off. Oland could see why. Villius, looking more enraged than Oland thought possible, appeared in front of them, wild-eyed. His hair was flat and damp against his skull, his face greasy and ghostlike.

"Villius," said Wickham, taking a step back. "Is everything—"

"What are you still doing here?" he roared. "I told you to go, didn't I? I told you to leave! Is it that whatever I tell people to do, they do the opposite now?"

"Of course not, Villius," said Wickham. "I was merely waiting to ask you if there were any territories in particular—"

"Everything *is* destroyed!" said Villius. "Everything is destroyed! Look!" He was holding up something small. "Look!"

Oland couldn't make it out in the mottled reflection.

"A button?" said Viande.

"You don't understand!" said Villius. "It's Oland Born's button! It was on the floor in my throne room! He was in my throne room! Everything has been destroyed!"

The intruder, thought Oland. *He must have ripped it off when he grasped my neck!*

"He left it unlocked!" said Villius. "He left it unlocked!" He was utterly crazed.

Oland was puzzled. The throne room door *had* been locked. He had heard the distinctive rattle behind him as he fled the intruder. But, as was often the case, paranoia had perhaps clouded Villius' judgement.

Of course, he had not been completely wrong. Oland *had* been in his throne room. But what could possibly be inside that would cause an intruder so much interest, and Villius Ren so much rage at its disturbance?

Oland's heart was pounding louder than the screaming souls, louder than the inhuman howls of Villius Ren, louder than his own footsteps as he ran down the hallway, ran through the stables, ran across the grounds and out into the world he did not know, but feared.

He knew that he was as dead as a boy with a still-beating heart could be.

10

CURSE YOUR SOULS

I N THE VILLAGE OF DERRINGTON, THE WET COBBLES OF Merchants' Alley shone. Smoky clouds coursed overhead, masking and unmasking the moon as they passed. The alley was a bleak and empty place after ten o'clock, bereft of the clamour of trade. Over the cries of the unsettled souls, a cough echoed down the street. Oland stepped out from the shadows as a second cough followed. He moved towards the sound and came upon a man curled in a doorway behind a wall of empty fruit boxes. The damp air was filled with the scent of raspberries. Oland looked down as the man squirmed under a shabby blanket that was so small, it would never fully cover him. At the man's neck, Oland noticed a sheepskin trim.

"Excuse me, sir," said Oland. He waited. "Excuse me," he said again. "Magnus?"

Magnus stirred.

"I… I came to find you," said Oland. "I've heard you saying that The Great Rains were coming."

"Please," said Magnus, "leave me be." He spoke quietly.

Oland began to crouch down. "I just wanted to know—"

"My body can't take another beating," said Magnus, shifting closer to the wall.

Oland stood up quickly. "I don't want to hurt you. Who hurt you?"

Magnus snorted. "The list would be as long as a Decresian night," he said, "except for the fact that no one can hurt me. Not any more." He still hadn't opened his eyes. "I know that The Great Rains are nigh; it's a fact. I know they are, and whether people believe me or not is no concern of mine. They can laugh at me, they can beat me in the shadows when no one is looking, but I know."

Oland lowered his voice. "Did King Micah tell you that?" he said.

Magnus went very still. "No…" He turned slightly and opened one eye to look at Oland. "Ha!" he said. "A spy from The Craven Lodge!"

"I'm not a spy," said Oland. "And I'm not from The Craven Lodge."

"I know you live up there with them." He laughed. "What fool mans my mill now?"

"Pardon me?" said Oland.

"Pardon you?" Again, Magnus snorted. "Twenty-eight years," he said. "For twenty-eight years, I was the king's miller. Along with my sons, long dead now. And my wife, long dead now. My beautiful Hester Rose." He paused. "And I no different," said Magnus. "Long dead now. Dead of heart."

Oland had no words of reply.

"And my beloved was guardian of the king and queen's one hundred beautiful acres. Every morning, safe from the winds and the biting rain, she would fill the throne room while all were sleeping. Flowers and plants and all manner of fruits and vegetables from our very own garden in the grounds." He paused. "And then came the craven…"

"I'm sorry—" said Oland.

"At night I lie here and I watch the blades of my mill go round and round up on that screaming hill and I wonder what fool mans my mill," said Magnus.

"It was a tragedy what happened to King Micah," said Oland.

"Not for you it wasn't," said Magnus.

Oland knew that his association with The Craven Lodge

would forever taint him. The fact that they had imprisoned him did not matter to a man who had lost his family, his livelihood, his home.

"Curse your souls," spat Magnus. "A thousand times, curse your souls." He closed his eyes again.

"Please," said Oland.

He waited, but the miller said nothing more… until Oland walked away. Then he shouted after him, "She's one of the souls! She's one of the souls! My love lies with the seeds she sowed! And you! You all trample the ground!"

When Oland glanced back, Magnus had his hands over his ears and his face was twisted in grief. Oland was sickened, but he knew he had no words to soothe this broken man. Instead, he walked back and set down beside him the small parcel of food he had brought from the castle, and he left.

There was no end to the poisonous reach of The Craven Lodge and Villius Ren's capacity for rage. Now that Oland was his master's focus, more than he had ever been before, the idea that he could perform the miracle of restoring Decresian made him laugh out loud.

I am no one, thought Oland. *I am fourteen years old, I achieved nothing by my tenth birthday and I will no doubt achieve nothing by my twentieth.*

But Oland Born had already achieved more than he would ever know. For somewhere in the filthy, dark and rowdy hallways of Castle Derrington, he had raised himself – a boy with a kind heart, a gentle soul. And, as he had only begun to discover… a fighting soul.

Oland Born, Oland bred.

11

DOWNFALL

OLAND MADE HIS WAY TO THE VILLAGE SQUARE AND found a bench under a silver birch tree. A shadow passed across a thin sliver of moonlight on the grass in front of him. Oland leaned forward. The shadow passed back and forth again. Something was swinging from branch to branch through the trees. Then it was gone. Before long, Oland could sense a presence behind him. He turned his head slowly, and was confronted with a monkey. It had golden grey fur and a hairless pink face. Before Oland could react, the monkey wrapped his arms around him and laid his head on Oland's shoulder. Oland slid away from him, and noticed a small silver medal swinging from the monkey's leather collar. A name was etched into it.

"Malben," said Oland, holding the medal to the moonlight. "Hello."

The monkey blinked and opened his mouth as if he were going to speak. Instead, he threw his arms around Oland one more time. Then he disappeared.

There was no more rustling in the trees. Oland looked around the square to see if the monkey would reappear. But he soon realised that he was alone. As for human company, Oland knew that everyone in Decresian was afraid of The Craven Lodge and that, from midnight, they locked their doors and hid away, terrified to draw attention to themselves.

As Oland stood up to leave, he sensed a strange vibration underfoot. He could hear the faint sound of metal on stone, and the steady blows of a hammer. It was his only sign that there was life in Derrington. He followed the dull noise through a maze of streets that brought him to a short row of ten cottages. He went around to the back and walked along the ragged laneway.

A red-haired boy burst out of a gate at the end of the lane and ran towards Oland, struggling on his chubby, turned-in legs. It was only as he passed that Oland recognised Daniel Graham, the butcher's son. The boy's eyes were filled with panic.

Oland walked down to the swinging gate and looked into a small backyard filled with a sombre crowd. More people were emerging from inside the house. The noise of the hammers had stopped and the only sound was the urgent whispers of the men in the doorway. Oland couldn't make out what they were saying, and the crowd was too thick to push through. Whatever was happening in this yard, Oland knew it was important enough that any fear of The Craven Lodge arriving had dissolved.

Intrigued, Oland left the yard and went into the neighbouring one. Like all the houses along the lane, it had a small room on each side of the back door. One was lit by the moon, the other by candle. Oland crouched down by the wall that divided the two yards. Through the candlelit window beside him, he noticed a huge shadow stretching up the wall inside. It was cast by a tall, blocky man with a bald, oval head. A row of shiny pins was gripped between his pursed lips. A line of heavy black garments hung on a rack in front of him. The floor was strewn with paper patterns. Oland's heart pounded. It was the Tailor Rynish. Villius Ren's private tailor.

"In a different world, it's a job of which my brother would be proud," came a voice behind him.

Oland jumped. He turned around and saw a man standing over him. He looked to be in his sixties, and was heavyset with a small round belly. He had thick sand-coloured hair that fell across his full face and bright hazel eyes. He grabbed Oland by the arm and pulled him into the shadow of the doorway.

"You're the boy from the arena!" said the man. "What are you doing here?"

"I… I… followed the sounds…" said Oland. "The Tailor Rynish… is he your brother?"

The man pushed open the back door and held it for Oland to walk through. "Come," he said. "You're not safe outside." He led Oland into a small darkened parlour and lit a candle.

"My name is Jerome Rynish," said the man. "What are you doing, risking coming to Derrington at this time of night? Oland Born, isn't that your name?"

Oland nodded. "Yes."

"Have they thrown you out of the castle?" said Jerome.

"No," said Oland. "I left of my own accord."

Jerome studied Oland's face.

"Why has a crowd gathered next door?" said Oland. "Is that Malachy Graham's house?"

"Yes, but that's not for you to worry about," said Jerome. "What brings you to Derrington?"

Oland didn't want to give too much away. "I am looking for someone to take me on a blind journey."

Jerome raised his eyebrows. "You?" he said.

"I need to go somewhere," said Oland, "and I need someone to take me there without question."

"And what, at such a young age, do you know of blind journeys?" said Jerome.

"In the castle dungeons, there are special cells for blind journeymen and their passengers…"

"Yet you are not deterred…" said Jerome.

Oland shook his head. "Like those who have gone before me, captured or uncaptured, I have no choice."

"Where do you want to go?" said Jerome.

"Does that mean you will take me?" said Oland.

"I saw what happened in the arena," said Jerome. "You defied and humiliated Villius Ren in front of the whole of Decresian. How he viewed you before, I don't know, but today you became his enemy." He paused. "I too am an enemy of Villius Ren's. And, if you want to get to safety, I will help you."

Outside, a commotion erupted in the neighbouring yard. Someone knocked on the back door of the Rynishes' house and pushed their way in. The draught caught the door opposite the parlour, and it swung open to reveal the Tailor Rynish scowling at the interruption. Oland noticed something he hadn't seen through the window: a remnant of sheepskin hanging on a peg. The Tailor Rynish must have made the mad old miller's sheepskin. Oland was now in a world where people helped the less fortunate. It felt shameful to have ever served men guided only by personal gain.

The back door closed, and the Tailor Rynish walked into the parlour, his eyes shining with tears.

"Our friend is dead, Jerome," he said. "Malachy Graham is dead. His heart couldn't sustain the shock." His voice cracked.

Jerome bowed his head. "His family will be ours now. Seven fine sons."

The tailor cleared his throat. "And I shall return to work," he said, "making their father's killer the finest, blackest clothing in the land…" He walked away and closed the door behind him.

"That was why a crowd had gathered next door," said Jerome.

"I think I passed his son, Daniel, in the laneway," said Oland. "He must have been running for a doctor…"

Jerome nodded. "Yes."

"This is all my fault," said Oland. "I… I was in charge of the animals at the arena. I knew that Villius Ren wanted them hungry, so I… I went to Malachy Graham's stall. I asked him for extra cuts. I told him why, and he gave them to me, all this week—"

"And he was happy to give them to you," said Jerome.

But Oland didn't hear him, and continued. "Villius must have found out. Malachy Graham was called into the arena because of me. It's my fault your friend is dead. I could see it in your brother's eyes. I could see his disgust."

"You saved Malachy Graham's life," said Jerome. "And whatever you saw in my brother's eyes, it was not meant for you."

"If I hadn't asked Malachy for help," said Oland, "Villius Ren would never have done what he did."

"Exactly," said Jerome. "Villius Ren did it. No one else. You are not to blame, Oland."

Oland stared into the empty hearth. It had no fuel stacked beside it, and the room was ice-cold. He was struck by the humiliating thought that he would never succeed on this quest without help.

"I found a letter from King Micah," he said, turning to Jerome.

"A letter? From King Micah?" said Jerome. "To whom?"

Oland hesitated. "To me."

"What did it say?"

"It said that I am to restore the Kingdom of Decresian."

Jerome's eyes were wide.

"I know it sounds foolish," said Oland. "It sounds foolish even to me."

"Well, not to me," said Jerome. "This is good news."

"I don't understand it," said Oland. "I don't know how, when King Micah never knew me, when he had never met me, when I was only born on the night he died, that a letter from him could come to me all these years later. And with such an extraordinary task. It must be a mistake."

"I knew King Micah," said Jerome, "and he was not a man to err."

Oland shrugged. "So I have heard, but… I don't know where to even start."

"Well," said Jerome, "at the very least, answer me this. To ensure that there was even a chance of restoring Decresian… what would you need to bring about?"

Without hesitation, Oland had the answer. "The downfall of Villius Ren."

12

CHANCEY THE GOLD

JEROME AND OLAND SAT IN SILENCE FOR SOME TIME.

"Oland…" said Jerome eventually. "If you are to bring about the downfall of Villius Ren, I think I should tell you about a man called Chancey the Gold."

"I've seen his name!" said Oland, his eyes bright. "In *The Sporting Heroes of Envar*." He paused. "Well, in the index. It said 'athlete, outstanding swimmer, named for all the gold medals he won in championships all over Envar…'"

"To watch Chancey the Gold swim was an extraordinary sight," said Jerome. "He moved through the water like a spinning ball through the barrel of an arquebus."

"I wanted to find out more about him," said Oland, "but, when I turned to the page, the entry was missing."

Jerome gave a wry smile. "Ripped out by Villius Ren, no

doubt… it's probably the only book he's ever opened."

"Why would he do that?" said Oland.

"Twenty years ago," said Jerome, "Villius Ren visited the Scryer of Gort to have his fortune told, and she told him that his downfall would be at the hands of Chancey the Gold."

Oland was dubious about the gifts of the scryer. All he knew was that she was imprisoned in a cave in Gort, and warriors and merchants from the surrounding lands would come to her to hear their future failings or fortune in battle or business. She asked each visitor to bring her water and, using a flame above the bowl, she saw visions reflected on its surface.

"Within a year of the scryer's prophecy," said Jerome, "Chancey the Gold put his name down for the Mican Games and Villius saw it as the beginning of the prophecy coming to fruition. Villius knew, because of Chancey the Gold's reputation, that he would be a formidable opponent, and he became fixated on defeating him. It was an unsettling obsession that yielded nothing; when it came to The Games, Chancey made it through the first eight events with little effort. It came to the second-to-last round, Aquatics, and, of course, Chancey won, breaking every record that was ever set. Villius came a distant second, but it still meant that they came face to face in the final round: Acuity. And, of course, in Acuity, Chancey the Gold beat Villius, as any man would.

"Villius was incensed. He believed that an athlete like Chancey the Gold, three years his junior, was no match for the warrior he considered himself to be. I'm guessing that what you did at The Games today reminded him of that defeat. It is more likely that Malachy Graham was meant to die in that arena, but that Villius Ren himself was to slay the beasts, then on to solo glory he would go. Villius Ren does nothing to help anyone else, Oland. Nothing. By doing what you did, I imagine you delivered quite the blow to his plans."

"What happened to Chancey the Gold?" said Oland.

"He left Decresian in the months before King Micah was overthrown," said Jerome. "Because of his skill in Aquatics, he was offered a job by the ruler of Dallen."

"But Decresian and Dallen are bitter enemies," said Oland.

Jerome nodded. "That is true. But Dallen's ruler made an exception for Chancey the Gold, because he is the only person who can guide travellers through Dallen Falls – travellers from Decresian who are of benefit to Dallen, or travellers from other parts who would have traditionally reached their destination by sea. They would pay to take a shorter route through Dallen Falls.

It was a job that never before existed. As you know, the waterfall is thundering and The Straits below it are wild. The currents move at a terrifying pace. But Chancey the Gold can navigate them. And in Dallen he was safe from Villius Ren."

"Has Chancey the Gold ever come back to Decresian?" said Oland.

Jerome shook his head. "No," he said. "There would have to be a very special reason for him to return. The Craven Lodge would surely kill him because of the scryer's prophecy."

"Was Chancey the Gold an ally of King Micah?" said Oland.

"We all were," said Jerome. "And, like Chancey the Gold, I was once champion of The Games – ten years before him. I was given a ten-acre farm by King Micah – for my service, and for my success in The Games. When Villius Ren came to power, he took my land away. He gave all my family jobs, except for me. He knew I would do nothing to harm my family's prospects; he knew that they could not afford to refuse his offer of employment. And he knew that if I had no job, and lived in a cottage he owned, in a village he terrorised, he had at least some control over me."

"Why did he want to have control over you?" said Oland.

"He saw me as a threat," said Jerome. "And you know Villius

Ren; he could find a threat in the eyes of an infant."

Oland smiled.

"So..." said Jerome. "If your aim is the downfall of Villius Ren... and it has always been said that Chancey the Gold was the man to bring it about, well... your next stop should be Dallen Falls."

Oland suddenly could not imagine being anywhere other than Derrington.

Jerome smiled. He took Oland's hands in his. "You were chosen, Oland. Do this. Do this for all of us. You have nothing to lose. Chancey the Gold is a good man, and to arrive to him an enemy of Villius Ren is to arrive to him a friend. As you are here."

Oland stared again into the cold hearth.

Jerome took a breath. "Oland, never forget the reign you have been asked to end: that of Villius Ren, a man among nine hundred and ninety-nine screaming souls, yet with no soul of his own."

They sat in silence for some time, Oland running King Micah's words over and over in his head.

But fear not – Decresian shall be restored. And it falls to you, Oland Born, to do so. On such young shoulders, it will prove astonishing how light this burden will be.

To Oland, the burden felt anything but light.

Suddenly, they heard a soft tapping at the parlour window. Jerome went to the back door.

"It's Villius Ren," someone hissed. "Alone! Not one of The Lodge is with him."

Oland stood up.

The Tailor Rynish burst through his workshop door.

"What's going on?" he growled.

"Villius Ren is in Derrington," said Jerome.

Oland felt a rough hand grab on to his arm. He turned to see the Tailor Rynish talking over his head to his brother. "I'll take him," he was saying.

"What?" said Oland, struggling against him. "Take me where?"

"Shut your mouth!" snarled the tailor. "Shut your mouth; they'll hear you." He looked at Jerome. "I'm going to collect The Craven Lodge's new cloth. Villius knows this so he won't stand in my way."

Jerome nodded.

"No," Oland managed to say. "No."

"It's your only hope," said Jerome.

"I'm not going anywhere!" said Oland. He turned to the tailor. "You work for Villius Ren; I don't know where you're going. This could all be a trick—"

"Go, Oland," said Jerome. "Just go. Unless you want to be in my parlour when Villius Ren bursts in."

Before Oland had a chance to say another word, the Tailor Rynish was dragging him down the hallway out into the cold night. He pushed him to the back of the cart. As he forced Oland in, a small figure jumped in from the opposite side. Oland could scarcely believe it. It was the monkey, Malben. It gave Oland strange comfort as they were both thrown under a length of tarred canvas.

Oland could hear Jerome's voice as he leaned down and spoke to him through a gap in the cover: "My brother has a keen eye," he said. "But do not fear, Oland. For he knows how to turn a blind one."

13

CENSUS

THE ROADS IN DECRESIAN WERE ROCKY AND UNEVEN, winding under trees that were once rich with leaves, but whose branches were now skeletal. Grubby fields, bordered by tangled hedges, stretched back from behind the trees, some with small houses at their far corners, others with just the stone imprint of what had once been. Oland imagined that, to the Tailor Rynish, every journey through Decresian was a solemn reminder of the glory of a different reign.

Oland could barely breathe. He was wedged between two thick bolts of wool, with another at his feet, and the layer of heavy canvas pressed down on him. He slid the cover from his face at intervals. It offered some relief, but was soon replaced by the chill of icy night air. There was some cloth beneath him, but it did little to cushion him.

Tired of hiding from empty roads, Oland eventually sat up in the corner behind the tailor, with his legs to his chest and Malben curled up, hidden, at his feet. Oland watched from the corner of his eye as the tailor's shoulders moved up and down, up and down as he worked the reins. Every now and then, he wiped his sleeve under his nose. But still, he drove on. He had not spoken one word to Oland since they left Derrington.

They had been travelling for three hours before Oland felt the horse slow. He slipped back under the cover.

The tailor guided them down a lane with a narrow strip of grass at its centre. The fields on either side were scattered with sheep. The cart came to a stop outside a small white farmhouse. The tailor jumped down and tethered the horse. He pulled back the covers and gestured to Oland to stay quiet and follow him. When he turned away, Oland tucked Malben under the cloth and gave him a look he hoped would make him stay put.

Oland and the tailor made their way around the back of the house to a row of barns. The tailor slid the bolt back on the middle gate and, as they walked in, they were hit with the rich stench of manure. They crossed the filthy floor to the back wall of the barn. The tailor slid a panel of shelves to one side, and pushed open a small door that was hidden behind them. He took off his boots and laid them on a shelf, before he unlatched the door. Oland did the same, and followed the tailor into a cramped, windowless room, lit by a half-melted candle. The floor was strewn with straw, but it had been sprinkled with pine needles, so the air smelled fresher than the barn behind them.

There were two chairs in the room, one bed and a table with a bottle of milk and a sandwich on it. Oland and the tailor sat opposite each other at the table. The tailor took a knife from his pocket and cut the sandwich, handing half to Oland.

"I'm Arthur," said the tailor. "And I want to say thank you for saving my friend's life."

"But I…" Oland paused.

"Malachy knew what he was doing when he agreed to help you," said Arthur. "But you had no idea what the consequences of your actions would be when you jumped in to help."

Oland nodded. "No. I didn't."

Arthur took a drink from the bottle. "What happened to Malachy tonight was a terrible tragedy," he said, "but he wasn't a very healthy man, we all knew that, and he had suffered a terrible shock. Despite what happened in the arena, I know Malachy was proud of the part he played in helping you. Giving you the meat to feed the animals was his quiet protest against The Craven Lodge's savagery, and his humble way of honouring King Micah. He was very grateful to you for what you did today – he just didn't get a chance to tell you himself. So I'm telling you now. It's important for you to know that Malachy Graham's heart was not your responsibility. It was his. Although, for the most part, he would say that it was his wife who protected it." He tried to smile.

Oland realised now that Arthur had been crying on the journey.

"Oland," said Arthur. "There is something different about you. What you did today was extraordinary. Where did you learn to fight like that?"

Oland stared at the floor. "I... don't know. I didn't."

"Where did you come from?" said Arthur.

"I don't know," said Oland. He could hear how his own voice cracked.

"I'm sorry," said Arthur. "I thought perhaps that your parents were from outside Derrington and you were sent to work at the castle."

"Wickham tells a story," said Oland. He paused. "Do you know Wickham?"

"I have never met him," said Arthur, "though I have been given his measurements, have made his clothes, have passed him several times in the castle hallways, yet never seen him in one of my garments."

"Wickham used to tell a story of a woman who gave birth the night that King Micah was killed," said Oland, "and that the father of the child was murdered, and that the woman left the baby in a crate with its name pinned to its blanket…"

"And you think that child might be you?" said Arthur.

"I had thought so," said Oland, "but then I found out that Villius Ren told Wickham all those years ago to make that story up. It sounded like it could be me. It… felt like it could be me. But I don't know – maybe some of it is true."

It was the first time he had spoken to anyone about the part he thought he might have had in the story, and he struggled to keep the emotion from his voice. "The mother was to come back to reclaim the boy," said Oland. "He wasn't just going to be left there forever."

"As you say, there may well be some truth in Wickham's story," said Arthur. "And, if your parents were at the castle the night King Micah was overthrown, there could be a record of their names. But only if they were there officially, if they were employed there or perhaps visiting. You see that night was also the night of the Decresian census. The king had dispatched his men to call at every house in the kingdom to take a record of the name, age and occupation of every person there at that time, along with details of the land that they owned, the crops that they sowed, and such. That was why there were scant men left to protect King Micah, and why a coward like Villius Ren saw that as his chance to strike."

"Where is the census now?" said Oland.

Arthur let out a breath. "It could be with the son of Archivist Samuel Ault. There is a bloodline of archivists who originated in Dallen, but who came to Decresian after the ruler of Dallen was overthrown. Samuel Ault's father was murdered the night of the Dallen uprising."

"That was the night they stormed King Seward's Hospital and set it on fire," said Oland.

Arthur nodded. "The uprising started with the founding of the hospital. King Seward thought he was doing the whole of Envar a great service building a hospital where the plague-stricken could be looked after. The ruler of Dallen at the time welcomed it."

"But his people didn't," said Oland.

"Neither their land nor their livestock had been poisoned,

so they wanted nothing to do with the infected patients, even though the plague wasn't spread from human to human," said Arthur. "Anyway, the night of the uprising, Samuel Ault's father had ensured his family's safe departure to Decresian ahead of him. But, as he was leaving his home, an angry mob descended on him. He was unable to defend himself, and he was beaten and left there to die. His son, Samuel, vowed that his own son, Tristan, would never become an archivist, that he would be trained as a warrior, so that he would always have the skills to survive in what Samuel Ault now came to see as a vicious world. Tristan had no interest in being a warrior – he wanted to follow in his father's and grandfather's footsteps, but his father insisted and, from the age of ten, the boy was trained in a special form of combat, Jandro. But, as if the family was condemned to repeat history, Samuel Ault was killed on the night King Micah was overthrown.

"The question is whether Tristan Ault chose to honour his dying father by becoming a warrior or, instead, if he thought that true honour was to be found only by following the Ault family's ancestral vocation."

14

THE ARCHIVIST'S OATH

OLAND KNEW ABOUT ARCHIVISTS FROM THE BOOKS IN the king's library, but he had found no mention of Archivist Samuel Ault having a son. His father must have wanted him undocumented, so that there would be no natural expectation that he would follow in his footsteps.

"This is what I know," said Arthur. "For years, Villius Ren had been King Micah's closest advisor in practical matters. In matters intellectual, it was Samuel Ault. He was King Micah's confidant, his scribe, his archivist, the trusted guardian of all the secrets of Decresian. At the time King Micah was overthrown, Tristan Ault was not much older than you are now. I suspect that he was sent away by his father with the history of Decresian – the only thing that could be protected from the treachery of Villius Ren. The last document Samuel Ault would have been working on that night was the census."

"So, Tristan Ault has the census," said Oland.

"Perhaps," said Arthur.

"And where is he now?" said Oland. "Did anyone see him leave the castle?"

"Well," said Arthur, "there is a story that travelled the length and breadth of Decresian, but no one can trace it to one witness. A boy of his age was seen fleeing the castle the night the king was overthrown. The Craven Lodge had been searing the initials of Villius Ren on to the nape of his neck, as they did to most of us, but this boy struggled, disturbing a lantern and sending oil spilling on to his shoulders. The oil went up in flames against the branding iron and, as The Craven Lodge jumped back from them, this burning boy took the chance to escape. The last he was seen, the flames had died and he was riding off in a carriage filled with chests."

"Did Tristan Ault abandon King Micah?" said Oland.

"Oh, no," said Arthur. "There exists an archivist's oath, a simple two-line oath. It supersedes all other oaths, including that which binds them to their master. Archivists believe that they cannot participate in any event that is to be recorded in the history of the kingdom. They believe that to become a participant would be to curse the future. Their only task is to truthfully chronicle events, and to guard these chronicles fiercely. That is why, if young Tristan Ault decided to take the oath that night and become an official archivist, he would have been compelled to leave the castle."

"And has Villius Ren ever tried to find him?" said Oland. "I've heard no mention of his name in Castle Derrington. And Villius constantly mentions the names of his enemies."

Arthur shook his head. "To cover the theft of the archives and the census, Villius Ren put the story about many years ago that he slaughtered the entire Ault family."

"But why, now, would this archivist not come forward?" said Oland.

"As you know," said Arthur, "archivists lead solitary lives. Samuel Ault would have dealt only with King Micah and Queen Cossima; his father would have dealt only with the ruler of Dallen. Archivists are known for having pride in their work and passion for it, but they seek no public recognition. Their only desire is to faithfully honour the king, the kingdom and its history."

"But who does Villius Ren say that the burning boy is?" said Oland.

"Oh, you know Villius," said Arthur. "'It was a burning rat, a burning weasel…'"

Oland nodded.

"It's a string of interwoven lies," said Arthur. "If Villius Ren admits that someone took away the history of Decresian, it would be admitting that King Micah had foreseen Villius' treachery; otherwise, the documents – of which there were thousands – would never have been packed away in a carriage, ready to be carried away. That would have taken a long time."

"So, if I could find Tristan Ault, maybe I could find out who my parents are and where I come from," said Oland.

"I'm afraid that is an onerous ambition," said Arthur. "Time and again, archivists have witnessed the devastating consequences of misplaced trust, so they trust few."

"Is there anything else you know about him?" said Oland.

"I have told you everything I know," said Arthur. He paused. "The only other thing I can think of is that the boy you are looking for, is a man now, close to thirty. And he will bear the scars of a liquid burn on his neck and back."

As Oland drifted off to sleep, he was occupied by the thought that, along with restoring a kingdom, perhaps he could restore himself, and the cloak of his dark past could be shed. Yet it wasn't all dark: now that he knew the story of his past was fiction, his father did not have to be a bad man; he was free to imagine an alternative.

He did not have to change his vision of his mother; he had always seen her as brave and strong and loyal. He conjured up a beautiful woman with a kind face, perhaps with his green eyes, perhaps his long fair hair. The comfort of her imagined warmth finally brought him to sleep, and on a makeshift bed in a strange room behind a stinking barn, he had the longest uninterrupted sleep he could remember.

When Oland awoke, he was alone. In the dim candlelight, he saw food on the table. He left it untouched. He went to the small door, and tried to open it. It rattled. It had been latched from the outside. Oland shouted for Arthur. He didn't care who heard; he didn't even know who might be there to hear him.

As the hours passed, hunger was turning Oland's attention to food, but, as the scent of pine needles faded, and the odour of the barn began to seep under the door, he was happy to remain hungry. He lay down on the bed, staring up at the ceiling. He realised he had left his bag in the cart. He patted his pockets. The king's letter was still there. But he had no book to read, nothing to distract him. At the castle, Oland's days were filled with dozens of tasks that he had to carry out for The Craven Lodge, after no more than four hours' sleep. Because he had slept long and peacefully the previous night, he was wide awake. And he was still alone hours later when the candle finally burned out.

A shaft of light eventually appeared at the bottom of the door, and the latch rattled again. Arthur Rynish, with a lantern in his hand, walked in.

"I'm sorry, Oland," he said. "It took longer than I thought."

"Where did you go?" said Oland. "Why did you leave me here?"

"There was something not quite right on our journey here," said Arthur. "It unsettled me. And I needed to make sure that we were safe."

"You could have left me a note."

"What you are doing is dangerous, Oland. Were I to have left you a note, and you were discovered, a link would have been made between us. And that cannot happen. For you to carry out this quest, it must be alone."

"King Micah's letter said that I was to have a companion," said Oland.

"I don't think you should," said Arthur. "But that's just my opinion. What I will tell you is that you cannot be connected to my brother or me. You don't know the Rynishes, you've never heard of them – do you understand?"

Oland nodded. "Why?"

"Stop," said Arthur. "Stop asking questions. I'm telling you things for your own good, for the good of everyone. Say as little as possible, and you will remain in as little danger as possible."

"Danger?" said Oland. "Why? Do you think anyone else knows where I am going?"

"Just my brother and I," said Arthur. "And… had you considered… whoever left the letter for you?"

Oland shook his head. "I hadn't, no."

"Regardless," said Arthur, "you are in danger, at the very least for leaving Castle Derrington – for running out on Villius Ren and The Craven Lodge."

Oland did not say that it had been very clear that Villius Ren wanted him dead.

The following morning, when Oland awoke, Arthur Rynish was sitting in the chair opposite him.

"Your bag," he said, pointing to the floor. "You left your bag in the cart."

Oland sat up and pulled the bag towards him. He wondered where the little monkey was. Was he still nearby?

"Eat and let's go," said Arthur. "We have many miles to travel before we reach the Dallen border."

15

BLACK AGAINST THE RISING MOON

As the nights passed, Oland's hope waned. Arthur Rynish's often sullen mood brought no comfort. Oland welcomed the brief stops in the deserted houses and outbuildings, and wondered who were the strangers that had left food for the tailor – always for one, never for two. Oland knew that, despite emerging from the shadow of The Craven Lodge, for now, he was still invisible. And when, over a week into their journey, they reached the official crossing between Decresian and Dallen, his invisibility was all he thought of as he buried himself under the canvas.

There was just one route from Decresian into Dallen, and it was carved through the vast forest that separated them. A group of border guards was stationed in a small wooden building at the official border, but every traveller knew that there were guards hidden everywhere in the trees.

As the horse slowed, Arthur whispered to Oland. "It's Terrence Dyer from Garnish," he said. "A merchant of misery, the greyest of men. Hard to believe he's the son of Gaudy Dyer."

Arthur brought the horse and cart to a stop.

"The Tailor Rynish," said Terrence grimly. "Welcome, again, welcome."

"Thank you, Terrence," said Arthur. "How are you?"

"In the throes of life," said Terrence.

"How's your father?" said Arthur. "It must be thirteen years since he left Garnish."

"Was *forced* to leave," said Terrence. "And not one day has passed without lament. The mines in Galenore are no place for an old man. Word has come in recent days that the smelting fires on the hills won't take, so there is much concern about the supplies of galena. Without lead, many territories will suffer."

"Let's hope for a change in the winds," said Arthur.

Terrence looked up at the sky. "The clouds are moving in strange ways. They have darkened and thickened. Look where they have blurred in places."

"There's a madman in Derrington who says The Great Rains are upon us," said Arthur. There was a smile in his voice.

"Great Rains, indeed," said Terrence. "Though my father himself would have me believe it." He slapped the side of Arthur Rynish's cart. "You must be keen to carry on your journey, but, as I am bound by law, I must inspect your papers, and your load."

"Of course," said Arthur. Oland could hear the rustle of papers as they were passed between them.

"All is in order," said Terrence. "And now..."

Oland heard more footsteps, fast-moving, crunching across the ground towards them. He guessed that there were at least four men, and they quickly surrounded the cart.

"Your load," said one of the guards.

Oland could sense the cold air as Arthur reached around and pulled back the canvas that covered the cloths, and then him.

"Wools and linens," announced the guard.

"Look," said another guard. "In the corner of the cart. Something is moving."

Oland's heart started to pound.

"A rat!" said another guard.

"It's bigger than a rat!" said the first guard. Oland could feel someone rummaging above his head. "There's a sack here," said the guard. He cried out. "It's… it's a monkey!"

Oland felt a surge of panic.

"A monkey?" shouted Arthur. "In the folds of my fabric?"

Malben let out a pained cry. Oland could sense movement again, and the smell of warm fur. "My linens!" shouted Arthur. "My linens will be destroyed! Out! Out! Get out!"

"It's illegal to bring monkeys across the border," said another guard.

Arthur erupted. "The notion! Is it not clear I had no idea he was there? Take him! Kill him for all I care, just get him away from my work."

"He's running for the hut!" said one of the guards.

The guards' footsteps moved away in pursuit of the shrieking Malben. Oland felt a sharp tug at his leg.

"Go," said Arthur, yanking Oland towards him, grabbing him roughly under the arm as he staggered down from the back of the cart. He handed him a small roll of tarred canvas. "For shelter, now run. Run, Oland."

Oland quickly gained his footing, then locked eyes briefly with Arthur. In that one moment, he felt the full force of his encouragement. He whispered his thanks to him, then sprinted for the bushes. He knew he should keep moving, but instead, he waited, unable to leave without knowing that Arthur and Malben were safe. He crouched behind a tree and watched as one of the guards broke away from the others to return to Arthur.

"What is your business in Dallen?" he said.

"What *was* my business, you mean," said Arthur. "My business, now, is to return to Decresian; my fabric has been spoiled by a pest, and I have important work to take care of at Castle Derrington."

"Ah, yes," said the guard. "Of course. After all, you are the personal tailor to Villius Ren. His loyal and faithful servant..."

The tone in his voice made the hairs stand up on the back of Oland's neck and he knew he couldn't wait any longer. Reluctantly, he turned and jumped for the patches of moss that disappeared into the woods behind him, using them as silent stepping stones to a safer place. But it wasn't long before the terrain changed and his boots were cracking the twigs on the forest floor and the sound was like thunder. In his panic, Oland ran faster, fighting his aching muscles and the searing pain across his chest. It was only when his legs finally gave way, when he collapsed to the ground, that he had the chance to think.

He lay on his back, heaving for breath. Parched and

disorientated, he watched the dark clouds pass over the narrow branches at the trees' spindly tops. There was no way to tell whether he had crossed into Dallen, or taken a circular route back towards the border. He thought about Arthur. He hoped that he had been able to leave unharmed, and that Malben, the curious little monkey, was able to find his way back to wherever it was he came from.

Oland was now utterly alone. He began to wonder whether he should have asked the Rynishes about the Crest of Sabian, or told them about the man in black who had come to the castle to take him away. If he had told them more, maybe he would have more information to help him on his quest. His only solace was in discovering the existence of the census and in the hope that his parents' identity would be preserved in its pages. He vowed to find not only Chancey the Gold, but also Tristan Ault.

He got up and walked on, and, as the darkness descended and the trees grew denser, that was all he could hope for. As the temperature dropped, he walked faster to stay warm, but he knew that, before long, the darkness would be complete. He planned to take shelter for the night under a tree, but, up ahead, he saw the outline of a large building, and the tips of eight spires – black against the rising moon. As Oland fought his way through the weeds towards it, he soon saw that, though it bore traces of a grander past, it had long been abandoned.

He stopped at the bottom of the building's stone steps, as did the weeds, as if, like him, they were reluctant to get too close.

16

THE HONOURED SON

OLAND WALKED UP THE STEPS AND STOOD IN FRONT of the two tall black wooden doors. On the arch above them, three words were chiselled into the stone – two on top, one underneath. Most of their letters had been lost to weather and time. All that remained was an N in the first, an EW in the second and an S in the third. He walked back down and went over to the left-hand wing. Through two huge broken windows, he saw a vast, empty room with high ceilings and ornate floors. It appeared to have been blighted by fire.

Oland crossed the grass to the first room in the right-hand wing, a ghostly room, strewn with wrought-iron beds. Piecing this together with the letters he had read above the front door, he knew that he was at King Seward's Hospital. And he knew then that he was in Dallen.

Oland thought of peaceful King Seward, and how he had built the hospital with the best of intentions. Before the year was out, he was forced to close it. His supporter, the Dallen ruler, along with most of the Ault family and many of the doctors and nurses, were exiled to Decresian where King Seward was generous in providing them shelter and jobs. It was the succeeding ruler of Dallen who severed all ties between the territories and set up the patrolled border. Ever since, the passage of travellers from Decresian had been restricted. Only those deemed of benefit to Dallen were allowed entry. The Craven Lodge were strictly prohibited, on penalty of death. To compound the nations' tense relations, Villius Ren had managed to poach some of the Dallen men for his army.

To Oland's good fortune, King Seward's Hospital remained an oppressive spectre to the people of Dallen; he had shelter for the night, with little chance of being disturbed. As for The Craven Lodge, they were called craven for a reason. They would not dare to cross the border into Dallen. Oland knew the tortuous routes they took to bypass it on their journeys to other parts.

Oland pulled himself up on to the stone sill of the shattered window. He had never been in a hospital. The closest he had come to sickness was tending to The Craven Lodge when they had succumbed to the excesses of eating, drinking or fighting. He would rather have tended the plague-stricken. He jumped down into the fire-damaged room and, despite the easy passage of the outside air, was hit with the smell of rot, and rain, and animals. He knew that he was walking through the symbolic core of the Dallen uprising: the desecrated room that marked its darkest night, when a flaming torch was fired through the window and raged through a good king's dreams.

The interior was illuminated by the moon. Oland stood, mesmerised; through a huge crater in the stone floor grew a towering oak. Its boughs, rich with leaves, had thrust their way upward, wrapping around the banisters and breaking through the roof; outside the grounds were a wasteland, yet inside, where the dying had lain, was this extraordinary display of life.

Oland climbed to the first floor through the twisted limbs of the tree, grasping them for support as he jumped the remaining steps of the crumbling staircase. At the top, he walked around the balcony, opening and closing each of the doors that lined it, revealing rows of empty, dust-filled rooms. He made his way downstairs through a narrow back staircase, and found himself in the infirmary hall. At the end, Oland stopped at a large mahogany door. As he opened it, something scraped along the floor, revealing a quadrant of clean stone under a thick mantle of dust. He bent down and picked up a foot-long wooden plaque with holes in each corner, and rusted nails hanging from two of them. The plaque was missing the gold plate where a name would have been. Oland glanced around. He had no doubt that he was in a doctor's office. All around him, gauzy spider webs stretched from the ceiling to the desk, to the second door frame behind it, to the floor, to the chair, to the bed against the wall, to the glass bottles and candlesticks and weighing scales.

Oland broke through the webs and cleared a path to the desk, where he carefully laid the plaque, as if the mystery doctor would come back from the dead to reclaim it. But, when Oland looked at the shining doorknob of the door to the rear, he knew that whether or not ghosts existed, he was not the first visitor to King Seward's Hospital in the past one hundred years. Or, by all appearances, in the previous week. There were large boot prints on the floor behind the desk, and a square clearing where something had once stood, but had recently been removed.

Slowly, he opened the door into the adjoining room, a smaller empty space that had nothing but more footprints – a trail he had no desire to follow. He stayed where he was and, when he turned around, noticed a large map pinned to the wall. He felt a surge of hope as he approached it. It was a map of northern Envar. The territories were in pale green, their borders marked in broken lines of black.

The area shaded in brown marked the path of the plague. It ran from the east coast of Decresian, bypassing Dallen, then southwest into the neighbouring territory. Then it ran south through Galenore, and onwards to its furthest point: Gort, midwest Envar, where the scryer lived. No part of Gort had survived the plague. The bermids had built towering nests there, but they had been unable to breed. Their only legacy were the empty shells of the nests that still stood tall.

Oland ran his finger from the top left-hand corner of the map to the bottom right, naming each town and village out loud, hoping that he would say the word Sabian by the time he reached the bottom right. But there was no Sabian. Oland folded up the map, nevertheless, and put it into his pocket. At least he now knew where to find Dallen Falls, and so Chancey the Gold.

He walked into the hallway and passed a small ward of beds that stirred a longing for sleep. But, when he thought of the sick, the dying and the dead, a chill crawled over him and he moved on. When he reached the foyer, he saw, for the first time, an inscription carved into the stone wall, preserved for almost a century.

To the people of Decresian, of Dallen, and beyond.

That no sickness, no fear and no death shall divide us. Through suffering, may solace be found within these walls.

Through healing, joy.
Through open borders, may we find welcome.
Through compassion, peace.

In fondness and faith,
King Seward of Decresian
(in honour of his son, Prince Roxleigh)

Oland was struck by a great sadness. King Seward had lost his own beloved son to madness. What solace was there for him to find? Yet still he offered to others the chance to find theirs. Signed 'In fondness and faith', like his grandson, King Micah.

There were men who sought to enrich the lives of others,

and those who sought to enrich merely their own. Oland knew who he would rather be. He polished the inscription with his sleeve then made his way around the trunk of the towering oak, discovering a stairwell under which he could rest. But, as soon as he lay down, he felt wide awake to his quest, to his responsibility, and to whatever the next day held, and the day after, and the day after that.

Despite the bad blood he feared might be coursing through him, despite the fourteen-year shadow of The Craven Lodge, Oland Born vowed to become a man of whom King Micah could be proud. Like the oak tree above him, he had come to life in a dark, forbidding place, and battled now to reach the light.

17

OILSKINS

THE FOLLOWING MORNING, WITH LITTLE SLEEP BEHIND him, Oland woke to a space alight with morning sun. Specks of dust danced in the shafts. As he made his way into the main hall, birds of all colours were circling the top of the oak tree and through the roof the sky was a dense bright blue. As Oland turned away from the glare, through the silver spots that dotted his vision he saw a small shape moving between the lower branches. The monkey, Malben! Persistent Malben. And he was carrying Oland's bag on his back.

Oland laughed, and it sounded loud to him, perhaps because of the acoustics, perhaps because it was rare. Malben jumped on him. Oland took hold of the monkey and held him at arm's length. Malben tilted his head and Oland found himself doing the same. At close quarters, Oland could see that Malben's eyes, clear and shining, were not brown, but a dark shade of green. His golden grey fur stood in flyaway spikes, but was soft under Oland's hands. Malben held eye contact with him and Oland could swear his tiny mouth almost smiled.

"It's time to go," said Oland. "As it is time for me to stop talking to a monkey."

The journey to The Falls had to be taken on foot, so they cut through fields and skirted the edges of villages and towns. Oland had decided that the only thing he was prepared to steal was food, though Malben was the better thief. He mostly stayed hidden in Oland's bag and jumped to the trees whenever he could. Oland missed the comfort of the roof over his head every night. Now, every evening ended with a search for shelter, or the task of building it. He had been wakened by short torrential showers and followed by more of the grey thickening clouds that Terrence, the merchant of misery, had mentioned. As the days dragged on, Oland began to miss even the scant conversation with Arthur Rynish. Unlike food, company could not be stolen. At times, Oland talked to Malben. There were times when he felt he would talk back. They were the times Oland decided to rest.

*

A week passed before they reached Dallen Falls. Oland had imagined its full glory being unveiled in daylight. Instead, they arrived at nightfall, and he heard the thunderous water before he could see it. As his eyes adjusted to the gloom, he saw, against the dark grey of the sky, the giant black shadows of the cliffs, and the cascades that plunged down from them. Oland took out his tinderbox and, with a few strikes of steel against flint, the charcloth ignited and he could light the lantern that Malben had found discarded on their journey.

One house stood by The Falls, clearly built from the stones of the cliffs beside it – grey and gold and white. Oland hadn't expected such a humble home for a man the Scryer of Gort had predicted would destroy Villius Ren.

The garden was overgrown, not with weeds, but with plants and flowers in bursts of bright colours. It was a curious sight beside such treacherous waters. Malben took to the trees. Oland went to the red wooden door of the house and knocked. There was no answer. He walked around the side. He shone his lantern into the small windows, but the rooms were empty. Then he heard a rattling sound coming from the back of the house. He followed it around and discovered another red door with splintered edges, held to its frame by a thick knotted coil of rope that had been loosened by the force of the wind. Oland knew that his knife was not strong enough to cut through it.

He looked towards The Falls. Suddenly, one of the cascades seemed to stop flowing. Oland kept watching, and the water flowed again. For almost an hour, Oland watched as all the way along The Falls, parts of the cascades stopped, then restarted, like keys played on a piano. When the spectacle was over, he sat down on the front step of the house, and watched as Malben swung back and forth through the trees.

"You lead a simple life, Mr Malben," he said.

As he fell silent again, he saw that the cascade closest to them had stopped. Too curious to ignore it, he walked down. It was a breathtaking sight. Malben, seemingly terrified by the roaring torrents, let out a yelp and disappeared. Oland moved closer to the water, mesmerised by its force.

He heard the sound of cracking twigs not more than six feet away.

He waited. Again, he heard the sound.

"Is… somebody there?" said Oland.

"Yes." It was a girl's voice, coming from behind a tree, where a light was glowing.

"Who are you?" said Oland, walking towards the tree and

trying to look around it.

"Who are *you*?" said the girl. "*You're* the trespasser."

"My name is Oland Born. I'm from the Kingdom of Decresian."

"My name is Delphi."

"What are you doing here in the dark?" said Oland.

She stepped out from behind the tree holding a lantern. Her dark eyes shone in the flame. She had flawless skin and choppy coal-black hair to the nape of her neck. The girls in Derrington had hair to their waists, and wore wool dresses to their ankles. Delphi wore loose grey trousers, with a black leather belt wrapped twice around her narrow waist and a grey top that slid off one shoulder. Over that, she wore a long, hooded oilskin cape that fell to the ground and almost covered her black boots.

"You're the girl from the arena!" said Oland. "The girl who was thrown out."

"I am," said Delphi. "No girls allowed."

"So what were you doing there?" said Oland.

"What were *you* doing there?" said Delphi.

Oland realised that she had not recognised him, and for that he was grateful. When he thought of what he had done, he felt nothing but shame at the ease with which he had killed.

"I… well, I was there to… watch," he said.

"As was I," said Delphi. Her eyes seemed to grow even darker.

"So…" she said. "Why have you come to Dallen?"

Oland hesitated. "Do you know Chancey the Gold?"

"I know of him," said Delphi. "In that he lives at one side of The Falls. I live at the other."

"Have you seen him?" said Oland.

"Many times," said Delphi.

"Have you seen him today?" said Oland.

Delphi shook her head. "Why are you looking for him?"

"I'd rather not say," said Oland. "Where has he gone?"

"I don't know," said Delphi.

"Has he got any family?" said Oland.

She shook her head. "No. He has no one. He lives alone."

"I… hadn't expected this," said Oland. "I came here just assuming I would meet Chancey the Gold."

"What made you think that?" said Delphi. "And, more importantly, how much time do you think you have on the border guards?"

18

THE OTHER GUIDE

OLAND WENT VERY STILL. "WHAT DO YOU MEAN?" HE said.

"Don't worry," said Delphi. "You don't look like a killer. I don't think you're that kind of criminal."

"I'm not any kind of criminal," said Oland.

"Just a border-crossing one," said Delphi.

"I wouldn't have crossed the border if I wasn't looking for Chancey the Gold," said Oland.

"Well, he isn't here," said Delphi. "I could take you through The Falls, if you like. I'm the other guide."

"I haven't come here to cross The Falls," said Oland. "I just need to speak with Chancey the Gold."

"Why?" said Delphi.

"I can't say," said Oland.

"Was he expecting you?" said Delphi.

"No."

"So what are you going to do now?" said Delphi.

"I don't know," said Oland.

"You could wait here until he comes back, which could be days or weeks or months," said Delphi, "or, if it's an urgent matter, you could go and look for him."

"But where?" said Oland.

"That's for you to decide," said Delphi.

"But I couldn't possibly decide that, I don't even know him," said Oland. "I'll have to wait…"

"It could be a very long time," said Delphi. She looked at him. "And don't forget the border guards…"

Oland considered his meagre options, and his thoughts again returned to the border guards. There was no way he could go back the way he came. "Maybe I should cross The Falls…" he said.

Delphi nodded. "Are you a strong swimmer?"

"No," said Oland.

"Me neither," she said.

Oland stared at her. "If you can't swim, how can you guide people through?"

"If you consider it," said Delphi, "who is the better guide? The person who has nothing to lose by falling into the water? Or the one who will die?"

"Die?" said Oland. "What do you mean, die?"

Delphi's voice was solemn. "Yes," she said. "That's what the Scryer of Gort says."

Oland was surprised to once more hear the name of the legendary seer. "*You've* been to the Scryer of Gort?" he said.

Delphi shook her head. "No. My mother visited her just weeks before I was born. The scryer laid a hand on my mother's belly and said, 'That child must never swim or her death will be assured.'"

Oland frowned. "But—"

"I can wash, I can get a little wet, I just can't be submerged in water," said Delphi, "or I'll die."

"But, if you could swim," said Oland, "surely your death wouldn't be assured, surely you wouldn't drown."

Delphi was silent for some time. "Maybe the scryer meant that I would swim to my death. Even excellent swimmers can swim to their death. If I swam in the waters of The Straits, for example, it could be hard to fight the currents. I could be swept away and drown."

"But… if you were warned not to swim," said Oland, "why do you live here?"

"You ask so many questions," said Delphi. "Well, I have one for you: do you want me to guide you through The Falls?" Her dark eyes danced with challenge.

Oland looked out towards the cliffs. He had never seen anything quite so beautiful and foreboding, anything quite so… entrancing.

Delphi sat down and gestured for Oland to sit beside her. "Let me explain," she said.

Oland sat at what he guessed was a polite distance.

"There are three ridges hidden behind The Falls," said Delphi, pointing towards them, "the low ridge, the middle ridge and the high ridge. They are ledges that you have to walk along to get through The Falls. And I can guide you along whichever one you choose."

"But why would I need a guide for that?" said Oland.

"Why do you think you are the only person in Envar who might *not* need one?" said Delphi, a swift spark of anger flaring in her eyes. "Look at them – the cascades are powerful, and sometimes the ridge runs directly through the flow of the water. I have the ability to turn the water off, which gives you enough time to make it through."

"It was you who did that?" said Oland.

"Yes," said Delphi.

"But how can you turn off a waterfall?" said Oland.

"I make dams," said Delphi. "If you look closely, there are ten Falls. They each flow from a spring on the top of the cliff. I take rocks of different weights and sizes and put them in a metal cage that hangs above the source of each Fall. The door of the cage is attached to a cable secured by bolts into the rock face. When we are down on a ridge and I am guiding you through, I untie the cable. The cage door opens, the rocks fall down and stop the flow of water… but only for three minutes, before the force of the water blows the rocks free. They're short minutes." She smiled.

Oland narrowed his eyes. "Couldn't anyone work those cables?"

Delphi stood up and ran to the tree she had been hiding behind. She grabbed the lowest branch, swung up and over it, then climbed, in seconds, to the top. She shouted down to Oland. "Yes," she said, "if the person knew how to scale the cliff face, if he knew the weights of the rocks, the timing, if he knew how to release the cables and how to avoid the falling rocks, then yes." Delphi tilted her head. "Anyone could."

Oland felt even smaller than he must have looked to her.

"So which ridge do you choose?" said Delphi.

"I haven't made up my—"

"Which ridge?" shouted Delphi. She paused. "The low ridge is the widest, but there are many, many caves, and three bridges. And, at one point, you have to stand under a strong cascade for several minutes. There is a row of iron rings that you can hold on to, to make your way across. You'll be swept off your feet with the force, but if you just hold tight…" She shrugged. "And, at least, if you're thrown off, your fall into The Straits will be the shortest." She held her thumb and forefinger up to show a distance the size of a pea.

Oland looked at it, and looked at her. "Thrown off?" he said.

"The water flows so quickly," said Delphi. "You can only let go of those rings exactly when I tell you to. And I can only do that from the spring above it, because the rest of the rock at the low ridge was too soft to secure cables to. The choice was rings or cables. And the rings are more important. So I have to release the cage myself," said Delphi. "It's the only point in the journey that you will have to be alone."

Oland nodded.

"The high ridge is the narrowest of the three," said Delphi, "but it's rocky and unstable, and were you to fall, the drop into The Straits is obviously the greatest. The high ridge offers the least work for me, but it's treacherous for someone crossing for the first time."

"Because you've left it until last, I'm guessing that the middle ridge is the one you want me to take," said Oland.

"Well, it creates the most work for me," said Delphi, "but it is the most rewarding. We can go into the Chalice. It's a cave, shaped like a chalice. You enter at the stem. Where it forks, you have to decide which route to take. They're both dark, low caves that fill with water as you travel through. When you come out the other side, part of the ridge is gone, so you have to jump across it. If you clear it, you have a straight run ahead."

"If..." said Oland.

"The Chalice is a special place," said Delphi. "That's all I will say. And you can make a wish at the fork." She put one leg on either side of the branch, then clamped herself around it. "You'll see," she said. She swung upside down, rotated in a full circle, grabbed the branch in front with her hands and, instead of climbing down the trunk, dropped to the ground and landed, almost with a bounce.

She stood, looking at Oland, her oilskins flapping behind

her in the wind. Oland studied the small hooded girl with her incredible strength and her huge smile.

"The middle ridge," he said. "The middle."

19

TEN FALLS

ELPHI CLIMBED UP AND DOWN THE CLIFFS OF THE Falls, hooking and unhooking cables, shouting to Oland over the roaring water. He was amazed that someone so small and slight could control something so wild and powerful.

It took them an hour to reach the Chalice. Delphi had no signs of the tiredness that Oland felt dragging him down. She moved quickly ahead of him through the darkness.

"Slow down," said Oland. "I can barely see."

He heard her stop.

"Can you see anything?" she said.

"I only know that you've turned to face me because of your voice," said Oland.

"Hold out your arm," said Delphi. She turned back around

as he touched her shoulder and they walked like that to the fork.

"You can go left or right," said Delphi. "Each way has its own magic. And, depending on the wind outside and the flow of the water, one side will fill with water quicker."

"Let's go right," said Oland.

"Side by side this time," said Delphi. "Take my arm. And don't forget to make your wish." She waited. But to Oland, wishes were pointless. He had forever wished for a different life, and, though the king's letter had delivered him a route to finding that, it came with an overwhelming challenge. Weren't wishes to be granted simply? Unconditionally? And what about his wish for his mother to return to claim him, the wish he had made over and over ever since he had first heard Wickham's tale?

"Come with me," said Delphi when she thought Oland's wish had been made.

The right-hand cave was hot and damp. It was filled with the sounds of moving water – trickling, flowing or falling in drops from the roof. Before long, the water was rising above their ankles. Oland didn't want to think of it moving much higher. But, as they walked on, he could feel his knees getting wet. Every now and then, he felt something bump against his legs.

"Now," said Delphi. "Stop."

"Why?" said Oland.

"Just stop."

Oland did as she asked and could hear Delphi climbing up the wall of the cave and breaking something away from the ceiling.

"Catch," she said.

Oland heard a splash as whatever she had thrown landed in the water beside him. He grabbed it before it floated away and picked it up. It was a sphere and, though it wasn't heavy, he held it cupped between both hands. It was no more than four inches in diameter, and its surface felt waxy.

"What is it?" said Oland. "Are these leaves on the outside?"

"Yes," said Delphi. "Feel for the rough part at the top, stick your thumbs into it to crack it open, then peel the leaves apart." There was excitement in her voice.

Oland did as she said, and immediately the space around them was illuminated. "What *is* this?" he said. He stared down at an extraordinary teal-coloured flower that had blossomed from the chalice-shaped cocoon of the leaves. Nestled at the centre of the petals was a tiny golden orb, the source of the incredible light.

"It's a camberlily," said Delphi. "Isn't it beautiful?"

Oland looked up. The small green spheres covered the entire roof of the cave.

"This is where they grow," she said. She plucked another one down and opened it, her eyes dancing in the light. "It's the seed that glows," she said.

But Oland was no longer looking at her. He was staring down, swaying back and forth, clutching at his chest. More camberlilies floated past him. He could see the reflection of his panicked face in the rising water. He desperately gasped for breath as he was overwhelmed by a series of terrifying, unsettling sensations, and his mind filled with a tumult of dark images he could barely absorb. All he knew was that he had to leave. He dropped the flower and began to run towards the exit of the cave.

"Oland," said Delphi, jumping down from the wall, splashing into the water, then following him. "Take the flower with you. Wait! You need light."

"No!" said Oland. "Leave it there! No!"

He splashed through the cave, drenching his clothes, banging off the walls as he staggered through.

Delphi dropped the camberlily, and caught up with him at the point where the tunnel was in darkness again. His chest was heaving.

"Are you all right?" said Delphi.

"I… I just need to get out of here," said Oland.

"Let me guide you," said Delphi, taking his arm. They moved as they had before, but this time in silence.

As they walked out of the cave on to the ridge, the unopened orbs washed over the edge and a high wind whipped around them. The harsh sunlight held no warmth, and their wet clothes turned ice-cold.

"Keep tight against the wall," said Delphi.

"I know," said Oland without looking at her. He pressed his back against the wall, and they both moved sideways along the ridge, their eyes narrowed against the intensity of the daylight. Before long, they came to an eight-foot gap in the ledge.

Oland turned to Delphi. "I didn't think it would be…" He struggled to keep his voice even. "I didn't think I'd have to jump this far…"

"You don't," said Delphi.

"But—"

"Tell me," said Delphi, "what happened to you in the cave?"

Oland was struck by the disturbing thought that he would never understand it, that the explanation was buried somewhere inside him – somewhere beyond his reach.

"I don't know," he said.

"But… did the flowers make you ill? Did the light?"

"I said, I don't know," said Oland.

She held her breath. Eventually, she spoke. "So, are you ready to go across?"

Delphi turned to the wall behind her and pulled a hanging vine from it.

"I'm ready," said Oland. He took a step forward.

"No," said Delphi, "Before you jump, you have to…"

Oland bent his knees.

"No," said Delphi. She tried to grab his arm, but missed. "Wait!"

But Oland had already started to jump. Delphi slid down the vine and caught him by his tunic, swinging him on to the ledge below. He landed hard, his head spinning, his neck raw from where his tunic had been pulled tight. Delphi landed lightly beside him.

"I was trying to tell you about the vines," she said. "Don't ever do that again. When I said, 'Before you jump,' I meant it."

Oland closed his eyes. His cheeks burned.

"Stay there until you catch your breath," said Delphi. "Don't move an inch."

After a long silence, Oland spoke. "I'm sorry for falling," he said.

"You should be sorry for jumping," said Delphi.

20

HOME

OLAND COULD SENSE DELPHI WATCHING HIM AS THEY sat on the ledge. He kept staring ahead.

"Do you wish you hadn't come here?" said Delphi. "Do you wish you were home?"

Oland laughed. "Home?" he said. "No." He paused.

"Are things that bad in Decresian?" said Delphi.

"Where I live, yes," said Oland.

Then, despite himself, he began to tell this stranger about Villius Ren, The Craven Lodge and his life as their servant in Castle Derrington. But, as the story continued, he realised what an unpleasant one it was, and he drifted into silence.

"I can't imagine how you could live with them," said Delphi. "From what I saw at The Games."

Oland thought of how strange it was to have someone willing

to listen to him. Conversation was rare in Castle Derrington. The talk of The Craven Lodge was restricted to the fulfilment of their basic needs: eating, drinking and whatever else it was that put smiles on their ugly faces. During their banquets, it was worse, the same grim stories going round and round like water on a mill wheel.

Oland told Delphi the story of The Mican Games, and how the Scryer of Gort had told Villius Ren that his downfall would be at the hands of Chancey the Gold.

"Chancey the Gold is to defeat the ruler of Decresian?" said Delphi. "How come I have never heard anything about this?"

"Why would he tell you?" said Oland.

"Just… because we are neighbours." She stood up suddenly. "Let's go," she said. There was an edge to her voice.

Oland followed Delphi along the low ridge. It was indeed the widest, and much easier to advance along than the others. But, up ahead, he could see the thundering cascade with the row of rings behind it, the one that Delphi warned him he would have to stand under alone, the one that would sweep him off his feet.

They moved as quickly as they could along the damp rocks.

"Now," said Delphi, raising her voice over the water. "Can you see the rings?"

"Yes," said Oland. They were spaced out in front of him across the rock face. "But how am I meant to—"

"Whatever way suits you," said Delphi. "You just need to use them to get across. Hold your breath, stay as close to the rocks as you can and I'll work quickly. You can hold on to them with two hands if you like… and move across that way… or you can hold on to one with each hand, and swing yourself across…"

Oland stared.

"You can do it," said Delphi. She started her climb up the cliff face.

Oland waited, then reached out and, with two hands, grabbed the first ring. He hung there as the intense force of the water battered his body back and forth against the cliff. Not for the first time, he was grateful for the heavy loads he was made to carry at the castle, for the stable work, for the scrubbing and scouring, for the running up and down stairs and across courtyards. His limbs were strong, and he knew they could carry him far. But he was soon dizzy and disorientated. Suddenly, he realised he had forgotten to breathe properly. His head began to loll forward, and it felt like his arms were beginning to tear away from their sockets.

He found strength from somewhere, momentary strength,

and moved blindly from one ring to the next. Mercifully, the water stopped. He took in a huge breath and made his way across to the other side. Before long, Delphi climbed down beside him.

"Quickly," she said, pushing him along to the next cave as the dam she had made at the top exploded, and the cascade restarted behind them.

21

THE THOUSANDTH SOUL

OLAND AND DELPHI SAT DOWN AT THE BACK OF THE cave to rest.

"There is one thing I've heard about Decresian," said Delphi, "about the screaming. Who screams there at night, Oland?"

"The souls of Castle Derrington," he said, and he told her about the failed experiments of Malcolm and Benjamin Evolent and the nine hundred and ninety-nine unsettled souls buried in the grounds.

"That is horrendous," said Delphi.

"And the Evolents are still alive," said Oland. "They're somewhere out there, walking the same land as us, breathing the same air." He paused. "And so is the Thousandth Soul."

"There is a *thousandth* soul?" said Delphi.

"In Decresian, we believe in the Fortune of Tens," said Oland.

"And, apparently, one thousand turned out to be fortunate for the Evolents: it was the one animal-human experiment that was a complete success. The creature, whoever or whatever it is, survived... but escaped. It's known as the Thousandth Soul, and the Evolents are desperate to find him, so that they can work out how their experiment was so successful. They want to recreate that success and use it for all kinds of evil."

"What will they do when they find it?" said Delphi.

Oland sliced his hand across his throat.

Delphi was silenced by the horror.

"Malcolm Evolent, Benjamin Evolent, Villius Ren..." said Oland. "They no longer speak. Not for years. Even the Evolent brothers have gone their separate ways. No one knows why."

As Oland spoke, a rope dropped down at the mouth of the cave and whipped from side to side, scouring the cliff face, sending stones pouring down.

Delphi reached out to Oland. "Quick," she said, grabbing his arm, dragging him backwards.

A man dropped to the ledge outside the cave. A second man followed. They were black silhouettes against the light. But Oland recognised their form and, when they spoke, their voices. It was Wickham and Croft.

"They're from The Craven Lodge," whispered Oland. "They must have come through Galenore."

Delphi put her finger to her lips and they retreated into the corner.

"This is like something out of one of your stories, Wickham!" said Croft. He was shouting over the water, the sound echoing through the cave. "What a surprise!" he went on. "What a dramatic turn of events! A midnight escape! Apparently, the boy was enthralled! What Oland Born did in that arena!" He shook his head.

Oland had never heard Croft so animated.

"You can see how it could all go horribly wrong," said Croft. "I'll say one thing—"

"You've been saying many things," said Wickham, his voice weary.

"I'll say one thing," Croft continued, "I have never seen Villius so wild with grief. Absolutely wild."

Oland's eyes went wide. *Wild with grief?* He waited for Wickham to confirm what Croft had said. Villius was wild with grief? Surely not.

"Well, I've done what he asked," said Wickham. "Chancey the Gold is dead.'

Oland went rigid. Beside him, he could feel Delphi do the same. He turned to her and, in that instant, her dark eyes had filled with tears. Why tears? Did she know her distant neighbour?

"We have sent word back to Villius about Chancey the Gold's death," said Wickham. "He may or may not seek mystic reassurance, but I don't think there is anything more for us to find here. It is time to go."

"There's more to this," said Croft. "Villius is just not saying."

"Whatever it is," said Wickham, "I don't expect that you would be Villius' first choice of confidant."

Croft snorted. "Well, if he told *you* anything, you'd only put it in a story and tell the whole world—"

"That's not quite how it works," said Wickham. "But maybe, to a man like you—"

"Too busy trying to be the next Archivist Whatever-his-name-is, that's your problem," said Croft. "Sitting about all day, making up stories…"

"Ault was his name," said Wickham. "Samuel Ault. He wrote facts. Anyone can write down facts. King Micah did this, King Micah did that. I have an imagination. I see things that no one else can see."

"That's how Roxleigh ended up being carted away," said Croft.

His laugh was a carnival of grunts.

Wickham stood with his arms on his narrow hips, swallowed into the heavy fabric of his long cloak. He looked child-sized beside Croft.

"It's rumoured," said Croft, "that the Ault son, Tristan, might be out there somewhere. You'd be no match for him. He's no pale little fellow like you, that's what I heard," said Croft. "He's built like a warrior, has the dark skin, the dark hair…"

"You sound enchanted," said Wickham.

Croft spun towards him, his fists raised. Wickham pushed him hard in the chest. The breath rushed from Croft's lungs. In a short terrible moment, both men teetered on the ledge. Croft fell first, but Wickham followed, their cries dissolving into the roar of the churning water below.

22

GRIEF

ELPHI SAT, SHAKING, IN THE CORNER OF THE CAVE. Oland walked over to the ledge and looked out over the cliffs. He saw tiny black dots disappearing into the raging white foam.

He felt a twinge of sadness at the death of Wickham. He remembered sitting beside him at the kitchen table, and Wickham running his finger under the words of a picture book called *The Boy Who Had Never Enough*. Even though Oland had been just four at the time, he remembered thinking that the book would be about him, because he had nothing. He was disappointed to find out that the book was, in fact, about a boy who had everything and who still wasn't happy. And Oland had found the story fascinating… and inexplicable.

Now it was Villius Ren's grief that was inexplicable. Every

encounter he had with his master was a deeply unpleasant one, even the ones that outwardly could appear civil. Was it the absence of a slave that troubled him? The idea that, until he trained another in his peculiar ways, he would be forced to fend for himself?

Lost in his confusion, it took some time for Oland to realise that Delphi was crying.

"Delphi," he said.

She didn't reply.

"Delphi," said Oland. "Are you all right? I—"

She bowed her head. "That's where you live?" she said.

"Pardon?" said Oland.

"They're the people you live with?" she said, looking up.

Oland frowned. "The people I was forced to serve," he said.

"I don't know how you could have done that," said Delphi.

"I am nothing like them," said Oland, struggling to stay calm.

Delphi paused before she spoke. "How do you know that?"

"Do you think I'm like them?" said Oland. "Have I given you some reason to think that I'm lying or treacherous or capable of—"

"No," said Delphi. "I'm sorry. I..." She started to sob. She wiped her eyes. "I know... I know... I don't even know you.

But… I have no one now, and—"

"What do you mean you have no one?" said Oland.

"Chancey the Gold," said Delphi. "He's… he's my father. He made me swear not to tell anyone." She turned and looked directly into Oland's eyes, and he saw, again, how black they were. But, when she spoke, her voice was soft. "Please don't ever tell anyone. For years, I thought he was simply my guardian. He told me that when I was a baby I was left at the entrance to The Straits, and that he took me in."

"And your mother?" said Oland.

"He has never spoken about her, only to tell me that I was so very loved," said Delphi. "There was so much pain in his eyes when he spoke of her…"

"How did he look after you alone?" said Oland.

"He brought in a wonderful couple: a groundsman and his wife…" Tears welled in Delphi's eyes. "Then one day, when I was nine, he told me that the couple who looked after me had had to go away. I cried for weeks. He said that there was no one else who could look after me."

Their childhoods were so different, thought Oland, but sorrow marked them both. He told Delphi about his own parents and how he hoped to find their names in the Decresian census.

He stopped short when he realised how insensitive he was being.

Delphi let out a heartbreaking sob. Oland turned away. It struck him that, on the rare times he had cried in his fourteen years, he had never felt the comfort of being taken into someone's arms, nor had he ever heard a quiet word of reassurance or understanding. He got up and walked over to the mouth of the cave, crossing his arms and staring out into the dark. The water of The Straits was sparkling. He glanced back. Delphi was still sobbing.

After some time had passed, her crying quietened.

"What you said before," said Delphi. "About me living so close to The Straits if it was so dangerous... my father was very careful, that was why. He was always warning me to be safe and he had marked out – with ribbons on the trees – how far I could go from the house if I was alone. Every year, I was measured for new oilskins to protect me from the water. He knew the currents of The Straits, so that's the answer to why I was allowed to live here: I was never in danger."

She burst into tears.

Oland let her cry, helpless in the face of her anguish. Delphi was alone, suffering the loss of the only person she had in the world, someone she loved. Oland knew that that was worse than his loss: a love conjured only from a story, or a vision of the future.

The following morning, Oland was wakened by the sense of light around him. He slowly opened his eyes and could see Delphi curled in the corner, still sleeping. Oland moved out of the cave and looked down on to The Straits, where a shoal of fish had turned the water to amber, its light radiating up the cliffs.

"Delphi," said Oland. "Delphi, wake up."

Delphi opened her eyes, and blinked several times, looking at him as if she were seeing him for the first time. "Oh," she said. "Yes. Hello."

"Look," said Oland. "Look at the fish."

Delphi joined him. "They're like amber waves."

Suddenly, Malben appeared from above, jumping down into Delphi's arms, sliding back the hood of her cape, rubbing her dark hair. She screamed.

Oland laughed. "It's only Malben. Malben, this is Delphi."

"Is he yours?" said Delphi, trying to pull Malben off her.

Oland shrugged. "I don't think he's anyone's. But he travelled with me. He… stowed away."

"A stowaway," said Delphi, narrowing her eyes at Malben. He

laid his head against her neck and pulled himself closer. Delphi laughed.

"He disappears, then seems to find me, wherever I am," said Oland.

"I've never met a monkey before," said Delphi, "but there's something about you that I like, Malben." She ran her finger down his nose.

"I thought I'd seen the last of you," said Oland, reaching out to stroke Malben's head. "Now, get down."

"Don't listen to him," said Delphi.

Oland looked back at the network of caves hidden behind the raging waters of The Falls, then out again over The Straits. He glanced at the girl beside him who dared to navigate it all, who could perhaps die if she put a foot wrong, yet whom he stood safely beside.

King Micah's words echoed again: 'Be wise in your choice of companion.'"

"Delphi…" said Oland.

Delphi turned to him. "Yes?"

He frowned. "I suppose we need to get to the end of The Falls, so that I can be on my way."

"Yes," said Delphi. She gripped Malben a little tighter, then led Oland along the ledge the short distance to the end of The Falls.

They climbed down the rocks, and stood looking at the fish moving through the water. Minutes passed in silence. The temperature had dropped, and the sky was beginning to darken.

"Those clouds are appearing more and more," said Delphi.

And Oland felt, again, the spectre of The Great Rains.

He strapped his bag on to his back. Malben jumped from Delphi's arms and slid into it.

A fleeting look of sadness crossed Delphi's face.

"So you're coming with me, Malben…" said Oland.

Delphi smiled. "Looks like he is." She paused. "Well, good luck on your journey," she said. "I have no doubt you will find what you're looking for."

"Thank you," said Oland. "Thank you for guiding me safely across. And good luck to you…"

He walked away. Before long, he glanced back, and could see Delphi making her way towards the amber waters of The Straits. He studied her, the tilt of her head, her strange, choppy black hair. He watched as she began to run towards the cliffs. She looked tiny and alone against them. Oland knew that there was no one waiting for her at the other side now, no one there to make sure she was safe. Just as she had made sure that he was.

"Delphi!" he shouted over the roaring water. "Delphi!"

Delphi stopped and turned around. She waved to him. The kindness and openness of the gesture blindsided him.

If Chancey the Gold was dead, Oland decided that he would honour him by honouring the daughter the great champion had so fiercely protected.

Oland waved Delphi towards him. She ran, her strides light and long, her cape flying up behind her. She stopped in front of him, smiling. He was drawn again to her eyes, dark and bright at the same time.

23

ABANDONED

The journey from The Falls to Galenore was across beautiful countryside, made richer by the waters of The Straits and the River Caminus it flowed into. But all the river's tributaries branched off before they reached Galenore, as though they knew the grey town had nothing to offer them.

"The deaths of Wickham and Croft will not sit well with Villius Ren," said Oland.

"Were they close?" said Delphi.

Oland laughed. "Like drogues…" It felt suddenly wrong to joke. The line had come so quickly, the story was so fresh in his mind.

Delphi shuddered. "When I was a child, they were the terror that woke me in the night."

"That woke every child," said Oland. He held his hands to his throat and quoted from *The Ancient Myths of Envar*, "'his final indignity was to be drenched in vile secretions vomited from the pit of the beast's insides; secretions that would quickly dissolve its prey, bones and all, without trace.'"

Delphi laughed. "I can see how they would remind you of The Craven Lodge," she said.

"Though even a drogue wouldn't kill its own," said Oland.

"Oh, yes, I remember that from the stories," said Delphi. "How honourable."

"The problem for Villius Ren losing two of his men is not about sorrow, it's about superstition: his faith in the Fortune of Tens is sacrosanct. He has nine men under him and, when he discovers that he has lost two, he'll be thrown into turmoil."

As he spoke, he felt that strange sadness at Wickham's death tugging at him and he hated himself for it. In some strange way, Oland could relate to Wickham. And how grim it was to relate to a liar and a killer.

Oland thought again of his unknown parents, and Wickham's words: *"Anyone can write down facts... I have an imagination."*

He wondered: was Wickham's creation better or worse than the reality of his birth?

Oland watched Delphi running up ahead, holding Malben in the air and rubbing his belly with her head. He couldn't understand her good spirits. Was she in denial about her father's death? She had been so protected from the world all her life that she had no idea how dark a place it could be. And Oland had no intention of showing her what her father had been loving enough to hide.

24

A MILLION STEPS

CARVED HIGH INTO A HORSESHOE OF MOUNTAINS ABOVE the galena mines, Galenore was the town of a million steps. It had winding streets, crooked turns, slopes and drops and alleyways, as if the buildings themselves wanted to hide from each other. Each one blended into the next, as grey as the lead buried deep beneath them. It was the only good to come from the plague – as the bermid ants destroyed the land, they uncovered the vast stores of galena that lay underneath. It was as if they took away one livelihood and left behind another. But it was not the livelihood the people of Galenore wanted. It had gone from being a prosperous and fertile land to the bleak, grey mining town it now was. The people of Galenore, who had so loved to work outdoors, were forced underground, and they were heartbroken.

Oland and Delphi arrived at dusk, when the air smelled of roasting meat, boiling vegetables, ale and cider. The streets were crowded with young miners, celebrating a break from work because of the high winds. Their older colleagues looked more troubled.

Malben uncurled from his sleep in Oland's bag and jumped into Delphi's arms, burying his head in her neck.

"Hello, Mr Malben," she said. He pawed her face gently and she laughed.

"That monkey is very fond of you," said Oland.

"And I of him," said Delphi. She let Malben down and he bounded across the street to climb up a rare bloom of ivy on one of the tavern walls.

"Delphi," said Oland, "I think we need to find out more about what happened to your father. It can't be a coincidence that he was killed at the same time I was sent to find the Crest of Sabian. It must have been to do with the downfall of Villius Ren. Maybe your father was looking for the Crest too. Maybe his visits to Galenore were part of this."

Delphi shrugged.

"Where do you think he would have gone if he were here?" said Oland.

Delphi stared down at the cobbles. "Well... just... around."
She shrugged.

"Around where?" said Oland.

Delphi didn't reply.

"Did he meet people? Did he eat here?" said Oland. "Did he go to the market?"

"I... think so," said Delphi. "I think he did all that. It's the evening, so the markets will be closed..."

"Where else might he have gone?" said Oland. "To a tavern?"

Delphi nodded. "Maybe..."

"Is everything all right?" said Oland. "There seems to be something bothering you."

Delphi stared at the ground. "It's just... truthfully, I haven't been to Galenore for years. I took ill here when I was eight, and there were no doctors, and my father had to take me home in a panic. I was terrified. So... he never really brought me back here since. That was six years ago."

"Then you're the same age as me," said Oland. "I doubt it was Galenore itself that made you ill, so you have nothing to worry about now."

Delphi nodded. "Thank you." She pointed across the street. "Maybe we could ask there."

The sign propped in the smoky window of The Lead Glass tavern read NO CHILDREN AFTER ANY O'CLOCK. Oland pointed to the side of the building. They walked around and saw an open back door. A large red-faced boy, no older than twelve, was gripping a huge saucepan, pouring water from a boiled ham down the sink. Oland and Delphi glanced at each other, feeling the hunger of two days without food. Malben climbed down the wall beside them and slipped into Oland's bag.

Oland and Delphi watched the kitchen boy move back to the oven, where he pulled out a tray of meat pies. Just then, the swinging doors beside the boy burst open and a man who looked like an older, slighter version of the young cook slapped some orders on the countertop. As the doors swung back and forth, Oland and Delphi saw the swollen purple faces of four men sitting at the bar, one of them hanging from a half-empty bottle of whiskey, his face smiling and sleepy.

"We need to speak to him," said Oland, pointing.

"Who is he?" said Delphi.

"The man most likely to answer a question," said Oland. "And least likely to remember who asked it."

Delphi smiled. "In that case, I have a plan."

*

Five minutes later, Oland watched from the tavern doorway as Delphi burst through, looking wildly around her.

"No children!" shouted the owner.

Delphi turned to him, her face earnest. "I have found something," she said, "that belongs to someone else. And it is someone very important."

"I said 'no children'." The owner grabbed a glass from under the counter and started to polish it with a dirty cloth.

Delphi walked up to the bar. "If I do not return this," she said, "I will be in so much trouble."

Out in the kitchen, the boy let out a cry and smoke billowed into the bar through the swinging doors. The owner ran into the kitchen, batting at the smoke with his cloth. Delphi turned quickly to the man with the whiskey.

"Sir," she said, holding up a gold coin, "for whiskey. But answer me first – did you see a man here recently, tall, broad-shouldered, flaxen-haired, sun-darkened skin…"

The man took moments to focus on her, his eyes shining like the gold in front of them. "No," he said, frowning.

"Please," said Delphi. "I need to find out if he was here in Galenore this week."

"I… whiskey," said the man.

"Please," said Delphi. "Please listen to me. I have to know if anyone has seen him."

She held the gold coin in front of the man's face, and made him focus on it. "Have you heard of a man called Chancey the Gold?"

The other men at the bar had started to lean towards her.

"What are you looking for, miss?" said one of them. He had parched curls of wiry brown hair around his ears, but nowhere else. His nose was narrow and sharp, his eyes yellow and watery.

Delphi glanced towards the kitchen and back to all the men. "I'm looking for news of a man called Chancey the Gold... the swimmer... the champion swimmer... do you know him? Did you by any chance see him?"

Two of them nodded, but it was a vague nod, born of the promise of gold.

"This is useless," said Delphi.

The kitchen doors began to open. As Oland saw Delphi turn to run out the front door, he did the same. She was right behind him, but there was someone right behind her too. A man, no taller than her, who had been sitting at a table by the entrance, had grabbed her by the wrist and was half lifting her into the cold air. Delphi cried out.

"Get out," snarled the man, pushing the door open and swinging her through it.

25

PINFROCK

OLAND STEPPED FORWARD, PREPARED BUT UNWILLING to attack. But the man's snarls appeared to be just a show for the tavern drinkers. For he didn't throw Delphi to the ground. Instead, he came outside with her and let her down gently. He was dressed in a flat grey woollen cap and a deep-green woollen coat to his knees. He wore a pair of metal-rimmed glasses, his white eyebrows arching high above their frames. He had sparkling green eyes and deep frown lines carved, like the number eleven, into the space above his nose.

"What are you doing?" said Oland.

"I'm sorry," said the man, addressing Delphi. "I was alarmed by what you said inside."

Delphi stared at him. "Why? Who are you?"

He lowered his voice. "Because you're not the first person to have asked for Chancey the Gold this week. And the men who were looking for him did not strike me as men a young girl like you would like to meet on a dark night."

"Please tell us who you are," said Oland.

"My name is Pinfrock. I work here in Galenore." He pointed down a side street. He glanced left and right. "Two men came here, it must have been four days ago… and the difference is that they found the man Chancey the Gold."

"What did these men look like?" said Delphi.

Pinfrock described Wickham and Croft.

"I'm warning you," said Pinfrock, "because… I know that they were Villius Ren's men… The Craven Lodge have been to Galenore before."

"Do you know why Chancey the Gold was here?" said Delphi.

"I expect you've heard that the smelting fires won't hold because of the high winds," said Pinfrock. "So the mines aren't operating. Many men have gone to the hills to try to fix this – to try to build shelters around the fires." As he spoke, he held his hat on his head with one hand. "They need to get the mines started up again."

"And you think Chancey the Gold came here to help them?" said Delphi.

"Certainly some of the older miners, ones who had followed Chancey the Gold in his competition days, mentioned that he had been there."

"Do you know where the men took Chancey?" said Delphi.

"I know merely the rumour," said Pinfrock. "These men were overheard saying that they would take him to Dallen Falls," he said. "But he resisted fiercely."

"And this was four days ago," said Delphi.

"Yes."

Suddenly, from around the corner the young cook appeared.

"Run!" shouted Oland, scrambling for Delphi's arm. "Run!"

They ran, the cook struggling behind them.

Delphi looked back at Pinfrock, as Oland swept her up in his panic. "Thank you, Mr Pinfrock," she said. "Thank you!" As she glanced to the right she was relieved to see Malen running across the rooftop, alongside them.

Oland and Delphi stopped when there was no more commotion behind them, and retreated into a quiet alley.

"What was that all about?" said Delphi.

"I employed Malben as a distraction and fetcher of food," said Oland. "Sadly, he appears empty of paw."

"Never mind," said Delphi, rubbing Malben's head. "Never mind."

"There is something about that Pinfrock," said Oland. "Something that I can't quite put my finger on."

"Something bad?" said Delphi.

"Something familiar," said Oland.

Delphi's thoughts had strayed. "If Chancey the Gold was resisting going back to The Falls, it was because of me... it was because he thought I would be there."

"That doesn't mean it was your fault," said Oland. "And Chancey the Gold made his own choice to come to Galenore in the first place, remember."

Delphi paused. "The thing is," she said, "My father was a very kind man, but I still don't know why he would have come to Galenore to help with the mines."

"This is us taking the word of a man we don't even know," said Oland. He paused. "Pinfrock!" he said suddenly. He jumped up, opened his bag and pulled out *The Ancient Myths of Envar*. Along with his play, *The Banon Servant,* it had been soaked on his journey through The Falls, but had since dried. The pages were now yellowed, stiff and rippled, but the ink was pristine. And on the back cover, clearly visible, was the printer's stamp: a small circle surrounding the words: 'Printer: Pinfrock of Galenore'.

Oland's heart pounded; if Pinfrock printed *The Ancient Myths of Envar*, it meant that he had worked for King Micah. It was an official publication of the Kingdom of Decresian, and it was printed during King Micah's reign. It also meant that, more than likely, Pinfrock was around in the time of Archivist Samuel Ault, and may even have met him or printed his writings. Oland wondered if Pinfrock could even know Tristan Ault, the possible guardian of the Decresian census and so the key to the identity of his parents.

"We need to go back and speak to Pinfrock," said Oland. "He pointed down a side street when he mentioned he worked here. It's the best place to start."

26

THE SAME HAND

THE SIGN ABOVE THE DOOR READ **PINFROCK & SONS: STATIONERS & PRINTERS**. The shop was in darkness. Oland and Delphi looked in at the mahogany cabinets that lined the walls on each side. They were mostly glass-fronted and filled with stacks of papers of different sizes. Where there was space on the walls, framed illustrations and print samples had been mounted.

Two glass-topped counters stood on the floor opposite each other. The one on the right held rows of quills, the one on the left, stamps and coloured waxes.

Candlelight glowed from the archway into a back room.

"That must be where the printing press is," said Oland. He turned to Malben. "You wait here." He gestured to a ledge above them. "It's a small shop. If we bring a monkey with us…"

"We might look roxley," said Delphi.

Oland smiled at her using a Decresian word. Malben tilted his head. Oland lifted him up towards the ledge and he jumped the rest of the way. Oland pointed a finger at him to stay.

Oland and Delphi knocked on the door. They could see the silhouette of Pinfrock in the archway as he leaned back into view from the desk he was standing at. He squinted towards them, then turned back to his task. They knocked again. Pinfrock approached the door slowly, but, when he realised who was outside, he hurried them in.

"I am nervous for you," he said to Delphi. "Why are you still here?"

Oland had taken *The Ancient Myths of Envar* from his bag. He held it out and pointed to the printer's stamp on the back.

"Ah," said Pinfrock.

"Did you know Archivist Samuel Ault?" said Oland.

Pinfrock stared at him. "Why do you ask?" he said.

"I used to live in Castle Derrington in Decresian," said Oland. "I am familiar with so many of the writings of the kingdom, most of which are written by hand. But of the pieces that are printed, yours is the only printer's name stamped on the back."

There was pride in Pinfrock's eyes, but he didn't reply.

"I believe that that means,' said Oland, 'if you worked for him, that you were loyal to King Micah... and that you might have known his archivist."

Pinfrock nodded. "I was loyal to King Micah, as were my ancestors to his."

"And... did you know Samuel Ault?" said Oland.

"Why do you ask?" said Pinfrock.

Oland pounced with his next question. "Or do you know his son, Tristan Ault?"

Pinfrock's gaze flickered. He looked nervously about him. "Please," he said, "why are you asking?"

"For many reasons," said Oland.

"To save the Kingdom of Decresian from Villius Ren!" said Delphi.

Oland frowned at her. He would have gone as far as telling Pinfrock about the census, about his own private quest, but he had no desire to tell him of the king's letter.

"Show him the king's letter!" said Delphi.

"What king's letter?" said Pinfrock.

"Show him!" said Delphi. "It will prove that you are telling the truth."

With reluctance, Oland took out the letter from King Micah.

"I'm sorry, but I'd rather not show you all of this, but I will show the first part and the signature, so you will know that I speak the truth."

He folded the letter and showed Pinfrock what he had promised.

"The writing…" said Pinfrock, frowning. He closed his eyes. When he opened them and turned to Oland, they were filled with resolve. "Follow me," he said.

He guided them into his workshop.

"You cannot breathe a word of what I am about to tell you," he said. "Not to anyone, not ever."

Oland and Delphi nodded.

"One morning, fourteen years ago, a letter was left at my door that said that, on the last Friday of every month, I was to deliver a bottle of ink and a ream of paper to the town of Hartpence in Oxlaven. It's close to the border with Gort. I was to place the ink and paper in a metal box under a statue of a woman who stands there. She's called the Spinster Caudelie Reilly.

"I was paid handsomely in advance for the ink, the paper, my time and my silence. Double my time. Who else would use so much paper and ink, other than an archivist? I know all my customers from near and far, and no one comes close to buying what this man does."

Oland thought about how strange it would be to follow instructions from someone you had never met and to do so every month for fourteen years. Then he realised that he was doing exactly that – but the person who had written *his* letter was dead, which made it even stranger.

"And you don't know who left you this letter?" said Delphi.

"No," said Pinfrock. "But… I am somewhat confused. If yours was written by King Micah, then how can this be?"

He pulled open a drawer and, from inside it, slid back a piece of wood and the envelope that was hidden behind it.

"I've kept the letter to this day," said Pinfrock. "I don't know why. And I don't know if I will ever be given instructions on when to end these deliveries…"

He slid out his letter. It was barely intact. He laid it flat on the desk in front of him.

Oland and Delphi leaned in.

Oland's face immediately darkened. "Both letters are written by the same hand. My letter can't be from King Micah. I've been tricked."

27

PROPHECY

ELPHI LOOKED AT PINFROCK'S LETTER. THEN SHE looked at Oland's.

"Yes, they're written by the same hand," she said. "So perhaps King Micah wrote both of them?"

"He couldn't have," said Oland. "He died that night. He couldn't have been collecting papers and ink after that."

Pinfrock shook his head. "This is an archivist's hand, but a youthful one. I believe that this, indeed, was written by the younger Ault. Tristan, did you say?"

"Yes," said Oland.

"If, as you say, the archivist died on the night the king was overthrown, then clearly his son did indeed decide to follow on the tradition. He could be doing that very well. I always remembered, from my dealings with King Micah, that his archivist was even more secretive than most. I would imagine that, if he had lost his life in the course of his duty, any son of his would take great pains to remain in hiding."

Delphi nodded. "Yes!" she said. "That makes sense, Oland."

Oland looked unconvinced. "Or it could all be meaningless. This entire..." He trailed off. He leaned into Delphi. "Let's talk about this later," he whispered.

They turned towards Pinfrock. There was a worried look in his eyes.

"Thank you," said Delphi.

"Yes," said Oland, "thank you for showing us your letter, and for telling us what you know."

Pinfrock handed him his letter and Oland put it into his bag.

Delphi pointed to some of the ornate writings that were framed on the walls.

"What beautiful coloured ink," she said.

"And they are no more," said Pinfrock. "It's all black ink now. My coloured inkwell has dried up, so to speak. Or has been misappropriated, ironically, by darker forces. Only one man is brave enough to work in colour."

Oland and Delphi had no idea what he meant, and Pinfrock

didn't elaborate. When he spoke again, it was clear that the conversation was at an end.

"Please, be careful," he said. "Mind how you go." He bowed.

Oland and Delphi ran down the cobbled streets and turned a corner into a deserted square with a fountain at its centre. A low stone wall encircled it. The night was filled with the winding-down sounds of late-night revellers.

"Stop running," said Delphi. "Where are we going?"

"I don't know," said Oland.

"Wait," said Delphi. "Wait. Listen to me."

He stopped. They sat down on the wall.

"So my letter was not from King Micah after all," said Oland.

"It had to have been!" said Delphi. "I have no doubt they were his words, dictated to someone loyal and trusted—"

"Did you know that Villius Ren used to be loyal and trusted?" said Oland. "Villius Ren was our age when King Micah took pity on him and rescued him from an orphanage. King Micah saved him from a terrible life, and gave him a privileged one. And still he was a traitor. We know very little about Tristan Ault and—"

"We know that his father was killed by Villius Ren," said Delphi. "And that Tristan likely took the king's records away…"

"We only know that because that's what we've been told," said Oland. "I'm tired of being told things, and having to act on them. The letter was the one thing that was different. It was in writing. It was fact... or so I thought."

"Oland, you've come this far," said Delphi. "Whoever left that letter for you believed in it and believed in you... can you not at least accept the possibility that the archivist wrote this on behalf of the king?"

Oland looked away. "I have no choice."

Malben suddenly landed in front of him.

"Malben," said Oland. "Did we forget about you?"

"Never!" said Delphi.

Malben climbed up the centre of the fountain.

"Oland," said Delphi, "the last Friday of the month is three days from now. Why don't we go to the border between Gort and Oxlaven and wait by the statue that Pinfrock told us about? If what he is saying is true, the archivist's son will come for his paper and ink. At least, if he does, we will know. He is the best person to tell us about King Micah. And perhaps about your parents. If you think about it, Oland, he is the only person we know of who can help..."

Oland paused. "If he wants to," he said eventually. But he was doubtful. His thoughts were tainted by the fear that he would never find the crest, by the inhospitable places they had stopped, by the obstacles that had already appeared in their path. There was so much to discover, and now the one person who could enlighten them was a man who had successfully hidden away from the world for fourteen years... yet what had they to lose by looking for him?

"All right," said Oland. "We'll go."

Suddenly, Malben jumped from the top of the fountain towards them. He landed hard on Delphi's shoulder and sent her toppling into the water. "No!" she cried as she went under. Oland jumped into the fountain. Malben cried out in fright, then darted away. Oland grabbed Delphi, turning her face up and pulling her out of the water. Her cape slipped from her shoulders. Malben reappeared, jumping up and down wildly, his small face panicked. Then he disappeared once more.

Delphi sat on the edge of the fountain, her head bent. "Thank you," she said to Oland. "Thank you." She took hold of her cape to pull it back on, but, before she had the chance, Oland saw three deep scars like slashes across each of her shoulder blades. He wondered what could have happened to her.

"You saved my life," she said.

"It was only a fountain," said Oland.

"Remember the prophecy," said Delphi.

"I never thought you were going to drown," said Oland.

"And yet still you came to my rescue."

"Delphi, you're perfectly fine – you're not even coughing or spitting up water," said Oland, "so perhaps this water prophecy is all nonsense."

"There is a way of finding out," said Delphi. "If we're going to the border with Gort, and we have three days to make it there, then we have time to visit the scryer."

Oland stood up. "Oh, no," he said. "No. We're not going to the scryer. No."

"Why not?" said Delphi. "She might even be able to tell us where the Crest of Sabian is. Does she not tell people their future fortune or failings?"

"You don't even believe that," said Oland. "You just want to know about the water prophecy."

"You'd want to know about your own death if someone warned your mother so fiercely," said Delphi. "I haven't asked for anything on this journey. Please just let me do this. I left the beautiful Falls," she said, "to come to miserable Galenore. There is nothing of beauty here, nothing. I feel so sorry for Galenorans.

I'm so lucky to live where I live. And yet the one part of the Falls that I can't truly enjoy is the water – the very essence of that beauty. You can't tell me that you don't believe in the Scryer of Gort, and at the same time stop me from going underwater," said Delphi.

"I think you can go underwater all you like," said Oland.

Delphi gripped the edge of the wall and leaned backward into the fountain, raising her legs straight up in front of her. Oland quickly put a hand behind her back and pushed her upright.

"Don't," he said. "Don't…"

Delphi turned to him, her eyes bright, water dripping from the ends of her choppy hair.

"We shall visit the scryer," said Oland. "Just to put an end to your taunts."

28

THE BRIDGE

IT TOOK A DAY AND A HALF FOR OLAND AND DELPHI TO reach the southwest border between Galenore and Gort – a dividing line between a barren grey landscape and one of barren bronze. It had scarcely rained in Gort in one hundred years and, as they walked, its dry hills seemed endless. The journey passed quietly. Malben had not returned since fleeing in fright at the fountain. Oland and Delphi appreciated even more the distraction he had brought to their journey.

No one could visit the scryer without bringing her water. Oland and Delphi had filled a flask from the fountain in Galenore. It was said that some merchants would bring the scryer gallons, as though the greater the volume, the brighter their future.

"What will happen here, do you think?" said Delphi. "Apart

from the water, is there something we have to do when we meet her? Bow or avert our eyes or—"

Oland stopped dead. "Gold!" he said. "I forgot about the gold."

"What gold?" said Delphi.

"Have you heard of the Bastions?" said Oland. "They guard the scryer. In Bastion culture, it's considered a great honour. They have little to say; their only concern is the fee: gold coins that they make into rings and chains, ornaments and charms." He let out a breath. "But I've got no gold to give them, so they won't let us in."

Delphi laughed. "But I'm a daughter of Gold." She rattled coins in her pocket. "Because of my father's name and reputation, no one paid him any less than in gold coins for his guide work. You can't give silver to a man called Chancey the Gold."

"I can't expect you to pay," said Oland.

"I'm the one who wanted to come here," said Delphi. "I'm sure my father would understand why." She walked on, "How do we know where to go?" she said.

Oland pointed to the hill in front of them. "We scale that and we see."

They stood and watched Gort spread out before them. There

was a huge valley ahead and, spanning it, a narrow rope bridge. Dark figures were gathered at either side.

"And there we have the Bastions," said Oland.

"You never said anything about a bridge," said Delphi.

"Because I didn't know there would be one," said Oland.

Four Bastions guarded the entrance to the bridge. They were ragged and rough, heavy-browed and heavy-limbed. Their leathery skin, their wild curly hair, the very air around them was dark, yet the Bastions were blinding. They did more than just make rings and chains from their gold. It appeared that their entire bodies were covered with belts, cuffs, chokers, earrings, nose rings, toe rings and anklets. Even the buckles of their sandals were made of gold. Yet not one piece was well-crafted – the shapes had no symmetry; the surfaces were pocked or uneven. Their inspiration had clearly come from the mottled landscape around them.

Oland and Delphi stood before them.

"We would like to cross to see the Scryer of Gort," said Oland.

The Bastions turned to each other and laughed, low and spiteful. One of them, dressed in a tunic studded with gold nuggets, opened his fat palm.

"Make shine," he growled, pointing into the sky. "Like sun." The other Bastions laughed.

Delphi reached into her pocket and pulled out two gold coins. A wide, crooked smile spread slowly across the Bastion's face as he closed his palm around them and shoved them into his pocket.

"What a shame – too young to see scryer," he said.

"That is ridiculous," said Delphi.

"Too many years ahead of you," said the Bastion. "Too many years."

"I have no fears for my future," said Delphi.

"Don't care," said the Bastion. "No entry. Rules."

"Rules that say you can chain up an old woman and take money for her gifts?" said Delphi.

"We've come all the way from…" said Oland.

The Bastion shook his head. "Spare you the sight. Ugly lady. One eye. Only one. Go. Go home."

"We're going nowhere until we speak with her," said Oland, stepping forward.

"No more sleep for you," said the Bastion. "Ugly lady." He gestured towards the other side.

"I don't know what sleep is," said Oland.

"Ah – Decresian." said the Bastion. "Souls screaming all night."

"Yes," said Oland.

"Long way," said the Bastion.

"That's what I said," said Oland. "So please allow us to pass."

"Your king… dead king. Good man," said the Bastion.

The other Bastions nodded. "Yes. Hate good men. All of us."

They laughed and took a step closer to Oland and Delphi. Delphi put her hand in her pocket and threw three gold coins on to the ground behind him.

"Sorry," she said. "I'm so tired, I dropped them."

The Bastion bent down, struggling to pick them up.

When he stood again, Delphi took a step towards him so she was six inches from his face. She reached out her arm.

Oland felt the hairs on the back of his neck stand up as he watched Delphi's delicate hand moving towards the face of this huge glinting monster.

Delphi didn't take her eyes off the Bastion. He stared at her, motionless. She ran her fingertips gently across his heavily jutting brow, and the row of tiny gold rings that hung over his right eye.

"Beautiful," she said. "Beautiful." She did it again. "Musical."

Oland was amazed at how she could get so close to such a man.

The Bastion slowly pulled his eyes away from her. He glanced at his friends, a fleeting, troubled glance. Then his stare again met Delphi's.

"Let us through," she said. It was as if she knew that her words would work, that there would be no question he would let them in.

It seemed that she was right.

"Warning," said the Bastion, holding up a finger covered from top to bottom with gold bands. "You see scryer after – when eyes close at night. You see her, eyes open, morning." He nodded. "Haunt you."

He stepped back and let them walk across the swaying bridge to where a row of Bastions sat, like rotten teeth, at the entrance to the scryer's cave.

29

RUMOURS AND FATHOMING

THE SCRYER'S CAVE WAS DOMED AND CLOSE TO FIFTEEN feet at its highest point. The surface was the same inside as out: amber-coloured and pitted. It was, in fact, a dried-out bermid's nest.

Delphi gasped when she saw the scryer, lying on the floor like a cowering dog, scarcely lit by the weak flame of her candle. Oland stood, silent and still. As his eyes adjusted to the dim light, her form became clearer to him. The scryer's head spun towards them, and they both recoiled.

As the Bastion had told them, the scryer had just one eye. In the empty socket was a puckered white stellate scar. Her eyebrows were wild and wispy. She was deathly grey and as thin as the winter branches of a silver birch tree. Every bone pushed against the skin that covered it. Her long, matted grey hair pooled out on to the floor around her. Her dress was a loose grey sheath over her skeletal frame. Frayed ropes shackled her at the neck, waist and ankles, stretching taut to dull metal rings in the wall.

Delphi took a step towards her. The scryer reached out her wizened arms.

"Let me see you," she said. Her voice had a dark lilt. Her breath seared the frigid air, turning it white.

Delphi's heart pounded. She walked forward and crouched down in front of her. Without opening her eye, the scryer pressed her palms against Delphi's face, then traced her bony thumbs over it.

She shook her head from side to side. "Beautiful girl," she said. "Beautiful and hiding."

Without warning, one of the Bastions charged into the cave, grabbing Oland by the arm and pulling him towards the entrance.

"One each time, witch!" said the Bastion to the scryer, using his free hand to lash his whip at her. Delphi swiftly raised her arm to protect the old woman, and the whip slapped against her oilskins. The Bastion tried again, and again Delphi blocked it.

The Bastion growled, then threw Oland from the cave, where he landed at the feet of the other men. They glanced down at him, then reverted to flaunting their gold. Oland sat back against the wall and kept his eyes on the ground, unwilling to indulge their vanity.

Before long, Delphi reappeared, blinking, into the light. Oland had no time to talk to her as the Bastions beckoned him to the entrance. Delphi's face was impossible to read as she passed him their flask of water.

Inside the cave, Oland handed the scryer the flask. He noticed that her hand was shaking. She poured some water into a stone bowl on the floor. She took the candle in her hand, and held it over it. She inhaled deeply and seemed to go into a trance. Eventually, she opened her eye and stared into the bowl. She screamed.

The anguished, tormented wail was like nothing Oland had ever heard, and it tore through him. As he staggered backward, the scryer's cries got louder. He ran from the cave out to Delphi.

A Bastion leaned back into the cave, pulled a whip from his belt and struck out. The scryer screamed again as the leather finally struck her.

Delphi stepped forward. "She's an old woman," she shouted. "How can you treat her this way? You are nothing but users. The only way you know how to make a living is by exploiting someone else's talents. And she gets nothing in return. Nothing!"

The Bastion laughed loud and low. "She gone soon. Next one come soon."

"Next what?" said Delphi.

"Next one. Two eyes. Maybe. See more." The Bastions all laughed.

"The next what?" said Delphi. "The next scryer? What are you talking about?"

"Come on, Delphi," said Oland. "We should leave." He hadn't realised how desperate he had been to hear something positive until the scryer had screamed at him. What had he done? He believed that he had been polite and respectful. Yet the scryer had howled as if he had drenched her in burning oil. He had never wanted to come here. He had thought, at worst, he would hear some nonsense. But the worst turned out to be the deep, unsettling feeling that was clawing at him.

He and Delphi crossed the bridge to the other side.

One of the Bastions stationed there pointed at them and laughed. "White face. Haunted now. Told you."

"Look at you all," said Delphi. "You have no gifts of your own. You rely on the scryer's. You are nothing—"

The Bastion stopped laughing. "Bad girl." He pushed his face into Delphi's, but she pushed too, and she seemed to push harder. She struck his forehead and he staggered backward. He howled, and, when he raised his head up again, blood was streaming down his eye, and three of the rings had been ripped from his brow.

Oland and Delphi ran.

Weighed down by their gold, the Bastions struggled to keep pace. They quickly fell away, returning to the bridge and the only job for which they were equipped. Oland and Delphi stopped once they were out of sight.

"What did you do to him?" said Oland.

"I... I don't really know," said Delphi. "He was coming too close to me, so I struck first and, before I realised it, he was bleeding."

"But how did you rip off the rings?" said Oland. "And what did you do to him when we arrived? He just let us cross."

"I did nothing," said Delphi. "I just stared at him. The rest was the gold."

"He looked stricken," said Oland.

Delphi laughed. "Good. What did you do to the scryer?"

"Nothing either," said Oland.

"You must have asked her something she didn't like," said Delphi.

"I didn't ask her anything," said Oland. "She may have sensed that I was doubtful…"

"You could have pretended you believed in her," said Delphi.

"Wouldn't she have known?" said Oland.

"Lucky I went first," said Delphi. "Otherwise we'd know nothing."

"And what do you know?" said Oland.

"What does it matter, if you won't believe in it?" said Delphi.

Oland smiled.

"She said she did meet my mother when she was pregnant with me," said Delphi. "She didn't say what she said to her, but then suddenly she said she could smell fresh water. She started to rock back and forth. Then she said she could see me in the ocean, but her face went dark and she said that I was never, ever to enter water, that I would draw something terrible upon myself."

"What did she mean 'something terrible'?" said Oland.

"That's all she said," said Delphi. "I asked her was my mother still alive and she didn't quite answer. It was all so strange…"

"Did you ask her where Sabian is?" said Oland. "Did you say anything that might help us? Did you say anything about the archivist?"

"She didn't mention the archivist," said Delphi. "She told me about King Micah and Queen Cossima. She said that they were very much in love and that, on the day they were married, King Micah brought her in a white carriage to Garnish and presented her with her very own private woods, filled with exotic trees and flowers and plants.'

"And?" said Oland.

"The next thing she said was that we would find someone 'by willow, by lamplights'."

"What does that mean?" said Oland. "Who?"

"I don't know," said Delphi. "I'm simply telling you what she said."

"None of it makes sense," said Oland. "She could say anything."

"How about this, then: she told me very clearly that, despite what everyone thinks, she did *not* tell Villius Ren that he would be defeated by Chancey the Gold."

"What?" said Oland.

"She said that she told him no such thing. She called it 'rumours and fathoming and guessing and lying'."

"But—"

"She told him that his downfall would be at the hands of 'a champion'."

"Chancey *was* a champion," said Oland.

"Villius no longer has to fear Chancey the Gold."

"I'm sorry," said Oland. "I… I wasn't thinking."

With Chancey the Gold dead, Oland thought of the only other man he knew to have been a champion of The Games: Jerome Rynish. Was he likely to bring about the downfall of Villius Ren? Oland thought about what Jerome had said: "It is more likely that… Villius Ren himself was to slay the beasts, then on to solo glory he would go." If Villius Ren crowned himself champion at The Games, then, in his mind, he would be reassured that there would be no new champion to defeat him. When he couldn't do that, he finally had his men kill Chancey the Gold. With Jerome Rynish beaten down, Villius Ren could finally be reassured. Then Oland thought of the flicker of fear in Villius Ren's eyes when he had stood before him at the arena. The crowd had chanted the worst possible word for Villius Ren to hear.

Champion.

30

ONE MAN DOWN

I AM NO CHAMPION, THOUGHT OLAND. BUT THEN VILLIUS Ren was a desperate, fearful man. Would he be determined to kill anyone with even a tenuous link to victory?

"Delphi," said Oland. "You're not safe with me."

"What?" said Delphi. "Of course I'm safe with you."

"There are things I haven't told you…" said Oland.

"What things?" said Delphi.

"Things," said Oland.

"That's very revealing," said Delphi. "I *am* safe with you. I *feel* safe."

Oland shook his head. "Please, you have to listen to me—"

"I don't," said Delphi.

Oland stopped. "That's true," he said. "You don't." But how could she believe in him? He had never been so unsure of himself.

But, though he had only just met this curious girl, he knew that he did not want them to part.

"I'm coming with you," said Delphi, as if she had read his mind. "All the way to Sabian."

Oland smiled, but his first thought was that they would never make it that far.

The sun beat down on Oland and Delphi as they walked. Oland's throat felt like the blade of a sword, and his pale skin burned.

"Delphi, I saw the back door of Chancey the Gold's house," said Oland.

Delphi tried to hide her faltering steps.

"I saw the bolt," said Oland. "It had been bolted from the outside. Someone broke the bolt from the inside. And now it's tied closed with rope…"

Delphi spun around. "What are you saying?"

"I saw you use the ropes at The Falls," said Oland. "I saw the knots you made. They were the same. You… you had been locked in the house, hadn't you? And you broke out, didn't you?"

"I've already told you how protective my father was," said Delphi. "He did his best, but…" She shrugged. "It was only in the past year that he has left me alone when he went travelling.

And, even though he wasn't there, I always obeyed his rules. He trusted me. And he was right to. I stayed safe, I didn't go far. But... over the past year, I started to get angry that he could go wherever he liked, and I had to stay at home. So, I started to go out to The Falls when he was gone, and it was then that I taught myself everything." She paused. "Just before The Games, some people from Galenore were coming through The Straits and were speaking of them. They had a friend who was coming from the Dallen border to meet them, and I stowed away in their cart. My father worked out where I had gone, and he followed me. He found me in Derrington after I was thrown out of the arena. He was furious. I tried to talk to him about how exciting The Games had been. I even told him about you, but he was still so angry. So... before he went away this time, he locked me in. Just that one time. He said that he would only be gone for a day. And that's why I was so worried. Because he wouldn't have locked the door if he thought he would be gone for longer. He wouldn't. I think he was scared for some reason..."

For a moment, they stood in silence.

"So you knew it was me at The Games?" said Oland.

Delphi nodded. "Yes," she said. "I just didn't want you

to think that I was only helping you across The Falls because you were a hero."

Oland's face burned. "I'm not a hero," he said. He quickly moved on. "So you've only been navigating The Falls for a year? And, even then, only at the times when Chancey the Gold was gone?"

Delphi smiled. "Yes."

"You could have killed us both," said Oland.

"But I didn't!" said Delphi.

"No wonder your father didn't trust you," said Oland. He smiled. "But Jerome Rynish did say that there would have to be a very special reason for Chancey the Gold to return to Decresian."

Delphi smiled back.

"Delphi!" said Oland. "Returning! I just realised, and I don't mean to sound harsh, but Wickham and Croft have rid Villius of his greatest threat, sadly, your father. But who warned Villius about Chancey the Gold in the first place? The Scryer of Gort. Knowing Villius, he will return to the scryer to be reassured. That was why, at The Falls, Wickham said that he might seek 'mystic reassurance'. He was talking about the scryer. Villius will want confirmation from her that his downfall will no longer occur. An open future is a terrifying thing to Villius Ren."

"What shall we do?" said Delphi.

"The death of your father is a recent one," said Oland. "Wickham and Croft sent word to Villius. I know how his mind works. He won't bide his time. So we wait, and I have no doubt he will appear."

"Wait where?" said Delphi.

"I'd like my curiosity satisfied on something," said Oland. He pointed towards a cave close by. "Look at that etching on the stone – does it not look like an eye?"

"It does," said Delphi.

"Would that not be the perfect sign to mark a scryer's cave?" said Oland. "I had always read that she lived in a cave. I think they moved her across to the other side of the valley, and that's why I had never read of the bridge or the strange place she now lives. I think she's now in one of the discarded bermid nests."

They went inside the cave. A small candle flickered.

"There," said Oland, "the metal chains that once shackled the scryer. They're rusted and worn. This can't have been used in a long time."

"Then, if Villius Ren were to return," said Delphi, "unless he knew differently, this is where he would come."

Oland nodded. They walked deeper into the cave and came across a row of beds against the wall, their covers disturbed, clothes strewn on top. There were various gold-embellished tunics hanging on pegs, and each bed had a locked box beside it.

Delphi's eyes went wide. "The Bastions' quarters," she said.

They heard a cough and followed the sound further into the cave. A cold breeze blew through. "There must be another entrance," said Oland. They moved forward and soon found themselves staring through an opening at the Bastion by the bridge whose rings Delphi had ripped off. He was alone now, sitting on a rock, clutching a bloodied handkerchief in one hand.

"Do the Bastions allow visitors at night?" whispered Delphi.

"No," said Oland, "but that will be of no concern to Villius Ren. And, remember, night time is when he roams."

Oland and Delphi waited in the darkness, until eventually, from the shadows, a dark form rode towards them. Despite the hat the man wore, despite the collar he had pulled up to meet it, he was unmistakable. It was Villius Ren. He dismounted his horse and tied it to a post beside the now-sleeping Bastion, who jolted awake.

Villius approached him and took a small pouch out of his pocket. He held out a palm glowing with coins.

"Who are you?" said the Bastion.

"My name is Villius—"

"You legend here," said the Bastion. "You smash scryer's cave, you break shackles." He shook his head. "Never come here again. Forbidden for you."

"Things have changed," said Villius.

"Yes," said the Bastion. "We have bridge now. Men like you go raging when bad future, we need way to kill you. We have rope bridge we shake, shake, shake, until unhappy men fall. Insane men…"

"You don't understand," said Villius. "I'm not insane. That was a long time ago… before you were even born."

"We all know your name from history," said the Bastion. "Go away."

Villius tried to push past him. "She will see me," he said. "I will give you all the gold you need."

"No end to gold I need," said the Bastion. "I need river of gold you no have. Sea of gold."

"How about I take you away from here?" said Villius. "To a place that is filled with gold? A castle in Decresian where everything is made of gold!"

Oland shook his head at Delphi to let her know this was a lie.

"Let me explain," said Villius. "I am the ruler of Decresian. And I am one man down. My men and I could make great use of you. If you agree to join us, you will be rewarded in many ways."

"Gold first, see scryer next," said the Bastion.

Villius Ren gazed across the valley. "Scryer first, then the gold."

"Only me here, this side," said the Bastion. "I die, you killed by Bastions other side. Shake, shake, shake. Show me gold castle, show me gold for all Bastions, we come back here, you see new future. May be bright, may be dark. But you like dark..." He paused. "For other people."

The Bastion smiled, and his small round eyes turned to ugly curved slits.

"You will be well met with my men," said Villius.

There was an eerie fixedness to the Bastion's smile. It stayed on his face as he took the coins.

"Meet me in The Lead Glass tavern in Galenore at midday tomorrow," said Villius. He nodded at the Bastion, climbed up on his horse and rode away.

Oland turned to Delphi. "It looks like there is a new member of The Craven Lodge..." He paused. "What I don't understand is why Villius said he's only one man down, when he lost both Wickham and Croft."

"It sounds like Villius Ren thinks and behaves in inexplicable ways," said Delphi.

"At least we know he is bound for Galenore," said Oland. "Which means we can get to the border with Oxlaven without fear of crossing his path."

When they arrived at the border, Oland and Delphi saw that it was nothing like the dense woods between Dallen and Decresian: here, the trees had worn, skinny trunks, surrounded by bushes at their base. At the top, the leaves were rich.

"Can you hear that?" said Delphi.

"No," said Oland.

Delphi ran through the trees. "It's water," she shouted back to him.

Oland followed her through to where a narrow stream flowed down into a small clear pool. Delphi was on her knees at the edge, drinking from her cupped hands. She made room for Oland.

"We need to find the statue," said Oland when he had finished drinking. "Then wait for the archivist to collect Pinfrock's paper and ink."

Delphi stood up and followed him through the trees.

A small shape came flying towards them.

"Malben!" said Oland. "Where did you come from? How do you always find us?"

"I think he smells us," said Delphi.

"Is that it, Malben?" said Oland.

"He follows the smell of roses," said Delphi.

They laughed.

"Look," said Delphi, "the statue!" She walked over to a giant intricate stone carving of a woman with round and beautiful curves, and a wide smiling mouth. The inscription underneath read 'The Spinster Caudelie Reilly, Beloved Mother to Men and Orphans'. She had been dead twenty-nine years.

"'To Men and Orphans'... isn't that strange?" said Oland. He thought again of his parents, and the census, and he felt a surge of hope at the prospect of meeting the archivist.

Nightfall came. Oland and Delphi hid for hours in the undergrowth, waiting for the arrival of the archivist. Malben curled into Delphi's arms again, and she quietly sang. Oland was the first to fall asleep.

Well into the night, in the distance, a horse and cart appeared, a lantern hooked on at the right-hand side at the front. Oland and Delphi sat up. The horse was weaving left and right, the cart behind it bouncing wildly on the stony ground. One of the wheels struck a huge rock, and the cart flipped into the air on one side, crashing back down again. Hundreds of white pages burst into the sky, and began floating down behind it. Oland and Delphi looked at each other, alarmed. They stood up, mesmerised by the speed. On it came, and the closer it got and the sharper the panic in the horse's eyes, the clearer it became that there was no rider to guide him.

"It's not going to stop," said Oland.

He grabbed Delphi's arm and pulled her back behind the trees. The horse and cart shot past them, the cart swinging wide, slamming into the monument, shattering the wooden bars that hitched it to the horse. Caudelie Reilly still stood tall. The horse, a simple brown packhorse, stumbled on the hard ground, but righted himself. He paused, his chest heaving. Then he turned and galloped back to where he had come from.

Oland and Delphi approached the cart. Pinfrock was in it.

Pinfrock was dead.

31

ALL THAT IS BURIED

F ROM HIS GRUESOME PALLOR AND THE DARK, DRIED STAINS of blood on his wool coat, it was clear that Pinfrock had been dead for some time.

"I think he was dead before his journey ever started," said Oland.

Delphi was crying. Even Malben looked troubled, and had retreated into a tree, wrapping his arms around himself.

Oland reached down to Pinfrock's body.

"Don't!" said Delphi.

"He's got some paper in his hand," said Oland. He turned to Delphi.

"Don't touch him!" she said.

But Oland pulled the paper free. It was the corner of a white page and, in the moonlight, he could make out the tiniest speck of teal ink.

"This was the archivist's letter," said Oland.

They stared at each other.

"It seems that this is what happens if you betray an Archivist Ault," said Oland.

With that, all thoughts of finding the census and finding his parents were gone.

"How could the archivist have known that Pinfrock had shown anyone the letter?" said Delphi.

"He must have been closer than we thought," said Oland.

"Which means, at least, he is still alive," said Delphi.

"And murderous," said Oland. "Someone who has put a dead body in our path to deter us."

"We can't stay here," said Delphi.

"Pinfrock was a good man," said Oland. "We shouldn't leave his body out here. He has a family."

"But what can we do?" said Delphi. "We can't bring him back to Galenore."

"We can do something," said Oland. "We have to."

Delphi shook her head.

"Let's rest for the night," said Oland. "We can go back to the stream, build a fire. We can decide in the morning the best thing to do."

"But… what if the archivist comes here," said Delphi, "and wants to find out who Pinfrock was telling tales to?"

"The archivist has no need to come here," said Oland. "He has sent his message."

They stood in silence for some time.

"Can we trust the word of a murderer?" said Oland eventually.

"But he has said nothing to us," said Delphi.

"Nothing but the words he wrote in a letter claiming to be signed by King Micah…" said Oland.

They sat, without speaking, by the fire, the stream the only sound in the forest. Delphi held Malben in her arms. Oland studied the map of Envar he had taken from King Seward's Hospital, hoping that there was something in it that would guide them closer to Sabian.

"There is nothing here," said Oland, "nothing that is telling me where to go, nothing that is giving me a sense of where Sabian is."

"I wanted to say I'm sorry about the census," said Delphi. "But I'm sure there's another way to find out more about your parents."

Oland nodded, then turned back to the map.

The heat eventually lulled Delphi to sleep. Oland got up and found a spot far enough away that he would not wake her, yet close enough that she was still in his sights. Then, with nothing more than a sharp rock and his bare hands, he dug a grave for Pinfrock, a name he had seen so many times in The Holdings, a name that had meant little then, but now meant more than he could bear.

Oland patted down the mound of earth covering Pinfrock's body. He stopped as he heard the sound of singing through the trees.

It was as pure a voice as could ever be, yet with its own spirited peculiarity. He realised it was Delphi, singing a tragic ballad about a woman and a man forced, by others, to part.

Oland walked back to where she sat, with Malben asleep in her arms. Delphi stopped singing when she saw him.

"Your singing is amazing," said Oland. I have never heard anything quite like it."

Delphi blushed. "Really? Chancey the Gold didn't allow me to sing anywhere else. He told me that singing was only for inside the house."

"Well, it shouldn't be," said Oland. He pointed at Malben. "Look at the effect it's had on him."

"What happened to your hands?" said Delphi, frowning.

"I… hurt them," said Oland.

"How?" said Delphi.

"From… from moving the cart."

"They should be bandaged," said Delphi.

"I have nothing to bandage them with," said Oland. He went to the stream and began to wash his hands. "You should really try and get some sleep," he said, "and I'll do the same."

The following morning, Oland woke first, after a fitful sleep. He looked down at himself. Though his hands were clean, the scratches, bruises and rawness of his palms were a sorry sight.

Malben was swinging back and forth between the trees, quicker than usual.

Delphi sat up, "What's wrong with Malben?" she said.

Oland looked over at him.

"He looks agitated," said Delphi.

Malben moved faster and faster, then he jumped, landing in front of Delphi, hugging her leg, then climbing up into her arms.

"I think he's perfectly fine," said Oland, smiling.

Delphi hugged Malben. He squeezed his paws against her cheeks and opened his eyes wide.

"Malben, you are so funny," she said.

He let go quickly and swung backward, his little legs still gripping her waist. Oland and Delphi laughed. Malben jumped down and started to pull at Delphi's hand.

"Are you bringing me to the trees?" said Delphi.

Malben opened his mouth then closed it. He tugged her arm.

"All right," said Delphi, "I will follow you."

"What about me?" said Oland.

Malben pulled Delphi's hand harder.

"I don't think I'm invited," said Oland, laughing.

"Well, we won't be long," said Delphi. "Maybe we'll find us some food."

"I'll come with you, then," said Oland.

"Yes!" said Delphi. "Do!"

"Why does it look like Malben is actually shaking his head?" said Oland. "Malben, have I offended you in some way?"

Malben gave him the closest to a sad smile he imagined a monkey could give.

Oland sat down beside the fire. "Go, then," he said. "Go without me." He laughed, but he was suddenly struck by how different his journey would have been if he hadn't met Delphi. Or Malben. He didn't want them to go, and it unsettled him.

Delphi held up her hand. "Shh!" she said. "I hear something."

Into the clearing charged a horse and cart, this time with a driver, one whom Oland recognised only too well.

It was the man who had come to Castle Derrington on the night of The Games, wrapped again in black gauze bandages – the intruder who had pulled him into Villius Ren's forbidden throne room. In one quick move, the man jumped down from the cart, grabbed Malben by the neck and threw him into a cage. Oland and Delphi lunged towards him. He swung the cage at Oland, knocking him to the ground. With his free hand, he pulled out a knife and held it to Delphi's throat.

32

BONES

THE MAN THREW THE CAGE IN THE FRONT OF THE CART and marched Delphi to the back, where he tied her wrists and ankles and secured them to the timber behind the driver's seat. He turned around as Oland was struggling to his feet. Pointing the knife towards Delphi, the man guided Oland, with little effort, into the cart and bound him alongside her. He unrolled a length of canvas to cover them. The man took the driver's seat, with Malben in the cage beside him, and they moved off, slowly at first, and then at an alarming speed. Oland and Delphi struggled to steady themselves against the motion.

Oland whispered to Delphi. "He came to the castle the night of The Games to try to take me away."

Delphi's eyes were wide. "Who is he?" she said.

"I don't know," said Oland. "I don't know."

"I know how to get free," said Delphi.

"Then do it!" said Oland.

"Not without you and Malben. When the cart stops, I'll have to find the keys to release you."

They travelled through the night and, within hours of dawn breaking, the cart finally came to a stop. The man jumped down from his seat and walked to the back. He untied the covering, and looked in at Oland and Delphi. He was carrying Malben, whose face was stricken.

Delphi tried to kick out at the man. "Give him back!" she said. "Don't touch him!"

The man laughed a low, throaty laugh, and he walked away.

Delphi turned to Oland. Her eyes were black. "I will kill him if he lays a finger on Malben."

Oland started pulling at the chains, rattling them hard.

"Shh…" said Delphi. "Let me do this."

Oland watched, wide-eyed, as she used her left hand to squeeze the fingers of her right, pushing it slowly through the cuff, squeezing again until she had pushed it further through. She stopped then wriggled her right hand the rest of the way out of the cuff.

"How did you do that?" said Oland.

"I have flexible bones," said Delphi.

"Flexible *bones*?" said Oland.

"Yes, I always have," said Delphi. "When I was a child, I could squeeze through the bars of my cot." She pulled her other hand free, then pulled her feet through the cuffs at her ankles. Oland couldn't bear to watch.

"I'll get your keys from the front," said Delphi.

"Grab my bag too," said Oland.

Delphi moved up to the front of the cart and unhooked the keys from where the man had hung them. She climbed back down to Oland and unlocked his hands and feet. She stopped when she heard the rattle of locks, and the piercing sound of rusted hinges. Footsteps rushed towards them.

Oland and Delphi froze. The cart jerked and began to move forward.

"Move!" the man was saying to the horse. "Move!"

The horse did as it was told and, from the back of the cart, Oland and Delphi watched the towering iron gates they had come through growing smaller and smaller, as they went deeper and deeper into peculiarly dark woods. The air was filled with the sound of birds, animals and insects in motion: beating wings, buzzing, scurrying feet, broken branches, rustling leaves.

With a sudden jolt, the cart began to move backward, and rock from side to side. The horse started to whinny.

"Shh," said the man. "Shh. Calm down! Calm down!"

But the horse was clearly trying to shake himself free. The cart rocked violently.

"Hold! Hold! Hold!" the man was saying. "Hold!"

But the horse gave one final thrust and the cart crashed to the ground, shattering the timber shaft. Oland and Delphi fell out and rolled into the undergrowth. They could hear Malben crying out. They could see a magnificent black horse galloping away. As the man followed, Oland and Delphi took the chance to escape. They watched from behind a tree as the man in black returned to the cart roaring that they had gone. There was no sign of Malben.

Oland and Delphi crouched, deathly quiet, in the hot darkness. A dark green shimmering snake unfurled slowly from a tree beside them. It spiralled down to the ground and, as it landed, a plume of violet feathers shot up from its head. It paused then slithered away.

33

PINCER

OLAND AND DELPHI STARED AT EACH OTHER.

"Where *are* we?" said Delphi. She knew Oland would have no answer. "Did you see Malben?" she said.

"No."

"Who's there?" said the man. "Is someone there?"

Oland and Delphi froze, but, as he walked slowly past them, they realised it was not them he heard. A muttering sound was coming from the clearing ahead. Oland and Delphi saw butterfly nets scattered on the ground, and a man dressed in a heavy green protective suit and a beekeeper's hat.

He stabbed a gloved hand towards the man in black. "Did you take the horse?"

"Yes!" said the other man. "And who cares, Benni?"

"Who cares?" said the man. "Who cares? And you think I'm the fool! And you can stop calling me Benni. Where is the horse now?"

"Gone!" said the man. "Gone!"

"You took him from the woods, Malcolm! Of course he's gone!"

Oland knew then the men who stood before him. His heart started to pound. His stomach churned.

"They must be Malcolm and Benjamin Evolent," he said, his voice low and trembling.

Delphi moved closer to him, gripping his arm.

"I brought him back!" said Malcolm.

"Why are you here?" said Benjamin. "Why aren't you on your own side?"

"I just wanted to—"

"You need to understand that the animals cannot under any circumstances leave these woods. You see the gates. You know that there are fences deep underground. I am beginning to build a cage over the entire woods. *The entire woods.* Can you understand that if you let out anything… even one creature – and they are *creatures,* you know this – that you have the potential to destroy everything?"

"Of course I do," said Malcolm.

"Then why do it?" said Benjamin.

Malcolm shrugged.

"And speaking of destruction," said Benjamin, "what happened to my watchtower?"

"Well, *you'll* have to tell *me*, won't you?" said Malcolm.

"It's gone!" said Benjamin.

"And what do you think I did?" said Malcolm. "Chop it down? Because one can hardly carry away a watchtower."

"It's completely gone," said Benjamin. "As if it never existed."

Malcolm frowned. "Oh…" he said. "Maybe there is one thing."

"What?" said Benjamin.

"A new insect I… discovered. It appears to have quite the appetite for wood."

"And you let this 'discovery' loose?" said Benjamin.

"No," said Malcolm. "I contained it. Well, there were two of them. Each in a glass jar… that they managed to knock over and smash. Quite a feat for such tiny things."

"Where were you keeping them?"

"In one of my timber buildings, unfortunately…"

Benjamin's eyes widened.

"I know!" said Malcolm. "We're both so used to you being the fool!"

"Did they damage the building?" said Benjamin.

"Well, they damaged the contents," said Malcolm. "The building, they simply devoured."

"What?" said Benjamin.

Malcolm nodded. "It took no more than minutes."

"For two of them?" said Benjamin.

Malcolm nodded, his eyes bright.

"This is nothing to be proud of," said Benjamin. "This is a catastrophe."

"Apart from your watchtower, I don't see anything else they've done," said Malcolm. "I'm sure their stomachs have exploded by now."

"You have no idea what has become of them," said Benjamin.

"But I will follow their progress with interest, said Malcolm."

Benjamin stared at the ground. "At least, for the sake of the larger creatures, go back and lock the gate," he said, his voice weary.

"Me?" said Malcolm. He snorted. "Don't be ridiculous. Get one of your minions."

"Fyles!" called Benjamin. "Fyles! Can you please go and close the gate? My brother saw fit to leave it open."

A man appeared from the building behind Benjamin Evolent. He had a long narrow body and short squat legs. He moved slowly, his body rolling left and right.

"Yes, doctor," he said, barely glancing up, his brow hidden under a filthy pile of dark hair.

"Look out for a horse!" said Malcolm.

Benjamin scowled at him. "Who knows what problems that horse might have!"

Malcolm readjusted one of his bandages. "That horse's only problem was—"

"Shh!" said Benjamin.

Malcolm ignored him. "I'm simply saying—"

"Fyles!" hissed Benjamin. "Fyles – stop walking! Don't move!"

Fyles turned towards him. "What?" he said. "What is it?"

"What is wrong with you?" said Malcolm. He looked to where Fyles was standing. Oland and Delphi did the same. Oland's eyes shot wide as a towering form peeled away from one of the tree trunks past Fyles' shoulder.

"What is that?" said Malcolm.

"I don't know," said Benjamin. "It's… it's… tall… over six feet tall…" He frowned. "It's the colour of the tree trunk, but now it's changing…"

Fyles started to shake. The creature moved closer. There was something so wrong about it. It seemed to appear and reappear as it changed with its surroundings.

Benjamin struggled to speak.

Fyles was quaking. Malcolm Evolent just stared.

"It's changing again," said Benjamin. "To… the colour of the leaves."

Suddenly, two arms shot from the creature's sides and two huge pincers started to snap at the air as it moved slowly towards Fyles.

Fyles stood, whimpering, his face contorted in terror.

"Oh, no," said Benjamin.

"What?" said Fyles. He was barely moving his lips.

"It's a scorpeleon!" said Benjamin.

Fyles' voice trembled. "Part scorpion, part chameleon?" he said.

"I'm sorry, Fyles!" said Benjamin. "I'm so sorry!"

Behind Fyles, the creature was rising to its full height. Its long black tail curved into the air behind it. A strange sound was building in the back of its throat.

"Oh, no!" said Benjamin.

"What?" said Fyles again.

"It's… it's just turned the colour of your tunic," said Benjamin.

With that, the scorpeleon pounced, swiftly latching a pincer around Fyles' waist, shaking him wildly and carrying him away through the trees.

34

ACQUISITION

ELPHI PRESSED HER HAND TO HER MOUTH TO STIFLE her screams. As the howling Fyles was being carried away, Oland and Delphi took the chance to run in the opposite direction. They charged ahead, ducking under branches, sidestepping the rocks and knotted roots. They ran until they could barely breathe.

"The experiments," said Oland when they stopped. "That giant scorpion. This is one big laboratory. That's why the Evolents said the word 'discovery' so strangely. It wasn't just a discovery – Malcolm had clearly experimented on those insects. How else could they have destroyed an entire building so quickly?" He paused. "Delphi – how long had we been travelling in the cart do you think?"

"I don't know," said Delphi.

"Long enough to have passed into Garnish?" said Oland.

"Yes," said Delphi. "Definitely."

"Then I think I know where we are," said Oland.

"Hell," said Delphi.

"No," said Oland, "I think where we are might, in fact, be useful. I think we're in Valle da Cossima, Queen Cossima's woods. Tell me again what the scryer said to you about them."

"She said that they were filled with all the beautiful plants and trees I told you about... and... oh, she said, 'Their myriad hues swathed the whole of Envar... and told us of their kings.'"

"That's it!" said Oland. "'Swathed the whole of Envar' – the Tailor Rynish told me that he used to get fabrics from a man in Garnish, Gaudy Dyer, who no longer provides them. He dyed fabrics, therefore he had to use plants, flowers and barks. And 'told us of their kings' – the scryer was talking about crests!"

Delphi's eyes were bright. "You're right!" she said.

"All along, we've been trying to find Sabian the place," said Oland. "What if we find out about the crest itself? I was told to find the crest, not necessarily to *go* to Sabian..." He paused. "If you were a heraldist, where would you live? In a place filled

224

with colour, where you have all the tools to make your dyes. Like here. That's why Pinfrock said that inks are no longer coloured and that only one man is brave enough to work in colour. Why would he say brave, unless, of course, it was a place he shouldn't be? A forbidden place? These woods are owned by Villius Ren and have clearly been taken over by the Evolents. Would it not be brave to trespass on the land of men so evil?"

Before they could continue their conversation, two dogs suddenly appeared from behind a tree. One stood in front of Oland, the other in front of Delphi.

"Don't move." Benjamin Evolent stood opposite them, holding a staff in his hand. He had taken off his beekeeper's hat. It had disguised how small his head really was, and how slim his neck. It was clear that underneath the protective clothes, he was a slight man, nothing like his older brother, Malcolm. Benjamin was short, with thinning fair hair combed flat, and damp with the heat. Skinny red veins covered his broad cheekbones. His eyes reflected the turmoil of the strange world he had created.

"Who are you, you fools?" he said. "Get inside! Get inside!" He pointed to a long, narrow stone building behind him.

"No!" said Oland. "We're not going anywhere with you!"

"You're in danger out here!" said Benjamin. "How did you get in here? What are you doing?"

"Your brother kidnapped us," said Oland.

"What?" said Benjamin. "Please, come inside. I don't want to harm you. You have to believe me."

Beside them, the leaves of a towering plant started to rustle with great force. Without another word, they all ran for the laboratory. Benjamin slammed the door shut behind them.

"Now, why would my brother want to kidnap you?" said Benjamin. "Who are you?"

"I don't know why," said Oland. "But it's the second time he's tried."

Benjamin frowned. "What happened in Decresian – the kidnappings, the experiments, the buried bodies – that was the work of my brother. All I wanted to do was good. I wanted to create beautiful creatures, the brightest humans, the best athletes." He gestured wildly with his arms, drawing their attention to a huge curved skeleton that hung across the wall.

"You worked with your brother," said Delphi. "You knew what you were doing was wrong."

"Not at first," said Benjamin. "He is the superior doctor, the

226

superior scientist. And, when I did realise what he was doing, it was too late. I was already tainted and I would be forever linked to his foul deeds. As is clear again from what you have just said."

"What has happened in these woods?" said Oland.

Benjamin Evolent grabbed a leather-bound book from a table beside him and clutched it to his chest. He began to tap on it, his fingertips working faster and faster.

From the cabinet behind him, a small white rabbit jumped out and stood at Delphi's feet, raising its two front paws, rubbing its nose. As Delphi crouched down to stroke its fur, Benjamin Evolent raised the huge book he had in his hand and struck the rabbit, throwing it towards the door. Delphi cried out.

"What have you done?" shouted Oland.

Benjamin's eyes were filled with an extraordinary panic. The doctor responsible for whatever creatures roamed the woods looked more terrified than Oland and Delphi. "That wasn't a rabbit," he said. "That wasn't a rabbit." His hands were shaking. He ran to the door, opened it and kicked the small creature out into the woods.

"It was a rabbit!" said Delphi. "You are insane!"

"It was a rabbidile," said Benjamin. "And it could have killed us all."

"Killed us?" said Delphi. "What's a rabbidile?"

Benjamin sprang towards her. He pushed his face into hers and hissed: "Nothing is what it seems here – nothing!"

Before Delphi could reply, Benjamin Evolent turned and ran out of the door. "Nothing!" he shouted again. "You will never truly know what hides inside the creatures of The Shadowed Woods!"

"These are not The Shadowed Woods," shouted Oland. "I've seen the map of Envar, this is Valle da Cossima. You don't own these woods!"

"No," said Benjamin. "I don't!" He looked around in fright. Then he started to run through the trees. "The creatures do. The creatures own these woods."

Oland and Delphi were stunned. Slowly, they made their way out of the door and walked over to where the rabbit's body lay slumped against a tree. Oland crouched down and reached out his hand.

"Stop touching dead things," said Delphi. She handed him a stick.

Oland used it to turn the body over.

"That is clearly a rabbit," said Delphi.

Oland glanced down at it. "Wait," he said. "There's something in its mouth." He took the stick and slowly prised the rabbit's jaws open. The first thing they saw was the chewed rattle of a rattlesnake.

"Rabbits don't eat snakes," said Delphi.

But then they realised what a rabbidile was. As Oland pushed up more with the stick, the rabbit's mouth opened wider and wider and its head bent back until it touched its spine… revealing oversized teeth and muscular, gaping jaws, like a miniature crocodile. It was only when it snapped that they realised the rabbidile was still alive.

Oland and Delphi ran.

"Benjamin Evolent was right," said Oland when they stopped. "Nowhere is safe here."

"We won't know what creatures we'll meet and what strange hybrids they might be," said Delphi. "And Malben is out there. Malben is all alone."

"At least he got away from the Evolents," said Oland. "Don't worry about him, Delphi. He's fast, and he'll be able to fly through the trees."

Delphi nodded. "I hope so."

"Surely Benjamin Evolent knows what each animal is," said Oland. "He's the one who carried out the experiments."

Delphi shook her head. "I don't think he does. Why did he look so terrified?"

They looked at each other as they both realised the same thing.

"Someone released his hybrid animals into the woods," said Oland.

Delphi nodded.

"And after that," said Oland, "they bred…"

35

MARSH LIGHT

OLAND AND DELPHI RAN, PLUNGING THROUGH THE undergrowth, reluctant to even pause for breath. They knew now that the woods were filled with beasts of all kinds, but they had no way of knowing what they would stumble across. The only thing that finally stopped them was a terrible stench, like the smell of rotten eggs. As they sucked in huge breaths of air, they began to choke on it.

A marsh appeared before them, stretching as far as they could see.

"It's the smell of the marsh," said Oland.

"It's terrible," said Delphi, holding her nose.

"Don't bother," said Oland, "it's best to get used to it."

At different points in the greenish water, lights glowed then faded.

"Oland!" said Delphi. "Willow! 'You will find someone by willow.' That's what the scryer said. She meant will-o'-the-wisps. Then she said 'lamplights'." Delphi pointed across the water.

They looked around and both noticed a long narrow jetty that stretched out into the marsh. It sloped upward, and at the end, perched high on green wooden stilts, was a tall, narrow, windowless shack, painted in red and green. A twisted strand of smoke rose from a red chimney in the roof.

"Look!" said Delphi, pointing to the back of the house, where a line of brightly coloured flags blew in the rising wind.

Oland turned to Delphi. "I don't believe it," he said.

Delphi smiled. "The heraldist!" She paused. "You were right."

"The scryer was right…" said Oland.

Delphi laughed.

They went to where the jetty started. It was so narrow that they had to walk one after the other.

"I'll go first," said Oland. He turned to Delphi. "Are you sure you want to do this?" He glanced at the water. "Maybe you should stay on dry land."

Delphi was shaking her head. "No. I'm not going to stay here alone."

As they stepped on to the jetty, the green water began to glow in front of them. Something slithered out of the water and crossed the jetty, slipping into the water at the other side. Oland went rigid. He turned to Delphi. She lost her footing on the slime.

He grabbed her by the elbow and steadied her.

"Delphi," said Oland, taking her by the shoulders, holding them tight and staring into her eyes. "Have you ever seen a lamprey?"

"No," said Delphi.

"It's like an eel," said Oland. "They're here, in the marsh. If you see one, don't look at it."

"Why?" said Delphi.

"Because – and this is no lie – they are one of the most hideous creatures you will ever see. *Willow. Lamplights.* That's what the scryer meant. A lamprey with the glow of a will-o'-the-wisp."

Delphi shuddered.

"They may not come near us," said Oland. "I'm just telling you not to look at them."

"But… what do they do?" said Delphi.

Oland shook his head. "Don't ask."

"Tell me, Oland, so that, if I need to, I can…"

"Delphi – they look like snakes. That's all you need to know. If one comes near you, kick it away. It cannot do you any damage unless it's extremely close to you. It can't strike out and bite. It moves swiftly, but not aggressively. But... just don't look at it."

"I don't think I can do this." Delphi's legs were shaking. "I want to leave. Now."

"We can't," said Oland. "Not yet. But, as soon as we get the Crest of Sabian, we will…"

Delphi nodded, sending tears spilling down her face. Oland reached out a hand towards her, but quickly pulled back.

"You can do this," he said. "I know you can." He paused. "Are you ready?"

"Yes," said Delphi. "Yes. Go."

Oland moved ahead. Every now and then, the water glowed to their left and right.

"What will you do with the crest when you get it?" said Delphi.

"I don't know," said Oland. "I'm hoping something in the design will tell me something… or lead me to something… or someone. All I was told about it was: 'depth and height, from blue to white, what's left behind is yours to find'."

Oland quickened his step. "We're nearly there," he said. He kept the fear from his voice; they were crossing a marsh, the deadest of water, yet it seemed to be moving and the level was rising. And a fog rose with it. Oland moved faster.

The heraldist's house was close; Oland could see that they would reach the lower of two walkways, spaced thirty feet apart, separated by a ladder. A second ladder stretched up to the house. Oland reached the end of the jetty.

"There!" he said.

He turned around to Delphi. For seconds that seemed endless, he watched as she stood frozen in the strange glow of the greenish light. Her fear had blinded her to the fog as it crawled slowly across the surface. But, as she looked up, Oland could see the panic in her eyes. He knew that the jetty in front of her was being swallowed up by the fog. A wispy strand of it floated across her legs.

As it disappeared, Oland could see a lamprey wrapping itself around Delphi's boot.

36

QUINTUS

OLAND BENT DOUBLE, CLUTCHING AT HIS STOMACH, releasing a terrifying moan.

"Oland," screamed Delphi. "What's wrong with you?"

As he fell to the ground, disappearing into the rising fog, he heard Delphi scream, "I'm coming, Oland, I'm coming."

She ran, ignoring the fog, the water, the glowing lampreys. In one final jump, she was kneeling at Oland's side, dragging him up from the ground where he had collapsed.

"Oland," she said. "What happened? Are you all right?"

He opened his eyes. His face was flooded with relief. "Delphi... you're alive." He glanced at her boot. The lamprey was gone.

"Yes," said Delphi. "Yes. Are you in pain? Do you feel unwell?"

Oland slowly sat up. "No," he said. "No. But are you all right?"

Delphi looked at him. The fear in her eyes tore at him. He could see that she was trying to be strong, but that some of the fire in her had died.

"What happened?" said Delphi.

"I… I…" said Oland. "I don't know."

From under Delphi's cape, the lamprey slid. Oland froze. As a child, he had seen the most intricately detailed watercolour of a lamprey, and it was burned into his mind. If it opened its mouth in front of Delphi, Oland had no doubt she would be so terrified, she would jump, and then she would fall into the water.

The lamprey disappeared; Delphi's oilskins were so stiff and heavy, she didn't feel it move under her armpit. But soon, from over her shoulder, by the choppy ends of her coal-black hair, the coal-black lamprey reappeared. Then it opened its mouth. Bile rose in Oland's throat. Once a lamprey's mouth opened, all that was visible was the lining – the colour of pale human flesh. There was no bony jaw, because it had no bones. Instead, there was a pale, fleshy circle, and inside it were concentric circles of pointed teeth with a dark chasm at the centre. Oland knew that lampreys clamped on to their prey and ate their way through the surface until they reached fluids and slowly sucked them away. Once they attached, they were impossible to remove. And one was ready to feed, inches from Delphi's face.

Delphi was talking and Oland had no idea what she was saying; he knew he couldn't do or say anything or the lamprey would be directly in her face if she turned. He had no idea how he would get it away. But the weight of it had begun to settle on to Delphi's body and, slowly, she became aware of it and, slowly, she turned around. The lamprey was right in front of her, its mouth open.

Delphi's eyes went black. She stared at it, as if she were more disgusted that it had dared to choose her as a victim than the fact that it was grotesque. It began to glow, its light reflected in the blackness of her eyes. Delphi's hand shot out with alarming speed. She grabbed the lamprey and, holding it at arm's length, squeezed it briefly then dropped it into the marsh.

She and Oland looked at each other. Delphi smiled.

Oland laughed. "I worried for no reason."

"You collapsed on purpose, didn't you?" said Delphi, suddenly serious. "You collapsed on purpose, so that I would rush to the other side."

"Would it be such a terrible thing if I had?" said Oland.

Delphi paused. "No," she said. She smiled. "Thank you."

Oland forced a smile – what he had just told her was a lie. But it was far better than telling her the truth. He had imagined Delphi disappearing underwater and it was a terrifying sight.

From the platform above they heard a deep hum that reverberated down through the timber. As it continued, the lampreys began to fall from the stilts into the water. Delphi and Oland climbed to the highest walkway, where a red ladder reached up to the house. A pale, bald man who looked to be in his sixties was leaning out over the gate.

"Goodness," he shouted over the wind. "Come up, come up. My guardian lamplights were doing what they do best… but I never imagined such young people would find their way into these woods. You must have got the fright of your lives."

He reached out his hand and helped Delphi the last of the way. Oland followed. Up close, the man's face, like the wooden shingles of the house, looked tired and weather-beaten.

"We have a baleful sky, pirouetting winds…" he said.

Oland thought again of The Great Rains. He had no sense of when they would come, nothing to tell him how much time he had left.

"Anyway, welcome, welcome," said the man. "Tell me who you are."

"My name is Oland Born. And this is my companion, Delphi."

"Well, hello, Oland and companion Delphi."

"Are you the heraldist?" said Oland.

"I absolutely am. My name is Quintus. Do come in."

Oland and Delphi looked at each other and smiled. Finally, they would uncover the mystery of the Crest of Sabian.

37

TRUTH AND LOYALTY

QUINTUS THE HERALDIST'S LOVE OF COLOUR WAS NOT just reserved for his crests; fine horizontal stripes of pale-to-deep shades of yellow, red, green, purple, gold, silver and bronze ran from his shoulders down to his wrists.

He led them into a long narrow room, bursting with more colours than Oland or Delphi had ever seen. The ceiling was neatly covered with hundreds of flags. Across three walls were hundreds of crests, all perfectly aligned. They were emblazoned with birds and animals, roses and swords and daggers. The fourth wall was unexpectedly made entirely of glass; every day, the inspirational colours of the woods were laid out before him like a palette.

"Everything is so beautiful!" said Delphi. "And so tidy!"

Quintus laughed. "Ah, but not in there," he said, pointing through a narrow doorway. Delphi and Oland went into the small room, where papers towered in crooked stacks, and books and ornaments and pots and pans were in haphazard collections on the floor, on shelves, on boxes and crates. There was a glass case mounted on the wall that held a row of dusters of different sizes.

"I rummage in there, and I create in here," said Quintus.

Oland and Delphi came back into the main room, but could hear the rattle of cups from a third room at the end.

"How on earth did you find me?" called Quintus.

"Oland worked it all out," said Delphi. "He thought about where cloth was made and dyed, why people no longer did that, how Villius Ren now owns these woods so that no one dared work with colours... except for one man. The Scryer of Gort told us more..."

"You have been on quite the adventure," said Quintus. He carried out a tray with three cups on it and a tall blue jug.

"Cinderberry," he said, about to hand them a cup.

Oland flashed back to the smell from the intruder's bandages on the night he came out from the throne room. "I can't," he said. "I'm sorry..."

"Ah," said Quintus, "did you suffer a burn?"

"No, not me," said Oland, "but let's just say I once met a terrible man with cinderberry-soaked bandages."

"Strange that a berry can taste so good as a juice, and transform into something so pungent as an ointment," said Quintus. "The patient man's ointment, as it is known."

"Why?" said Delphi.

"Well, there are more effective ways to treat burns, ways that heal them quicker. Cinderberry takes many years, but will ultimately leave no trace of a scar. None whatsoever." He looked from one to the other. "So shall I make lemonade for you both?" he said.

"I'll try cinderberry, please," said Delphi.

"Lemonade for me," said Oland. "Thank you."

"Bad memories spill from all the senses," said Quintus as he left the room.

"Is it true that you have made all the crests of all the lands?" called Oland.

"In the last fifty years," said Quintus. "Yes."

"And before that?" said Oland.

"My ancestors did," said Quintus. "Where are you from?"

"Decresian," said Oland.

"Aha!" said Quintus. He reappeared with Oland's drink and handed it to him. "Come with me."

They went to a table in the corner, where a giant book lay.

"What a fine king you had in King Micah," said Quintus. "I was saddened by his passing."

He heaved the book open.

"Here I have all the crests ever made – in Envar and beyond."

He beckoned Oland and Delphi to his side as he opened up the contents page. He held two bony fingers to the corner of the book and flicked so quickly through the pages that they became a blur.

"Here we are," he said. "The Crest of Decresian, and its beautiful gold and teal. This was a very special crest, designed by my grandfather," said Quintus. "Did you know that the teal and gold of Decresian was to mark King Micah's birth? When his mother, Queen Amber, knew that she was with child, she wanted the official colours of the kingdom to change to reflect his birth, and she wanted a colour that had never before been used. My grandfather travelled the length and breadth of Envar, and he returned with the most magnificent teal dye. It was used for the king's robes when he was born, and for the Crest of Decresian. That was over one hundred years ago…"

Delphi pointed to it. "Where did he find the colour?"

"From a flower, I was told," said Quintus.

"I know the flower," said Delphi. "It was taken from the petals of a camberlily." She paused. "Well, that's the name I gave them."

Oland was nodding as she spoke. "It's that exact colour."

"Well, that's extraordinary!" said Quintus. "Are you from Dallen Falls?"

"Yes," said Delphi.

"Well, would you believe, my grandfather went back there – we've all been back there to look for them, every year – and we've never seen them since."

"They're there now," said Delphi. "In one of the caves."

"That would be them indeed," said Quintus. "My grandfather found them in the cave, quite by chance, floating by. How could we have missed them, in all our pilgrimages?"

"I only saw them for the first time a few months ago," said Delphi.

"Well, I might take a trip to Dallen Falls once more," said Quintus. He smiled, and his eyes sparkled with all the glorious colours around him.

"Thank you for showing us the crest," said Delphi.

"But we've been sent to find the Crest of Sabian," said Oland.

Quintus frowned. "Sent?" he said. "By whom?"

"King Micah," said Oland.

"King Micah? But surely he died before you were born…"

"He left a letter for me," said Oland. "That is all I can tell you."

"Sabian, you say?" said Quintus.

Oland nodded. "Yes. We came here because we wanted to see the crest, or find out where it is."

Quintus' face fell. "Oh, Oland Born, Delphi, dear," he said.

Oland felt a stab of panic.

"It is with a heavy heart I tell you: there is no Crest of Sabian," said Quintus. "There is no Sabian – not any more. Sabian is the land that fell into the sea."

Oland stood, motionless. It was as though he hadn't heard Quintus' words, yet had heard them so loudly that they became unbearable. He was surrounded by more crests than were imaginable, yet the room might as well have been bare. It was not that he was here to prove that he had achieved something, or reached somewhere, or deciphered something. He had left an entire kingdom behind, and though its people scarcely knew him, and certainly did not know of his quest, he had a loyalty to them that he could feel like a flame burning inside him. He had never envisaged a future that the past had already destroyed.

"Hundreds of years ago," said Quintus, "there was a battle for control of Sabian. It lasted for many, many years and it was the ruin of many. Only one army was left standing, led by a man named Obuled – a dangerous and ignorant man. For years he ruled Sabian with a crazed mind and a violent hand.

"One night, during a banquet he threw in honour of himself, Sabian was plunged into darkness. The ground started to tremble. Cracks broke out all across the land and, before long, they became huge crevices. Within minutes, every last trace of Sabian disappeared into the sea.

"So I would imagine," said Quintus, "that there was little chance that a crest survived and little chance that anywhere outside Sabian the crest of such an evil man was ever preserved." He paused. "I am sorry, Oland, Delphi."

"But... the letter says... it's a blue and white crest."

"There *are* no crests of blue and white," said Quintus. "In heraldry, blue represents truth and loyalty and white represents peace and sincerity, but, at that time, hundreds of years ago, it was the colour of the flags used by the army of Obuled. Of course, it was a mockery: Obuled was an evil man, who knew nothing of truth and loyalty. He lied, cheated and betrayed his way through life. He found it amusing, therefore, to have a blue and white crest. My father, my father's father and every generation of heraldists before me refused to allow blue and white to be used in a crest ever since."

"But where was Sabian?" said Oland. "I've never seen it on a map."

"But you may have heard of it," said Quintus. "Or what's left of it."

"No," said Oland. "I haven't."

"It used to be the southernmost tip of Envar…" said Quintus.

Oland knew then where Quintus meant. He closed his eyes. "It can't be."

Quintus nodded gravely. "I'm afraid so," he said. "Sabian is now Curfew Peak."

"Curfew Peak?" said Delphi. "The prison? The drogues…"

Oland quoted his book. "'One mythic beast was four engulfed: vulture, bull, bear and wolf.'"

"If the crest is there," said Quintus, "it should remain there. As it is said: 'If you disturb the grounds of Curfew Peak, the grounds of Curfew Peak will disturb you tenfold.'"

38

COLLAPSE

QUINTUS' SHACK SUDDENLY KEELED SHARPLY TO ONE side, sending him, Oland and Delphi sliding along the floor, crashing into the wall. They could hear the sound of the wooden stilts creaking, and the window frames start to rattle. Quintus edged closer to it, ignoring Delphi's pleas to stop.

"What's happening?" said Delphi.

"I don't know said Quintus.

The house shifted and this time all three struck the glass, Quintus head first. Blood poured from a cut above his eye. Delphi cried out. The house shifted again, and all the stacks of papers collapsed. Quickly, Oland and Delphi blew out all the candles, and they were plunged into darkness. Again, the house tilted sharply. Delphi and Oland grabbed on to each other. Quintus grabbed on to his giant book.

"Go," said Quintus. "Please, go."

"But… you're coming too…" said Oland.

"Yes," said Quintus. "But please, go first. I need to collect some of my things."

"We'll help you gather," said Delphi.

"Yes," said Oland.

"Thank you, but no," said Quintus. "I will follow you. Please. Please take yourselves to safety."

The house rocked again, throwing Oland and Delphi to the floor.

"Run," shouted Quintus, dragging his precious book towards him. "Run."

"We can't leave you," said Delphi. "We're not leaving without you."

"You have to," said Quintus. "Go. Please. There is a boat tied to my cabin that I can drop into the water if I have to. I can make it to safety in that. You can climb down the ladder faster; you can run along the jetty to the bank. I can't fit you both in my boat with all my books. You'll be doing me a great service."

Oland and Delphi looked at each other.

"Will you be safe?" said Delphi to Quintus.

"Yes, go," shouted Quintus.

Oland pulled Delphi by the hand. "You can't fall into the water. We have to go. Now!"

All around the room, the wooden crests began to drop from the walls. Plates and glasses and tankards shattered on the wooden floor.

Oland turned to Quintus. "Thank you for your kindness," he said. "We will meet you on the bank."

"Until then," said Quintus. He bowed. "And good luck to you both."

Oland and Delphi ran, pushing their way through the creaking door out into the night, sliding halfway down the ladders and running along the walkway. They heard a huge crash behind them. They turned and saw Quintus' boat falling from where it hung at the side of the shack. It shattered as it struck the water. They ran faster and heard the creak of the stilts, then a crack, then another, and the deafening sound of Quintus' home crashing down into the wild waters. When they looked back, they saw the jetty begin to break up behind them.

"Faster," roared Oland. "Faster."

Everything was a blur as they fled the collapsing jetty. The sound of shattering timber grew louder behind them. Delphi was running ahead. The plank of wood behind Oland's heels exploded. Oland pushed Delphi hard, sending her flying through the air towards the bank of the marsh. There was no more jetty beneath Oland's feet and he tumbled into the water, crying out when he hit the surface. He plunged quickly down into the darkness. When he reappeared, he could see Delphi standing by the edge, her face stricken.

"Oland," she screamed. "Swim! Swim!"

Though Delphi was close, the distance between them felt insurmountable as Oland struggled desperately to escape the viscous, stinking water. As the last of his strength began to slip away, Delphi reached out towards him, but her feet slid closer to the edge. The only way Oland could stop her was to get to her first. Just when he thought he had no more fight left, he gave one final burst, and he collapsed, exhausted, on to the bank beside her.

39

A TRUANT KINGDOM

OLAND LAY AT THE EDGE OF THE MARSH, STARING UP at the sky. Delphi sat beside him, picking at the damp grass. "When I get back to The Falls," she said, "I'm going to take a camberlily and let it float through The Straits in honour of Quintus – through beautiful water, instead of this."

Oland could hear the crack in her voice.

"Curfew Peak," he said eventually. "I can't believe it was once part of Sabian." With his arms outstretched above him, he held out the map. "The southernmost point in Envar is a place called Pallimer Bay. Maybe there is a crest of Curfew Peak…"

"You're not thinking of going there?" said Delphi.

"Why? The drogues?" said Oland, laughing. "You do know they're not real? But, from the illustrations in my book, they are ferocious." He laid down the map and held up his hands like claws.

Delphi laughed. "I know they're not real. It's just the idea of them…"

She stood up. "Oland," she said. "Look!"

Oland looked out across the marsh to where the contents of Quintus' home floated across the surface.

"Can you see?" said Delphi.

Oland nodded. "I can," he said. "There is not one remnant of Quintus' shack or the jetty."

Suddenly, Delphi slapped her own wrist. She cried out. When she pulled her palm away, she could see that something round was embedded in her skin. She pinched it between her nails, pulled it out and held it up. It was a plump, orange insect with a bloated brown abdomen the size of an acorn. Its head came to a sharp point.

"So this is Malcolm's creation," said Oland. He put the map in his bag, then grabbed a branch from under the tree beside them. Delphi lay the insect on top. In seconds, the entire branch was dust, and the insect was gone.

"We need to leave," said Delphi. "Now. Let's retrace our steps, then, when we reach Benjamin Evolent's laboratory we go straight ahead, instead of going left like we did the last time."

They disappeared into the trees and walked on in silence.

"To think," said Delphi eventually, "that Valle da Cossima was a beautiful gift that must have been filled with love and with happiness. And this is what it has become."

Oland nodded. "Do you think we're going the right way? Is there anything here that's familiar to you?"

"Not yet," said Delphi.

They reached a clearing.

"Look!" said Oland.

At the centre of the clearing were Benjamin Evolent's gloves and mask. There was a terrible twitching sound from the trees, like the flapping of the wings of a trapped bird. Oland and Delphi looked up slowly. Three thick-snouted boars hung upside down like bats from one of the tree branches. Blood dripped on to the ground from their fangs.

Delphi held her hand to her mouth.

In front of them, each boar dropped slowly to the ground. What looked like wings were just stretched flaps of flesh that the boars snapped out like a cape, and they sped, on hooves, through the trees ahead, flying only at intervals.

Oland and Delphi stood, shaking in the hot darkness.

"What have the Evolents done?" said Delphi. "What have they done?"

Oland pointed to a small pool of light on the ground in front of them, where they saw the battered leather-bound book that Benjamin Evolent had been clutching earlier. It was titled: *A Truant Kingdom: Dark Crossings.*

Oland took the heavy volume and opened it. A map stretched across the inside cover. It was divided by a forest that snaked down the centre. To the right was a vast area bounded by a curved path, with four paths running off it towards the centre to sections numbered one to four.

"It's a map of the woods," said Oland.

The key to the map was in the bottom right-hand corner under the heading 'Animal Enclosures'.

"One: snakes/lizards," said Oland, "two: birds/insects, three: primates, four: lions/tigers." He paused, then turned to Delphi, his eyes filled with horror. "And we're here."

He pointed to a fifth area, coloured in red, that spread like a pool of blood across the map, larger than all the others combined. Arrows pointed from all the other areas towards it. There was no key for number five. Instead, across the crimson expanse, was one word: 'Unknown'.

Oland turned the pages slowly, but his pace accelerated as he moved through the drawings and diagrams and notes.

"These are Benjamin Evolent's notes on the creatures," he said. His face had turned white. He closed the journal.

"Oh, Delphi. It's worse than we could ever have imagined."

Delphi tried to take the book from him.

Oland pulled it back.

"Let me see," said Delphi.

Oland shook his head. "No. You don't want to see."

"I do!" she shouted. She took the book and flipped past the map to the following page. "This book is volume three?" she said, her eyes wide.

"Yes," said Oland. "There appear to be three volumes. This one is about what lives in the red area on the map."

"There aren't many entries," said Delphi.

"Yet," said Oland.

"What about the humans they experimented on in Decresian?" said Delphi. "And the screaming souls? And the Thousandth Soul?"

"Maybe they never documented them," said Oland.

"What were they trying to do to the world?" said Delphi.

Oland was reminded of how safe Delphi's life had been,

where the only world she knew was one carefully constructed by Chancey the Gold. Even if, at times, she had felt trapped, at least she knew that she had always been safe.

"Let me take that," said Oland.

Delphi handed him the book and he put it in his bag.

They walked on, side by side.

"I want to go home," said Delphi suddenly. Tears welled in her eyes. "I want to go home."

Oland too felt the urge to be in The Holdings, master of a battle of his own creation. He wished that he was standing as the powerful leader of a fearless army. He could guide his soldiers across familiar terrain to face an enemy he knew, an enemy whose actions he could predict. Outside that tiny room, there was nothing or no one for Oland Born to trust. The world was a bleak and hopeless place.

It was at his darkest moment in these darkest woods that Delphi reached out and took his hand.

They walked, hand in hand, for some time. Oland was extremely conscious of the fineness of Delphi's bones. Despite himself, and despite her strength, he had never felt she was so breakable.

"Look!" said Delphi, releasing his hand. "It's a dog. He's been hurt." She started to run towards a small slumped shape up ahead.

Suddenly, Malben jumped from the trees and landed in front of her. His eyes flashed with fright. He opened his mouth. "Delphi, no!" he cried. "Don't touch it! It's poisoned!"

All Oland and Delphi could do was stare at him. He had looked so close to speaking so many times, and now, finally, he had.

40

DYING BREATH

MALBEN STOOD IN FRONT OF OLAND AND DELPHI, holding up a finger.

"You cannot interrupt me," he said. "My power of speech is like a bee's sting and, once it's released, I will die. So, with my dying breath, I want you to know that I have betrayed you, Oland. I am the animal who is closest to the perfection of the Thousandth Soul. The Evolents didn't think that they would fail with me, so they called me Malben – the perfect combination of their names and their work.

"I was healthy for a time, but within weeks of my birth…" Malben shook his head. "I displayed behaviour that concerned them. They called me 'wild and two-sided'. The world is a battle of good and evil and is won and lost across different terrains. But, for me, the fight was in my very soul; a fight so intense that it became unbearable. Sometimes good triumphed, sometimes evil. But the unpredictability was devastating for me and everyone around me. The turmoil in my soul could not be sustained by my heart, Oland. The turmoil is breaking my heart.

"Unbeknownst to Malcolm Evolent, on my anguished nights, a young woman was brought to the laboratory by Benjamin Evolent to watch over me. She thought it was nothing more than a hospital for sick animals. She had no fear – no matter how restless or distressed I was, she would take me in her arms, hold me and sing me to sleep. And one day she was gone. Malcolm Evolent told me that he had sent her away, and that I would probably be dead by the time she returned. And so I was in a cage, with no hope of anyone to come and comfort me.

"It was not long afterwards I heard that the Thousandth Soul was created, and I knew that the Evolents would have little use for me. But then the Thousandth Soul disappeared, and they turned their attention back to me. Fearful of what they would do, I decided to help them find the Thousandth Soul. I believed that they would be grateful and, if they studied the Thousandth Soul, that they would be able to fix me, make me one spirit instead of the two that fight inside me. The night of the Villian Games, when you fled from the castle, Oland, I followed you. On our journey, when I disappeared, it was to return to Malcolm Evolent and show him on the map where you were or where I had heard you plan to go…

"When I returned after fleeing Dallen Falls, you had found Delphi. And, on the way to Galenore, when I heard her sing, it was so beautiful, so pure… and it stayed with me… but… then, then I let Malcolm Evolent know you had gone to Galenore. I couldn't help myself! This is the fight I speak of! And then I left Pinfrock's to tell him where you were!" He looked as shocked at his own actions as Oland and Delphi were. "I didn't know what Malcolm would do!" Malben continued. "I knew he would come for you, Oland, but… not that he would kill Pinfrock! He killed him! Just like that! To make you think it was the archivist… he wanted you to mistrust everything and everyone… he followed us to the Oxlaven border. I tried to pull you into the woods that day, Delphi, to spare you being taken away by Malcolm Evolent. I knew he was coming. I tried to, but then Malcolm Evolent appeared. When I saw how you only went with him because he had a knife held to my throat, I could no longer bear who I had become…

"I betrayed you, but it may not be too late to save yourselves from him. You must leave the woods immediately. There are creatures who hibernate here, and you do not want to be here when they awaken. It will be within the hour. Come with me; there is a horse waiting for you."

Oland and Delphi struggled desperately not to interrupt Malben, not to ask him a hundred questions after what he had just revealed.

"Villius Ren and the Evolents know things about each other that each uses against the other. I know that Villius Ren encouraged them to start the experiments; he was nineteen years old at the time, and believed himself to be sick. He wanted their help. The Evolents began their experiments, but ten years later, King Micah uncovered their work and called on a magistrate to try them in court and send them to prison. Villius Ren saved the Evolents from this fate when he overthrew King Micah. It meant that the Evolents could leave Decresian, and that no one would ever know that it was Villius' idea to start the experiments. But King Micah took something away from Villius Ren before he died. He protected more than just the history of Decresian from him. Whatever it is, they all want it. It's something to do with the experiments. It's something to do with extracting the traits of animals. There are distillations, extractions, essences and infusions. They don't require breeding in a laboratory. These are simple liquids, Oland. They are in vials, they can be injected, they can be drunk, they can be... devastating. They have never been used," said Malben. "All I know is that they are volatile, that in order to survive, they have to be kept in a controlled environment. And where they are, no one knows. But, in the wrong hands, they could destroy Envar. Whatever your quest is, Oland, wherever it shall lead you, you must find them, wherever they are."

Malben's breath was failing him. Oland panicked. "But why was Malcolm Evolent looking for me?" he blurted.

Malben howled in sorrow. He spun round and round in frantic circles, his eyes wild with pain. It was too late. He had lost his power of speech. He started to run, gesturing for them to follow him. The three moved silently through the woods, but by the time they reached the gates, Malben was trailing weakly behind them. And, as they turned to thank him, he was lying curled on his side on the grass as if he were sleeping.

41

BLACK TO THE CORE

OLAND AND DELPHI RAN THROUGH THE EASTERN GATES of The Shadowed Woods and stopped to catch their breath.

"I can't believe that Malben reported back to Malcolm Evolent," said Oland.

Delphi was crying. "Poor Malben. It wasn't his fault. He was… just… used. And now he's gone."

Oland's thoughts turned to what Malben had told them. He could barely believe that there were transformative liquids out there that were the result of such grotesque experiments. The weight of being told by Malben that he must find them felt like too great a burden.

He heard the stamping of a foot behind him and turned to see the black horse that had fled from Malcolm Evolent. He was tethered to one of the bars, his head held high. They went over to him.

"What *is* this?" said Delphi. From the base of the horse's neck to the tops of his legs, he was encased in the hardened plates of a pangolin.

Oland ran his hands the length of the horse. "He has his own natural armour. He's incredible."

"He needs a name," said Delphi.

Oland smiled. "Standback," he said. "His name is Standback."

Delphi stroked his mane.

"Climb up," said Oland, holding out his hands, boosting Delphi on to the horse's back.

Without thinking, she pulled Oland up in front of her. Neither said a word, but they were both surprised at the strength in her skinny arms.

Oland had never ridden a horse with another rider, and it took him some time to move his elbows away from his side so that Delphi could put her arms around his waist.

Standback began tentatively, but quickly reached his full potential, carrying Oland and Delphi away at an unimaginable speed.

*

When they reached Pallimer Bay, Oland and Delphi looked across at the black island-mountain that was Curfew Peak. Standback stood quietly by their side. The remaining light overhead would soon leave, and Curfew Peak would be in darkness. A sailing boat was nearing the pier from the east.

"This is one place the Evolents will not expect us to go," said Oland. "Malben never heard us saying we're looking for the Crest of Sabian; perhaps he doesn't even know that Curfew Peak was once part of Sabian."

Delphi stepped a little closer to the edge of the pier. Under its calm, glassy surface, the water was beginning to churn. Delphi beckoned Oland over. They watched as pockets of dark sand began to burst under the surface.

"Something is happening under there," said Delphi. "It's like the marsh."

They looked again at the distance they had to travel to Curfew Peak.

"We're not going," said Delphi.

"We have no choice," said Oland.

The sailing boat pulled up alongside a stone boathouse to their right. As it docked, they could see a sign on the side: CURFEW PEAK. NO BOARDING WITHOUT MAGISTRATE'S PAPERS.

The captain jumped down on to the pier. He had smooth, rich-brown skin and green, copper-flecked eyes that appeared to change colour in the fading sunlight. He had the build of a man who hauled heavy loads. He frowned when he saw Oland and Delphi, and how they were gazing out towards Curfew Peak.

"Surely you're not volunteering," he said, smiling.

Behind him, forty young men and women, all dressed in white, disembarked and stood beside the boat in four parallel lines of ten.

He turned to them. "Go, eat, and I will join you shortly."

Without a word, they walked up the slipway, disappearing out of sight.

The captain turned his attention back to Oland and Delphi.

"What are you doing here?" he said.

"We need your help," said Oland.

"Who are you?" said the man.

"I'm Oland. And this is Delphi."

"My name is Bream," said the man. "Tell me how I can help you."

"We need to get to Curfew Peak," said Oland.

Bream's eyes widened. "Why?"

"Because…" said Oland.

Bream waited.

"Because I have to find something there," said Oland. "That's all I will say."

Bream shook his head slowly. "I have lived on Pallimer Bay for twelve years, so you better listen carefully."

His tone was enough to make the hairs on the back of Delphi's neck stand up.

"Curfew Peak is called Curfew Peak because the sun goes down early, earlier than anywhere else," said Bream. "The island itself has a curfew. At six o'clock it plunges into darkness. But," he said, "can you see how dark it is now, even in daylight?"

Oland and Delphi nodded.

"The island is covered in a fine black dust," said Bream. "Finer than sand. And that dust is stirred up by the wind and it will blow into your eyes and will be sucked into your nose and mouth and lungs. It is an unpleasant dust with unpleasant effects. If a person holds anger within, this dust will give it an easy path to the outside world and, once released, it will be directionless.

"The only lights that can burn on Curfew Peak are along its shore," he continued. "They are lit by the Pyreboys. They descend from the mountain top at dusk and light a row of torches along the shore to keep any boats from crashing there."

"Who are the Pyreboys?" said Delphi.

"The criminal children," said Bream. "Any child who commits a crime gets shipped off to Curfew Peak from the age of twelve to twenty-one. If they're under twelve, their name is written in a magistrate's ledger and they are collected on their twelfth birthday and off they go – to stay there until their twenty-first. Oh, they can roam somewhat freely, but, if they are caught by the guards making any attempt to escape, they are jailed in cells on the northwest of the island for the rest of their lives." He paused. "Not that you could really call them guards; they're paid handsomely to work there, but they have little to do... the wild waters that surround the island might as well be bars. It is said that some Pyreboys have escaped, but I've yet to see proof...

"Anyone unfamiliar with the island and unfortunate enough to end up there is told that, once they leave the shore, they are never to light their way."

"Why?" said Delphi.

"Drogues are attracted to light," said Bream. "But they don't approach the shore lights, because they too fear the wild waters."

"Drogues?" said Delphi. "But drogues are not real."

"Not real?" said Bream. His gaze drifted out towards the island.

42

ROTTING

OLAND AND DELPHI STARED AT EACH OTHER.

"I can't say whether or not a drogue is real," said Bream. "The most I can say is that I've seen strange things. Inexplicable things."

"Like what?" said Oland.

"Movement," said Bream. "Shadows."

"But… have you been on the island?" said Oland.

Bream shook his head. "Apart from the prisoners, anyone who has to go there goes no further than the shore."

"Can you please take us there?" said Oland.

Bream shook his head slowly. "Travellers have gone to Curfew Peak," he continued, "and never returned, and for that reason I won't be taking you there," he said. "You're too young and I couldn't have it on my conscience were you not to make it back alive."

"But we will make it back alive," said Oland.

Bream shook his head. "There is something terribly wrong with Curfew Peak," he said. "There is a dark secrecy that seems to come from the earth itself. It's as though an illness is rotting the island from the inside out." Bream pointed to the sky. "Not to mention The Great Rains are coming... the weather is too fraught."

"What?" said Oland. "The Great Rains?"

"Yes," said Bream.

"When?" said Oland.

"It won't be long. Days..."

"Days?" said Oland. They had travelled for so long that even if they took a more direct route back to Decresian it would be too late.

"Why don't you join us for supper?" said Bream. "There's nothing more for you to do here."

"Thank you," said Oland. "But we won't stay here for much longer."

Bream paused, then nodded and left them behind to join his crew.

Oland turned to Delphi.

"So are you coming to Curfew Peak with me?" he said.

"To the drogues?" said Delphi.

"Movement and shadows are not drogues," said Oland.

Delphi shook her head. "This is where my journey ends."

"No," said Oland. "It can't… we are right there." He pointed across at the island. "We can't give up now after everything we've done."

"Curfew Peak is not a stinking marsh or a scryer's cave, Oland. It's much worse," said Delphi. "I have the worst feeling in the world about Curfew Peak and I think Bream is right. I don't think we will make it out alive. Please, please, Oland, don't go. Because I won't be coming with you, and I don't want you to go alone."

"I'm sorry, but I have to go, whether you come with me or not," said Oland. "This feels like my last chance to find the Crest. I won't give up."

"Please," said Delphi. "I have never begged for anything in my life, but I am begging you now. Do not go."

"I have to," said Oland.

Delphi gripped his arms. "You are making a huge mistake."

Oland pulled gently away from her. "Will you wait for me?"

Delphi paused. "But what if you don't come back?"

"I will come back," said Oland.

"But how are you even going to get there?" said Delphi. "Bream will never take you."

Oland lowered his voice. "I'm going to find another boat…"

"But… do you even know how to sail?" said Delphi.

"A rowing boat," said Oland.

"But what if there are drogues?" said Delphi.

Oland shook his head. "That's just to deter people from going there. I can't understand why there are no boats here. There would have to be boats on a pier like this."

"You're not listening to me," said Delphi. And she knew he hadn't even heard that.

Oland and Delphi sat on the edge of the pier. Minutes passed in tense silence.

"Surely people deliver supplies to Curfew Peak,' said Oland. "Or… people sail from here to other places." He paused, then he shifted backward and lay on his stomach so he could look under the pier. "I knew it!" he said. There were five rowing boats sheltered underneath. He reached down and started pulling at one of the ropes.

"Please, Oland," said Delphi, "we can't do this."

"I have to," said Oland. "I have to continue on my quest."

"Yes – your quest," said Delphi. "Not mine. I just helped you."

"And have stopped helping me when it mattered most," snapped Oland.

"It mattered most every step of the way," said Delphi. "It always matters when someone's life is at stake. And yours is at stake now." She stabbed a finger at the sea. "And mine too, Oland. Mine. You want me to travel across water for you, in a boat you have never helmed. On a strange, strange sea." She turned and walked away.

"I'm sorry, Delphi," said Oland. "I can't come this far, be within reach like this, and just walk away…"

She could hear his footsteps on the timber behind her and the sound of them landing in the boat below. She turned back and watched as it pulled away from the pier. The oars looked huge in Oland's hands.

Delphi took a deep breath… and ran as fast as she could the length of the pier, jumping high and landing behind him.

43

BENEATH THE SURFACE

THE BOAT ROCKED WILDLY FROM SIDE TO SIDE AS DELPHI landed. It tipped down into the ocean, taking on water as it righted itself. An oar slipped from Oland's grip with the fright. Delphi caught it before it fell. But there was no laughter. Oland knew that Delphi had just risked her life by jumping across water on to a moving boat. And Delphi had just encouraged Oland to carry on with a journey she felt was doomed.

"Thank you," was all Oland said.

"I hope Standback will wait for us," she said. Then she looked out at the sea, quietly troubled by the pockets of black sand bursting beneath the surface.

They reached Curfew Peak as darkness was falling. Their faces were rough with sea salt, their eyes stinging. Their arms ached from rowing, but still they pulled the boat to the shore and secured it in a sheltered cove. A line of wooden stakes stretched along the beach, just below the dunes. As the sky was turning its darkest grey, the sound of half-broken voices drifted down from behind them.

"The Pyreboys," said Oland.

Oland and Delphi crouched down and watched as six skinny boys in long grey robes appeared at the stakes. They all looked to be somewhere between twelve and nineteen years old, with straight hair to their shoulders, alabaster skin and dark shadows under their eyes. They wore red kerchiefs tied in a knot around their necks.

Each had a bag filled with birch twigs slung across his body. They collected sticks and branches from the dunes and set them in a pile by the rocks not far from where Oland and Delphi were hiding. One of the Pyreboys took out a tinderbox and, before long, the fire was lit and the boys' faces were illuminated.

They each held a twig to the flames, then set about lighting all the torches along the shore. They returned and gathered around the fire. One of the boys, who looked to be about seventeen, sat cross-legged, clutching his ankles. His hunched shoulders and sunken chest making him appear more timid than he sounded when he spoke.

"Welcome," he said dramatically, and as if he had never met his fellow Pyreboys before. He raised his eyebrows, and looked each one of them in the eye. "Have you ever heard the legend of... Praevisia?" He said the name in a whisper.

"No," said the other boys.

"Blaise, it's my turn to tell a story," said the smallest boy. He was waiflike, like something carved as an almost life-sized figurine. As he turned, it was clear that he was missing his right forearm.

"It's not your turn," said Blaise. "The last time you told a story, Frax, it was about the drogues. Again. Not tonight. Tonight you need to listen to a different legend."

"Sorry, Blaise," said another boy. "It is Frax's turn." He gave Blaise a worried look over Frax's head, as if it would be wise to do what the small boy wanted.

"Frax it shall be!" said Blaise, his eyes wide in mock enthusiasm.

Frax leaned into the circle and began, his lips barely parting as he spoke. "On a wild, hot night, a prison ship rocked up on an island shore, and a stowaway emerged from below deck with a box under his arm. He was met by a band of dastardly boys! But then he knew he would be met by them! They were no surprise. They were exactly what he was here for. They were the Pyreboys of Curfew Peak.

"'For the volunteer brave among you,' said the man, opening his box and revealing rows of glass vials, filled with a cloudy liquid. He pulled one out. 'Try this,' he said. 'It has the power to transform your miserable lives. If the magic captures you, you shall have the chance to leave this island before your sentence ends.'

"Four boys stepped forward and each drank a vial. The man smiled, and it was a terrible smile.

"'But what do we do next?' said one of the brave boys.

"'You simply wait, and you will know,' said the man. 'Ownership of Curfew Peak has passed on to me. I will return, and I will assess your… transformation.'

"'What kind of transformation?' said one of these four boys.

"'If I told you that you would forever be free,' said the man, 'what would you say? If I told you that you could go to places where no one else had been, what would you say?'

"'I would say "yes",' said two more boys, stepping forward to join the others. Only a handful remained behind – they were the older ones, close to being released, with no need to take a risk.

"The man with the magic began to leave, but turned towards the peak instead of the sea.

"'Wait,' said one of the boys, 'where are you going?'

"'To explore my island,' said the man.

"'No one explores Curfew Peak,' said the boy. 'It's not safe.'

"'I'm not afraid of criminals,' said the man.

"'There are more than just criminals to fear,' said the boy.

"The man laughed. He grabbed a bunch of birch twigs from one of the boys and took a light from the fire. Away up the peak he walked with his makeshift torch. Before long, he was just a shadow."

Frax turned and traced his hand across the dunes behind him.

"But," he said, as he turned back to them, "the story was not over yet! For, high on a ridge above him, one by one, six silhouettes slowly filled the dying white circle of the moon; drawn to him like... drogues to a flame."

The Pyreboys gasped.

"You just threw in that last part about the drogues!" said Blaise.

"And what of it?" said Frax. "Did I not end it in style? Or do you want to hear what happened after the drogues pounced?" Frax's eyes moved as if they were each travelling to different parts.

Blaise stood up. "I'm hungry," he said. "Let's go."

"But wait!" said Frax. "Don't you want to hear the cruel, cruel trick that the magic man played—"

"Why would we want to hear that?" said Blaise, turning on him. "You are insane!"

"Oh, Blaise, we all know it has a happy ending!" said Frax. "After, of course, the six brave boys were caged. Yes! Can you imagine? The magic man offered them freedom, but when he saw how well his magic worked, how free they would really be, they were all caged... them and all the brave boys who followed them!" He howled with laughter.

"Blaise, sit down, tell us your story," said another of the Pyreboys.

"Later, Stoker," said Blaise. He began to walk away.

"I'm sure it will be gripping," said Frax, darting in front of Blaise, shooting forward and clutching his throat with his one hand.

Blaise pushed him away, knocking him off balance. "Get away from me, you lunatic."

But Frax was already running ahead, laughing a high, curious laugh.

44

HOPE

THE PYREBOYS DISAPPEARED, LEAVING THE LIGHT OF THE shore behind them.

"If that boy Frax just added that last part," said Delphi, "does that mean the first part was true about the magic man?"

"There is something unhinged about that boy," said Oland. "As for the first part of his story, I have no idea."

"None of the Pyreboys acted like it was new," said Delphi. "What could the magic have been, I wonder." She paused. "Does it not sound like what Malben spoke of: the distillations, extractions, essences and infusions?"

Oland had no desire to answer that, because he thought that to answer yes would be of no reassurance to either of them.

"For now, all we know is that it's a story," he said.

"I wonder what happened to that boy's arm," said Delphi.

"Maybe he was snatched by a drogue," said Oland, laughing. He paused. "Now, how are we to know where to go in the dark?"

"By taking a torch?" said Delphi.

They laughed. The wind whipped up and blew black dust into their eyes and mouths. They coughed and wiped at their eyes.

"This dust is terrible," said Oland.

"We can only hope that the wind dies down," said Delphi. She paused. "We should have approached the Pyreboys."

"We're not supposed to be here," said Oland. "And you're forgetting they're criminals."

"What can they do?" said Delphi.

"Any number of things," said Oland.

"They don't seem like they would hurt us," said Delphi.

"Even if they didn't," said Oland, "who knows what else is on Curfew Peak?"

"I'm not listening to you when you talk like this," said Delphi. "You brought us here. I was the one who didn't want to come, so you are obliged to stay positive. Otherwise, we have no hope." Delphi had already started to walk ahead. "I'm following them," she said. "Because they are the only people we have seen."

Oland caught up with her and they walked the path the

Pyreboys had taken. The wind did not die down as they had wanted. Instead, it continued to rise in gusts, swirling the dust around them. They turned away from it, but it seemed to encircle them. At first it made them cough, but, as the dust was so fine, they became used to inhaling it and it was only their eyes that seemed to be affected. They bowed their heads and kept moving.

"This won't end well," said Delphi.

"Stop," said Oland.

"But it won't," said Delphi. "I feel like this island is crawling all over me and pulling me in."

"It's just an island," said Oland.

"It's not just an island," said Delphi. "I have a bad feeling." She walked faster.

"What would you know?" said Oland. His voice was like a whip.

Delphi stopped dead. She turned to him, her eyes flaming red, her pupils huge. She drew back her hand and slapped Oland hard across the face.

He gasped.

"What did you say to me?" she said.

"Delphi…" said Oland. He moved towards her, his eyes wild. He was suddenly overwhelmed with rage. He pushed her hard.

She fell backward on to the ground, throwing up a cloud of black dust. All Oland could see through the darkness were Delphi's eyes, burning like flames. She jumped towards him and kicked him hard in the stomach. Oland gasped as he rolled on to his knees, coughing and spitting. His heart was pounding, his hands shaking. He rose slowly to face Delphi. Water streamed from his eyes and nose. Delphi wiped the back of her hand across her face and spat on the ground. She stepped towards him, her fists already raised.

"I said," shouted Oland, "what would you know? You've barely been outside your door all your life!"

Delphi went to punch him.

Startled, Oland blocked it, grabbing her wrist and holding it firm between them. Delphi stood staring through him, almost in a trance.

"Get out of my way!" she roared, pulling her arm back. Her eyes bored through him. A shiver ran up his spine.

"No wonder your father had to lock you up—"

"Because he was worried!" said Delphi.

"And did you believe that?" said Oland. "Did you believe everything that Chancey the Gold told you?"

"Of course I did!" said Delphi. "Why are you asking me that?"

"You told me that you fell ill in Galenore when you were young, and that there were no doctors there to treat you," said Oland. "We passed three doctors' rooms—"

"They might not have been there six years ago!" said Delphi.

"They were!" said Oland. "They were all established at least nine years ago – it said so on the plaques beside their doors."

"I was only telling you what I remember…" she shouted.

"Or what you made up," said Oland. "Or what Chancey the Gold told you. Maybe you're both liars!"

Delphi's eyes widened. "I'm telling you the truth," she said. "You don't know what it feels like to have no freedom, to be forced to stay—"

"Everything I *did* I was forced to do!" said Oland.

"You've never had a father to answer to," said Delphi. "And The Craven Lodge never cared what you did. You had the run of a castle, you could come and go as you pleased as long as you polished their boots—"

"Polished their boots!" said Oland.

He stood watching Delphi, feeling the anger that radiated off her churning with his own rage. It was disturbing. He wanted her to get away from him. He couldn't comprehend it.

"Well, whatever you did for them, you were free," said Delphi.

"Oh, yes," said Oland. "How wonderful it was to be able to run free in the pitch dark of a miserable kingdom—"

"Then why didn't you leave?" said Delphi. "I don't understand why you didn't run from that life if it was so terrible."

"I don't expect you to understand after the cosseted life you've led!" said Oland, his voice rising. "Are people slaves because they choose to be? You have no idea how The Craven Lodge can torture a mind. And it's not just mine. It's the entire kingdom! Why didn't the whole of Decresian just leave?" He paused to draw breath, sucking in more dust. "And on top of everything, I have drawn the wrath of Villius Ren even more than usual, just by going into his private room. And let's not forget his reaction to me slaying those panthers—"

"And weren't you lucky," said Delphi, "that glory was the prize?"

"A man's *life* was the prize," said Oland.

He remembered how Malachy Graham had lived for just one more day after what happened in the arena. Everything that Oland had been trying to bury came rushing back to him.

"Why does it matter to you whether I left the castle years ago?" he said.

"Because it would have shown that you were—"

"What?" said Oland. "Brave?" He had begun to shout. "And what if my mother had come back? What if my mother had come back to find me? And I was gone! Then what?"

They stared at each other. Moments passed.

"Go away," said Oland. "Just leave me alone."

Delphi turned around towards the peak. Oland watched as she pulled up her hood and ran ahead, the wind with its swirling black dust sweeping her oilskin cape up behind her. He called to her. She didn't turn around. She didn't even break her stride.

The wind whipped at Oland's hair and stung his eyes. Then he remembered what Bream had said. It was the dust. The dust was causing their anger! The Pyreboys had kerchiefs around their necks. They must have been to wrap around their mouths to stop them inhaling it.

Oland ripped a strip of fabric from the bottom of his tunic.

"Delphi!" he shouted. "Delphi!"

He started to walk towards her, but she had moved so quickly ahead, his words were being carried away. "Delphi!" he shouted. There was no reply. He couldn't tell where she had gone. He pulled out his tinderbox and, using the flint and steel, showered sparks on to the sand. He wanted to make her laugh; he wanted to see her face. Delphi turned around and smiled. Oland waved the fabric at her and pointed at his face. She watched as he wrapped it around his mouth. She ripped a piece from the bottom of her top and did the same. Oland was relieved to see that she stood waiting for him. He could feel his own anger ebb away.

But, drawn by the smallest of sparks, a band of drogues leapt from the darkness. It was Delphi they were closest to. And it was Delphi they encircled.

45

ENGULFED

THE BREATH RUSHED FROM OLAND'S LUNGS AND HIS head filled with a terrible icy weight. He was transfixed. These creatures that they had only ever thought of as myth stood before them, dark and grotesque: *'One mythic beast was four engulfed: vulture, bull, bear and wolf'*. In the flesh, they were beyond their worst imaginings. They towered over Delphi, stamping their sinewy, hoofed front legs, their eyes small and shining, casting a hazy silver light in front of them in the darkness. Their long snouts were covered in short sharp spines that looked like a thousand tiny needles..

Oland, stirred from his paralysis by the drogues' snarling and grunting, began to run towards Delphi.

"Delphi!" he roared, the sound muffled by his mask. But right before him, Delphi disappeared, screaming, into the circle of beasts. He could scarcely make out the shapes and shadows ahead, but he ran desperately towards them. It was too dark for him to see what was happening, but he was overcome with a terrible sickness at the rawness of the sound. If the drogues were everything it was said they were, Oland knew that there was no way they would make it away from this alive. Overhead, a dark cloud drifted from the charcoal moon and, for an instant, he watched as one of the drogues reared up on its hind legs and dived into the circle. Oland heard Delphi roar. A cloud of dust exploded from the earth, engulfing her, engulfing the beasts.

"Delphi," Oland shouted. "Delphi!" All he could hear were her cries, and the desperate howling of the drogues. As quickly as the violence erupted, it ended. There was an eerie silence, followed by the sound of the creatures darting from the scene towards the top of Curfew Peak. Oland ran to where Delphi lay, her small body limp and covered in blood.

He knelt by Delphi's side. Her cape was twisted around her, one of the sleeves was ripped and her hood was pulled to the side of her head. Her hair was matted and stuck to her face. Oland turned her head towards him, smoothing the hair gently back. Her eyes were closed. The material that had covered her mouth was in shreds on the ground beside her. But Oland could see that her chest was moving up and down. She was breathing. They were shallow breaths, but she was alive. She was still alive. Suddenly, her eyes flickered open. Oland jumped, and staggered backward. Delphi sat up. Her face was filled with terror. As she looked down at herself, she cried out, wiping at the blood on her face, streaking it with her panicked fingers.

"Quick," said Oland. "Don't breathe in any more dust." He ripped off more of his tunic and wrapped it around her mouth.

She twisted and turned, searching her body for wounds. They both gasped when they saw one of the drogues, lying still behind a huge boulder beside them.

"What happened?" said Oland. "What happened?"

"I don't know," said Delphi. "They must have turned on each other."

"How strange," said Oland. "According to the stories, they don't to do that."

"I don't know why they attacked each other," said Delphi, "but I'm grateful they did. I… I can't believe I'm alive."

"Are you sure you're not hurt?" said Oland. "Stand up… slowly."

Delphi stood up, and Oland turned her around to see if there was a wound that she had missed.

"Your oilskins may have saved you," said Oland, trying to

smile. He could barely look at her. He took a flask of water from his bag. "Do you want to wash your face?" he said.

"Thank you," said Delphi. She held her breath, then pulled off her mask, and stared at the ground as he poured water over her hands and she washed the blood away. Oland helped her put on her mask again.

"Do you still want to go on?" he said. "We can go back, if you like. I'd rather that you were—"

Delphi shook her head. "Let's go. Let's keep going."

"I should go first," he said. "If I had gone first the last time, you wouldn't have been in danger…"

"You can barely see where you're going," said Delphi. "That's the only reason I went first. I'm used to the darkness of the caves; my eyes have adjusted."

Oland again followed her, almost kicking her heels as he walked. Despite his covered mouth, he was trying desperately not to choke on the terrible stench of the drogues' blood that Delphi was trailing behind her.

46

THE LEGEND OF PRAEVISIA

OLAND AND DELPHI REACHED THE RAGGED STONE path that led to the Pyreboys' cabin. The air was clear and there was only a sprinkling of black dust on the ground. They untied their masks and returned them to Oland's bag. They could hear a faint voice inside the cabin. They walked up the path and listened.

It was Blaise. "Finally!" he was saying. "I shall recount the Legend of Praevisia. And not a word from any of you."

Oland looked at Delphi and shook his head. Now was not the time to call on the Pyreboys.

"Hundreds and thousands of years ago," said Blaise, "a baby girl was born, arriving, bawling, into the world, like every other baby born before and since. The midwife handed her to her mother and the baby quietened. Satisfied, the nurse smiled and left the two alone, promising to return the following day. When she closed the door behind her, the baby opened her eyes. The mother stifled a scream. For the baby's eyes were like two pools of crystal water. There appeared to be no end to their depth and there was no dark pupil at their centre.

"Although the mother did not sleep one wink, the baby drifted in and out of sleep all night. But each time she opened her eyes, they were the same deep pools of crystal water, and the mother saw images in them: she saw herself, she saw family, friends, people she knew. When the nurse arrived the following day, the terrified mother told her everything. But when her daughter opened her eyes, the pools of water were gone, and she simply had two beautiful eyes of blue. The nurse told the mother that her tiredness had led her to see things that were not there. The mother, relieved, named her beautiful baby daughter Praevisia.

"It was later said that for the first twenty-four hours of her life, the baby's eyes were pools to be filled with the futures of many, and that these visions would pass across them, for anyone fearless enough not to be repelled by the aberrance. For Praevisia was a scryer, born with the power to see things before they came to pass."

Blaise continued. "It first happened during a thunderstorm two days before her tenth birthday. The sky grew dark and rain started to pour from the skies. Lightning would not be far behind.

"Praevisia had been playing in the garden, but her mother soon called on her to come into the safety of the house. Overhead, the thunder built to a deafening crescendo. Seconds later, a huge bolt of lightning struck the tree in front of Praevisia as she ran to her mother. It exploded into flames. But this was not what terrified Praevisia. What terrified her were the hundreds of images that flooded her mind as the flames shone in the water at her feet. She saw fragments of her mother's future, her friends', and all the noblemen for miles around.

"Praevisia fell to the ground, screaming, her entire body rocking and shaking with the power of what she had just seen. Her mother rushed to her side, throwing herself on the ground, dragging her daughter into her arms. The flames raged behind her, the rain poured down, but she held her daughter there until the last embers died.

"'I saw everything,' said Praevisia to her mother. 'I saw the future. Strange pictures have been coming to my mind since I was eight years old and now they make sense. I can see the future.' She jumped up. 'I must tell my friends.'

"But Praevisia's mother stopped her and made her promise never to speak of her gift to another person as long as she lived. For who would believe that someone could see the future?

"But," Blaise continued, "someone did believe. Praevisia's mother took her to a strange medicine man to cure her. It turned out that even Praevisia's own mother did not believe that Praevisia could see the future, the medicine man believed. He bided his time until many years had passed and Praevisia's mother had died. He returned on the day of her funeral to take Praevisia away and lock her up in a cave to tell the fortunes of others in exchange for gold.

"But," said Blaise again, holding up a finger, "Praevisia had a true love that no one knew about and, before this medicine man had come back to take her, Praevisia had borne her true love a son and a daughter and her gift was passed on. And over the years, while she was locked away, her son and daughter met true loves of their own, and their gift was passed to the next generation and the next and the next.

"And it is said that an old woman – the Scryer of Gort – who lives in a barren land, is in her ninety-ninth year of telling the fortunes of those who have the gold to see her. She tried to poke out her own eyes when she discovered her gift, so only one eye remains. She is the longest serving scryer and, if the next scryer is not revealed soon, the spell will be broken, and never again will a fortune be told. The men who guard this scryer, the Bastions, will do anything to find the Rising Scryer, so they can lock her in a cave for a hundred years and continue to collect their golden reward."

"Is that a true story?" came a Pyreboy's voice.

"As true as I sit here tonight," said Blaise. "As true as the fact that only the scryer herself will know the Rising Scryer, because—"

Delphi lost her balance and, as she steadied herself, her boot raked across the stony ground.

Blaise stopped suddenly. "Shh!" he said. "Shh! Stoker, go!"

There was silence inside. Oland and Delphi froze. They could hear footsteps on the floorboards. They had no time to react, as the door burst open and Stoker stood staring down at them.

47

FRAX

STOKER FROWNED. "WHO ARE YOU?" HE SAID TO OLAND, but his focus quickly became Delphi alone. He smiled. It was a remarkable sight – the counterweight to every bleak, washed-out, charcoal corner of a Pyreboy's existence.

Delphi smiled back.

Stoker had an almost feminine face, long dark hair, sculpted cheekbones and long eyelashes. His face and neck were coated in an even layer of soot. His hands were black and his fingernails blacker.

Oland stood up. "I am Oland Born," he said. "This is my friend, Delphi."

"I'm Stoker," he said, his eyes only on Delphi as she stood up.

From behind Stoker another Pyreboy appeared, pushing in front of him.

"Where do you come from?" he said, spitting out the words. "What do you want?"

"Flint..." said Stoker, his voice appeasing.

Flint pushed him back.

"What do you want?" said Flint again.

"Well," said Oland, "we are from the Kingdom of Decresian. We are looking for something. And this something may be found here..."

"Do, please, come in." Flint bowed graciously and led Delphi and Oland into the room. It was dimly lit by half-melting candles and the windows were shuttered. There were armchairs all around the room, draped in dull grey sheets and blankets. A Pyreboy lay slumped on each one, his eyes heavy, his body limp. Along the wall by the door was a row of hooks, each holding the bag the Pyreboys used to carry their birch to the shore. Underneath, each had a crate that held a tinderbox, cloth and a jar of wax to make the torches. The Pyreboys' names were on the top of each hook: Blaise, Flint, Brennen, Stoker, Tallow and Frax.

"Pyreboys," said Blaise, "welcome these visitors from Decresian. They are looking for something, though can't say what, and won't say why."

Everyone but Stoker laughed.

"Now," said Flint, turning to Oland and Delphi. "How may we help you to find this something that may be on Curfew Peak?"

"I... we... it's a crest," said Oland.

"We need to find a crest," said Delphi.

Flint frowned. "For Decresian? Why would—"

"No," said Oland. "Not for Decresian. For Sabian."

Flint let out a long breath. "There is no Sabian," he said. "This is Sabian." His tone was cruel. He threw his hands up in the air. "You are standing on Sabian ground. Curfew Peak is all that is left of Sabian."

"We know that," said Delphi, "but we thought maybe that there might be a Crest of Curfew Peak, and that—"

Flint laughed. "A Crest of Curfew Peak? A prison crest? Are we to travel the land planting our flags and claiming territories? Who told you that there was? And what has it got to do with you? We are hundreds of miles away from your miserable kingdom."

"Curfew Peak is miserable!" shouted Delphi. "A miserable place! If this is what is left of Sabian, good riddance to it. Maybe Curfew Peak can go the same way and take its hideous beasts with it. And the criminals who live in the half-darkness—"

Flint stepped towards her. "Get out! Go live your lives. What are you doing here, if you haven't been condemned here? I've got one month left and I am doing nothing for no one to jeopardise my freedom. None of us is."

He pushed them out of the door. The last thing Delphi could see from inside was a look of apology on Stoker's face before Flint slammed the door. Delphi pounded on the door with her fists until Oland dragged her away. She pulled up the hood of her cape.

From the side of the cabin, they heard the crunching of stones. The smallest Pyreboy, Frax, stuck his head out. "Girl," he said. "Girl!"

"Yes?" said Delphi.

"Did you see the drogues?" said Frax, shifting from one foot to the other, the stump of his right arm twitching. His skinny left forefinger was pointing to her ripped clothes.

"Yes!" said Delphi.

Frax's eyes went wide. "Were they scary?" he said, walking over to them.

"Yes," said Oland. His voice was firm. He was trying to guide Delphi away from Frax.

"Haven't you ever seen a drogue?" said Delphi.

Frax shook his head violently. "No," he said. "None of us has! In all these years!"

"Here," he said, taking two clean kerchiefs from his back pocket. He handed the first to Delphi, the second to Oland. "For your journey back," he said.

"Thank you," said Delphi. "Why were you sent here?"

Oland squeezed her elbow, again trying to pull her away.

"Where are you from?" said Delphi.

"Quisknee," said Frax. It was pronounced *quiz*-nee. "The place with the funny spelling."

"Why were you sent here?" said Delphi again.

"For spelling it wrong," said Frax. He paused before he laughed, which he managed to do through pinched lips so it shot through his nose. Then he jumped from one foot to the other as he half sang, half spoke: "Q is for Quick! U is for You. I is for Me. S is for Show. K is for Knowing, N is for No, E is for Easy, he's Eager to go."

He pointed at Oland for the last part. He had clearly been a street performer of some kind. Oland's face was set. He had no time for cheap tricks.

"Girl, I was sent to Curfew Peak for stealing," said Frax. "Two slices of Quisknee's finest bacon slices. From a live pig. And also for beating the farmer I stole them from. And for picking the pocket of the person who came to help him. And for burning down both their houses." He smiled a black-tipped, tiny-toothed smile.

Delphi felt the hairs on the back of her neck stand up. "Well," she said, "we better be on our way."

"Good luck," said Frax, nodding furiously, his eyes wide. He threw his head back and laughed. "Good luck. Run for the shore," he said. "That's what I'd do. Run for the shore."

A sudden gust of wind swept Delphi's hood from her head.

Frax recoiled when he saw her face. He struggled to speak. "Stay away from me!" he managed to say. "Stay away!" He began to walk backward.

"Pardon?" said Delphi.

"Stay away from me!" roared Frax.

"I'm sorry," said Delphi, alarmed. "I didn't mean to—"

"Mean to what?" said Frax.

"I don't know… to… to frighten you…" said Delphi.

Frax stepped forward. Delphi froze. He grabbed her with his one hand, then jerked her close. He whispered into her ear. "You didn't mean to frighten me when you ripped my arm off, either, did you?"

Delphi pulled away from his grip. "Let me go!" she shouted.

"What do you think you're doing?" shouted Oland, putting himself between Frax and Delphi.

"What do I think I'm doing?" said Frax. His eyes were wide with fright.

"You can't just grab a girl like that," said Oland.

"A girl?" said Frax. "A girl?" He snorted. "She ain't no girl. She's a roxling witch."

48

STAKES

FRAX GAVE ONE LAST PANICKED GLANCE BEHIND HIM before he disappeared into the shadows.

"He called *you* roxling..." said Oland.

Delphi was too stunned to speak.

"He's clearly mad," said Oland.

"That was... the strangest... we need to leave here, now," said Delphi. "Bream was right about this place. We should have listened to him. And there's no crest here anyway..."

Delphi and Oland made their way down to the shore to the cove where they had left the boat tied.

"They imprisoned a firewild on an island where his only job is to burn things," said Delphi, untying the rope from the stanchion. "How is that meant to teach him anything?"

"I would venture that no one is meant to learn anything on

Curfew Peak," said Oland, taking the rope and beginning to pull the boat into the water.

"We certainly haven't," said Delphi. "What a hideous place."

Suddenly, Oland grabbed for his bag and opened it. He stared inside. He shook out the contents. "The little runt!" He jumped up. "He's taken King Micah's letter! He's taken my knife!"

They both stood up.

"When he was handing me the kerchief, he was distracting you," said Delphi.

"Singing his stupid song." He started to walk back towards the cabin.

"We can't go back up there," said Delphi.

"Oh, we can," said Oland. "I'm getting that letter back…"

He fell silent. An ominous sound was building at the far end of the shore, its deep tone mounting over the sound of the water.

Delphi looked towards the source. "Oh, Oland," she said.

A wave taller than the highest tower in Castle Derrington rounded the cliff on the furthest end of the shore and moved in a way that they had never before seen water move. Oland felt as tiny as one of his tin soldiers.

It was a tornado of water, swirling and foaming, spinning towards them, half in the ocean, half tearing up the beach. They watched as its vicious, twisting force quenched the first torch that the Pyreboys had lit, then the second, then the third. It moved rapidly towards them.

"Look!" said Oland, pointing. "The stakes are still standing! The water has quenched the flames, but the stakes are still there. Run for the stakes! We must climb the stakes!"

He turned to Delphi, a girl whose whole life had been spent facing dangerous waters. He thought about her strange existence – the fact that she knew so well the thing that could kill her. And here it was in a terrifying incarnation, bearing down on her, hostile and insurmountable.

They reached out for each other's hands as the water came their way, the white ridges of the waves foaming and spitting.

"What about the boat?" shouted Delphi.

"Forget the boat," said Oland. "Run!" He pulled her towards the closest stake. "Wrap your arms around it," he said. "You'll get wet, the water will be powerful, but you will not be submerged."

Delphi grabbed on to the stake. Oland ran to one that was twenty feet from hers, closer to the swirling water that was charging their way. He wrapped his arms and legs around the timber, pressing his cheek against the weathered wood. The last thing he saw before he squeezed his eyes shut was the wall of water, building in strength and height the closer it came.

The strange tornado hit Oland with breathtaking force. Delphi screamed as the water washed over him, but he held his grip on the stake.

Seconds later, Oland opened his eyes and turned to Delphi. The stake where she had stood was still there, but Delphi was gone. Oland's heart jumped. He looked towards the shore and saw one of her boots where it had been torn from her foot. But worse than that, when his eyes moved out to sea, he saw the turmoil of the water and, at its height, Delphi. Her tiny body was being thrown around with the force.

But still, she did not go under. Oland couldn't predict what the water would do next – maybe it would spin back towards the shore and drop Delphi at his feet. Instead, he watched in horror as the water started to calm and each rotation of the tornado got slower and weaker. And, as it did, Delphi was dropped lower and lower until, eventually, she was submerged.

"No!" screamed Oland. "No! Delphi!"

He ran into the waves until the water was up to his waist. "Delphi!" he roared. He could see nothing except miles of merciless water and the white tops of its waves. "Delphi!" He roared and roared until his throat burned. And, as the water rose around him, he was forced to swim. It was a monstrous battle to stay afloat. He fought for as long as he could, but soon, part of him wanted to succumb to the waves. As their force waned, he finally washed up, shattered, back on to the shore of Curfew Peak.

49

RECKLESS

CURFEW PEAK WAS THE DARKEST PLACE IN THE WORLD when its torchlights were quenched. Oland sat on the shore for hours, waiting for Delphi. He ached in every way possible, but he refused to lose hope, if only because Delphi believed in it. He had never thought it was her life he would be hoping for.

The water had calmed, and it seemed cruel that it could rise up so violently, and now stretch out before him, almost serene. It was as though it had gone back to sleep after a nightmare. For Oland, there was no nightmare, just a horrifying reality. He fought sleep. If there was a chance that he could go into the water again, that Delphi might appear and that he would have another chance to save her, he wanted to take it. But, as he listened to the gentle, lapping, lying ocean, exhaustion finally took over.

After a short troubled half-sleep, he woke up, desolate. The sun had come up and was cruelly shining on the bare shore. His best friend, his only friend, was gone. He was the one person who could have saved her. And he had failed. There would be no second chance. He looked out again at the mocking calm of the sea. There was just undulating water, no waves, no white crests.

Oland felt something stir at the edges of his consciousness, an idea beginning to form. Something to do with waves, their rage and their calm. *No white crests.*

Oland sat up. "Waves!" he cried. King Micah's riddle rushed back to him. "Depth and height. From blue to white!" A wave!

"I have found the Crest of Sabian," he said. *The giant wave that struck the shore of what was once Sabian.*

Oland realised that it had never been a heraldic crest they were searching for. It was the crest of a wave.

"Delphi," he shouted, running back towards the water. "Delphi – it was the wave. The Crest of Sabian… Delphi… Delphi…"

He had discovered the Crest of Sabian. But it was gone, and it had taken Delphi with it. Powerful gusts encircled him. An unfamiliar pain burned in his chest. He struggled to breathe. But he could no longer blame the wind for that. The fact that he had found someone like Delphi and so quickly lost her was what was truly taking his breath away.

Distraught, Oland backed away from the sea and walked up towards the dunes. He thought about the crest; he wondered, could a wave really be lost? Or was it just swallowed up by the sea and returned again in a different form?

He let out a breath as a feeling slowly crept over him. All of nature had been stirred up: the high winds at Galenore, the sea off Pallimer Bay, the terrifying height of the Crest of Sabian. Oland could feel the ground, unsettled, beneath him.

He considered the rest of King Micah's riddle:

'What's left behind is yours to find.'

He looked around the beach. The only things that the wave had left behind were the stakes. And him. The boy who was to save the Kingdom of Decresian. He felt like a fool. The boat they had stolen had been washed high on to the dunes, and made his efforts seem all the more pathetic.

But then he noticed something, something that had only appeared after the wave had struck. It was a deep channel that had been filled with seawater, and it wound into darkness through an archway in the cliff. Oland wondered if this was where he should go. He looked further up Curfew Peak. In the gloom, he could see the place where the drogues had attacked Delphi; he recognised the silhouette of the boulder where Delphi had lain.

Delphi. With the recklessness that comes with loss, Oland ran up the dunes to the boat and dragged it towards the channel. He set it in the water and climbed inside. He had no reason to do anything else. He had nowhere else to go.

He rowed up the channel. Before long, it ended in a pool, and from its centre rose a giant, craggy, triangular rock. The only sound was the echo of the lapping water. Oland sat in the boat, feeling like he had reached the end of the world. Cliffs towered around him. The only way out was the way he had come in. He had truly reached a dead end. The cliffs were so high and curved at the top, it was almost as dark as night. Oland looked up at the sky, and willed even a sliver of sunshine to appear. But he knew he had no power to alter the dark world of Curfew Peak.

Suddenly, a shaft of sunlight shone through the opening. Oland straightened. He stared up, but it was no longer just the sun that had captured his attention. Halfway up the rock, at the centre of the pool, there was a metal door. Oland rowed closer. He tied the boat to a stanchion, and climbed up.

The door was bolted shut in two places. Oland's heart pounded wildly as he slid back the first bolt, then the second. He pushed open the door. The tiny cell glowed with candlelight. As he stood in the threshold, a figure came into focus. Oland's legs were weakened by a rush of recognition. For before him a man, a portrait, had come to life.

The man rose to his feet.

Oland could not understand how this could be. He could not understand how now, years from his birth, and years after his death, stood roxley Prince Roxleigh… the lunatic prince.

50

BANISHED

PRINCE ROXLEIGH SMILED. ALTHOUGH HE HAD AGED, HE seemed youthful. His smile was as warm as Oland had been told and there was a charming curve to his mouth. His limbs were skinny, his neck slender and his grey hair was like tumbleweed.

"Now, who might you be?" he said.

Oland struggled to reply. He'd had no time to process the loss of his only friend, and now he had to process the reappearance of a dead prince.

"My name is Oland Born." he finally managed "I am from Decresian."

"And did you come looking for me or did you stumble across me?" said Roxleigh. His brow furrowed as he spoke and one eye opened slightly wider than the other. It was an endearing quirk.

"But…" said Oland, "you're…"

"Mad?" said Roxleigh. "Dead?"

Oland didn't want to answer.

"Both?" said Roxleigh. He smiled. "I'm sane and very much alive."

"But everyone thinks you went to an asylum," said Oland.

"Oh, I did. But that was a very long time ago…"

"I know," said Oland.

"It is sad when a father thinks his son has gone mad," said Roxleigh. "Sadder still when everyone appears to agree."

"But people only ever speak fondly of you," said Oland.

"Ah," said Roxleigh, raising a finger, "but also mockingly." He paused. "Have you ever called someone roxley?"

Oland nodded. "Yes… I'm sorry…"

Roxleigh smiled. "Now, back to the questions…"

Oland was hesitant. "Why are you here? Why are you imprisoned?"

Roxleigh smiled. "Please don't worry, Oland. I'm on your side. I'm on the side of Decresian."

"Who keeps you here?" said Oland.

"I keep myself here," said Roxleigh. "I came to Curfew Peak for my own reasons, and then I decided to stay. Now, tell me, Oland – how did you come to be here?"

Oland told him about finding King Micah's letter, without mention of the archivist's hand, which might have diminished the letter's importance in the prince's eyes.

"Would you mind showing me the letter, Oland?" said Roxleigh.

"A Pyreboy stole it..."

"Frax?" said Roxleigh. "The firewild? It is ash by now, I imagine. He used to spend a lot of time in Galenore when he was younger. Before he fell under the spell of fire, he was a street act, a thief. Shameless. He once stole the emerald ring from a magistrate and had the gall to wear it himself. He used to steal anything from anyone – he wasn't particular..."

"What happened to his arm?" said Oland.

"He tried to steal from the wrong person is what I heard," said Roxleigh. "Now, to the king's letter..."

"I remember it all," said Oland, "I've read it so many times." And he recited the king's words:

"'You live in the ruins of a once-proud kingdom destroyed by greed and misguided ambition. But fear not – Decresian shall be restored. And it falls to you, Oland Born, to do so. On such young shoulders, it will

prove astonishing how light this burden will be.

Your quest is to find the Crest of Sabian before The Great Rains fall, lest the mind's toil of a rightful king be washed away.
In life, a father's folly may be his son's reward.

In case this letter were to fall into the wrong hands, to guide you, know this:
Depth and height
From blue to white
What's left behind
Is yours to find.

Be wise in your choice of companion and, by nightfall, be gone.

In fondness and faith,
King Micah of Decresian'"

Roxleigh went very still. It was some time before he spoke. "I don't quite understand all of that, Oland. But... tell me, have you heard anything from anyone else about The Great Rains?"

"A madman," Oland paused. "I mean… a man in the village of Derrington says that The Great Rains are nigh."

"Who is this man?" said Roxleigh.

"His name is Magnus—"

"Magnus Miller?" said Roxleigh.

"Yes!" said Oland.

"What about the Roses?" said Roxleigh.

"Hester Rose?" said Oland. "That's his wife, who tended the gardens of Castle Derrington."

"And the Dyers?" said Roxleigh.

"Gaudy Dyer?" said Oland.

Roxleigh nodded. "Are they saying the same thing?" he said.

"Yes," said Oland, "and a man called Bream who we met at Pallimer Bay. But how do you know these people?"

"Decresian is a land of tradition," said Roxleigh. "They're all, I would guess, descendants of the group of great thinkers I was once part of, along with my dearest friend, Rowe. The Great Rains nearly destroyed Decresian, so it became one of the subjects we studied. No one had predicted them. We looked for signs… anything that might have foretold them."

"Such as?" said Oland.

"There were teal flowers that only bloomed right before The Great Rains came," said Roxleigh, "shoals of amber fish, particular types of cloud formations, high winds, shipwrecks, cyclonic waves—"

"I don't know about shipwrecks, but the rest have all happened," said Oland.

Roxleigh's eyes widened. "In that case, we must return to Decresian at once," he said.

51

HEARTBREAK

PRINCE ROXLEIGH BLEW OUT THE CANDLE, AND THEY left the cell. Carefully, they made their way down the rocks and into the boat.

"Why did everyone think you were insane?" said Oland.

"From a very early age, I had knowledge beyond my years," said Roxleigh. "Effectively, I could see things that other people couldn't, maybe a link from one thing to another, or a future for something that seemed unimaginable or impossible. My father, King Seward... well, he thought I was a genius." Roxleigh laughed. "He was a wonderful man, kind and generous and loving. He indulged me; he allowed me to build a laboratory in the dungeons of Castle Derrington. And so, while my peers were overhead in the arena learning sword skills that could end lives, I was learning skills that could enhance the lives of men.

"When the bermid plague struck, everything changed. As you may know, my father, King Seward, vowed to contain the plague within Decresian, despite not understanding how it had come about. He tried what he could, but nothing worked and he was devastated. The plague raged on.

"My very best friend, Rowe, and I were 'joined at the brain' as we used to say. We worked night and day to find a way to stop the plague. We focused on how these strange ants worked. And they literally worked, almost like soldiers. They were like hybrid insects – they behaved like ants, but they were also like bees, like scorpions. We had heard the myth of the drogues, and thought that perhaps there was something to it, which is often the case with myths: they contain elements of the truth or they're exaggerated versions of the truth. We thought that perhaps on Curfew Peak there was *some* kind of hybrid beast. We didn't expect something quite as fantastical as a drogue." He paused. "Of course, that was exactly what we found. Or rather, what Rowe found. While I manned the laboratory at Derrington, he went alone on that journey. He was always the adventurer." He smiled. "Rowe studied the drogues for weeks, unobserved. But one day, he let his guard down, and a pack attacked him. He slew a drogue, and the rest of the pack fled."

Oland thought of Delphi, and it sickened him. "Or the drogue was attacked by one of his pack," he said, with new authority.

Roxleigh shook his head. "No," he said. "Remember, I have studied these beasts for years. I have never seen evidence of that."

"But how was Rowe able to slay a drogue?" said Oland.

"Clever man that he is, he found their weak point. Because the vertebrae of the drogue are so pronounced, Rowe had observed that the seventh one down from the head was much smaller than the others. He struck that point and, indeed, it felled the beast. He returned to Derrington, triumphant. Between Rowe's research and mine, we had discovered how the ants worked. The problem arose when I approached my father and told him how to tackle the plague. My father was sceptical, to say the least. I think his pride had been hurt and, regardless of how intelligent he believed me to be, he couldn't accept that I was right. He thought if a king could not control this plague, how could a boy of nineteen?

"And then tragedy struck. Rowe disappeared. I was distraught. We all were. Weeks passed with no sign of his return and, after much consideration, I confided in my father that Rowe had gone to Curfew Peak and had slain a drogue and that, perhaps, for some unknown reason, he had returned there." Roxleigh took a deep breath. "I will never forget the look on my father's face

– one of pity and heartbreak. It was the expression of a loving father coming to the conclusion that his son was insane, after all my time holed up in my dungeon laboratory. 'Your beloved friend succumbed to the plague, my dear Roxleigh – nothing more fantastical than that,' he said. 'You must understand that to believe in drogues is madness, and to say so outside the walls of this room will undermine both my rule… and your future rule.'

"I was horrified. Nothing was more important to me than Rowe. I pleaded and begged with my father; I tried to convince him. I gave him all the details I possibly could. This is what people went on to describe as 'wild ramblings'. It was just because they didn't understand my ideas, because they were too advanced. At first, my father appeared to listen. But it transpired that he had simply become resigned to my insanity; the following night, doctors came for me, I was taken from my bed, strapped into a carriage and brought to an asylum."

"How did you escape?" said Oland.

"I was eventually released," said Roxleigh. "After my father died. He had signed me in for as long as he lived. Unfortunately, he lived for a very long time. And, once released, I came here, to Curfew Peak. It was, after all, the last place I thought Rowe had gone. I hoped to help him. While locked away in the asylum, I had much time to think, and I realised that Rowe's behaviour changed only after his visit to Curfew Peak. When I asked him about slaying the drogue, he appeared haunted, even though he was the victor, the one who had triumphed.

"I thought of the drogues and how curious they were and about the mongrel blood that coursed through them. I came to the conclusion that Rowe in some way had been poisoned on Curfew Peak – poisoned by the drogues. Despite the years that had passed, part of me hoped that my research was still in Castle Derrington, so I planned to travel back and search for it. Before I had a chance to, I was discovered here," said Roxleigh. "Prison or no prison, I was still trespassing. And those who rule Curfew Peak did not want me to roam free, to reveal the secrets of the island."

"How did King Micah know you were here?" said Oland. "How did he know to send me here?"

"A Pyreboy took pity on me," said Roxleigh. "He had started out as my guard, but we had become friends, of sorts. Certainly, he was miserable with his life on Curfew Peak, and, like me, he wanted to be free. Though he was not from Decresian, he had ancestors there. He understood me. He was a very bright young man, who was innocent of the crime he was banished here for.

He told me that King Micah, who was my brother Stanislas' son, was now ruling Decresian. It gave me hope. Stanislas, who was only a child when I was sent away, looked up to me. He always believed in me, which of course meant nothing to anyone, because he was only a boy. Of course, it meant the world to me.

"So my Pyreboy friend stowed away on the prison boat and made his way to Decresian to take my message to King Micah. It must have been fourteen years ago and I haven't heard from him since. I know now that he must have reached King Micah, because, as you said, how else would he have known where to find me? I'm trying to work out how you figure in all of this, Oland. Clearly, you are a capable young man; after all, here you are. But why did King Micah himself not come for me?"

"I'm afraid King Micah was overthrown fourteen years ago," said Oland. "He was killed by his most loyal counsel, a man named Villius Ren."

Roxleigh bowed his head. "Most loyal, indeed," he said. "So King Micah may well have taken the secret of me to his grave, then," he said. "Though he left a letter for you."

"Why didn't the Pyreboy come back and rescue you?" said Oland.

"I don't know," said Prince Roxleigh. "I fear that he was killed.

I always expected him to come back here, of course… that was the plan. Especially as, in his absence, his youngest brother lost his way, and he himself was sent to Curfew Peak. He would have wanted to be reunited with him."

"I've met the Pyreboys," said Oland. "Which one is his brother?"

"Blaise," said Roxleigh. "The Pyreboys have real names, but, as you may have noticed, when they arrive here, they are all given names connected to fire or flame, bestowed upon them as soon as they arrive on Curfew Peak."

"And his brother – the Pyreboy who helped you?" said Oland.

"I never knew his real name," said Roxleigh, "but his Pyreboy name was Wick."

52

THE EVIL THAT SHONE

OLAND WENT RIGID.

"What is it?" said Roxleigh. "You look like you have seen a ghost."

"I'm sorry," said Oland. "But there is a Wickham who joined the ranks of The Craven Lodge, the savages who support Villius Ren. They have taken over Castle Derrington; they have destroyed Decresian."

"My beautiful Decresian," said Roxleigh. Tears welled in his eyes.

"It has become a ruin," said Oland.

"And Wick…" said Roxleigh. "He is still alive?"

Oland shook his head. "He fell to his death, not long ago, at Dallen Falls."

"Do you mean he drowned?" said Roxleigh.

Oland nodded. "Yes."

"Did you witness it?" said Roxleigh.

"Yes," said Oland. "Well... not exactly. I saw him disappear into the water."

"Wick is from Kaltoff," said Roxleigh. "The land of rivers, the place where Chancey the Gold was born. Not one child from Kaltoff is anything but a superior swimmer. I wouldn't put money on your Wickham not having made it out of there alive."

"That was why Villius Ren told the Bastion he was only one man down! He knew that Wickham was alive!"

"Blaise will help us," said Roxleigh. "We'll wait until night falls. The Pyreboys will be going back to the shore to light the stakes. We can speak with him then."

Delphi ran along the shore of Curfew Peak, the cold wind biting at her flesh. She had no idea how long she had been gone, but it was beginning to grow dark again. She had lost her cape in the water at the other end of the shore, and her loose grey top slid off one shoulder. She was desperate to find Oland, terrified that he too had been taken by the wave. All she wanted to do was to tell him everything that had happened, how the water had taken her under, dragged her into a blinding eddy, how she had been filled with horror. And how, when she tried to move, it had proved effortless. She had glided with the current; she felt like she was dancing. It was exhilarating, like nothing she could have imagined. Chancey the Gold, the scryer, her mother – they were all wrong. Why anyone had feared for her safety, she could not understand. How could such a terrible mistake have been made? She was free. There was nothing to hold her back.

As she ran along the hardened sand, it began to rumble beneath her, and before long she heard the dull sound of hooves. In seconds, the hot breath from a horse and rider turned the air white in front of her. Before she could move, a lantern, strapped to the horse's saddle, lit up the unmasked face of Malcolm Evolent. Delphi screamed.

He wore no bandages. Delphi recoiled. They had clearly been there to hide the deformity of his skull. His face looked like it had been carved from a block of bone and covered with dried parchment. His heavy brow jutted out over his nose, and his thick, wide chin curved up to meet it. A vein bulged along the side of his face. His eyes were deep-set and entirely white, like his long hair, his eyebrows, his lashes. The only dark part of Malcolm Evolent's face came from the evil that shone from inside him.

He jumped down from the horse, landing hard in front of her. He was dressed in layers of heavy leathers and cloths with crisscrossing straps and buckles. He yanked hard on the reins of his black horse. He reached a finger out towards her.

"Don't touch me," said Delphi, whipping her head away. She couldn't understand how he had got here. But, by the shore, she could see the sails of Bream's boat whipping in the wind. She knew that it was unlikely he was still alive.

Malcolm raised his hand, covered in a heavy gauntlet, and struck Delphi across the face. She landed hard on the damp sand. Malcolm leaned slowly down to her, inching his face towards her. He reached out and shoved his hands under her armpits and picked her up, holding her in front of him like a doll.

"So," he said, setting her down. "Do you know who you are yet?"

Delphi stared at him.

"After the swim you were warned never to take?" said Malcolm. "Are you enlightened?"

Delphi frowned.

Malcolm smiled. "Why, Delphi," he said. "You are my most treasured possession. You are my Thousandth Soul."

53

SIX SCARS

ELPHI WAS PARALYSED. "WHAT? NO…" SHE MANAGED to say. "I'm not the Thousandth Soul! The Thousandth Soul? You are insane." The Thousandth Soul was a monstrosity, an experiment, part-human, part-animal, the creation of two evil doctors who only wanted to find it so that they could kill it.

"I'm not the Thousandth Soul!" said Delphi. "I'm not!"

Malcolm Evolent laughed, and it was a grotesque, choking sound.

"I'm not the Thousandth Soul!" screamed Delphi.

Malcolm Evolent laughed louder.

Delphi stood, fighting tears and the terrible sickness that was rising in her stomach. "I'm not!" she said, over and over.

Malcolm Evolent raised his hands in the air as if he were powerless to say otherwise.

"That would mean…" said Delphi, "that would mean…"

"Well, that would mean that I'm here to take back what is mine," said Malcolm. "I created you; you are mine."

"That's not true," said Delphi. "That's not true."

"Oh, but it is," said Malcolm. "Don't you know?" he said. "Don't you know what creature we crossed you with?"

"I'm not crossed with anything," said Delphi. "I'm a person."

"I'm tired of your protestations," said Malcolm. "Tired."

Delphi stepped towards him, despite herself. "But—"

"I thought Oland Born was my Thousandth Soul," said Malcolm. "When I heard a slave of just fourteen, with no training, no experience, no reputation for bravery, dived into an arena and slew three panthers, I thought it was him! I thought that I had instilled in him some extraordinary powers of strength. I followed you to the border, lost you in the woods, but what wonderful dogs we have. How they trailed your familiar scent all the way to Pallimer Bay. I arrived here, all ready to steal Oland Born away. You see, like everyone else, we believed that the child was a boy. We had seen only enough of the newborn to know that it was perfect in terms of what we had created. So it was to my surprise… that my Thousandth Soul turned out to be… well… you." He paused. "Tell me, Miss Delphi… did you enjoy your swim?"

Delphi stared at him.

"Didn't you find it strange that the Scryer of Gort told your mother never to let you go underwater?" said Malcolm. "Yet tonight you find out, not only *can* you swim, but that you are quite an accomplished swimmer. In fact, the most proficient swimmer I have ever seen? For a *person* who has never before swam?"

"But my father is—" said Delphi, before she stopped herself.

"Chancey the Gold!" said Malcolm. "Now, how would I know that if I didn't know all about you? But it's not just the blood of Chancey the Gold that makes you swim." He let out a breath. "Do you know what creature we crossed you with?"

"You didn't!" shouted Delphi. "You didn't cross me with anything!"

"The six scars on your back," said Malcolm. "Three on each shoulder blade. Have you ever seen them?"

Delphi was horrified that he would know anything about them.

"Did you feel them when you were underwater?" said Malcolm.

"Stop!" she said. "Stop!" Her panic was rising.

"I could hold you under the water to show you," said Malcolm, "or you can take my word for this: they're not scars. They're gills."

Delphi's legs went weak.

"Now," said Malcolm. "Before we go to find and kill your friend, please take a guess. A wild guess. At what creature you were crossed with…"

Tears welled in Delphi's eyes.

Malcolm laughed loudly. "Come on! Guess… guess!"

Delphi shook her head, and tears spilled down her face.

"Well, what has gills?" said Malcolm. "Answer me that."

Delphi spoke through her sobs. "A… fish? A fish… has gills."

"Oh, Delphi," said Malcolm. "Would we have wasted that much time on a simple fish?"

Delphi stared at him, puzzled.

"You can see in dim light, can you not?" said Malcolm. "You had no problem seeing your way around Curfew Peak. Haven't you got thick skin that can't easily be cut?" He leaned down and whispered to her. "I chance you didn't tell your friend Oland what you did to the drogue… they didn't sink *their* teeth into each other at all, did they?"

Delphi stared down at the ground.

"Have you unsettled young Oland with your black-eyed stare?" said Malcolm. He laughed. "Oh, Delphi, didn't you see the beautiful white *shark* skeleton on the wall of my brother's laboratory? Yes, shark, Delphi. That skeleton is one of our treasured possessions… as are you. Well, at least until we've studied you… and created more. After the autopsy…"

Delphi screamed so loud, she thought her throat would rip apart.

Malcolm Evolent laughed. "Carry on," he said. "Scream." He looked around. "There is no one here—"

"Oland Born will find me!" said Delphi. "Oland will find me—"

"Ah, your protector?" said Malcolm.

Delphi hesitated.

"Just like Chancey the Gold protected you?" said Malcolm, smiling.

"Yes!" said Delphi. "Yes!"

"Oh, Delphi, you don't understand, do you?" he said. "All this time…" He let out a long breath. "Chancey the Gold wasn't protecting you from the world. Chancey the Gold was protecting the world from you."

Delphi's head started to spin; she remembered it all now. She remembered that day in Galenore when she took ill. She was eight years old. Chancey the Gold had gone to the chandler's. She was wandering down a side street when someone ran up behind her. She could feel someone pulling at the silver amulet that was around her neck. She spun around and there was a boy there, she remembered a boy, a thief, with his mean, twisted little face. His arm reached out towards her, his hand gripped on to her amulet, and he wouldn't let go, and there was a ring on his finger, an emerald ring... and... and then everything was red, and he was screaming and she was running the other way, and she ran into the arms of Chancey the Gold, and he scooped her up, and they ran away and over Chancey's shoulder as they moved up and down, up and down, she could see the now one-and-a-half-armed boy zigzagging, screaming down the street... and later that night, when she was crying and coughing and choking, and Chancey the Gold rubbed her back, she remembered... she remembered now... she spat something round and gold with an emerald centre into the pewter tray he held to her chin.

54

HIDDEN

MALCOLM EVOLENT LEANED DOWN AND LAUGHED IN Delphi's face. "Scream again. Scream. You can run too, if you like. Go on, run. Run."

Delphi turned and ran, her head filled with terrible images. Malcolm Evolent's laughter was ringing in her ears. She could soon hear the thunder of the horse's hooves closing in. Malcolm Evolent reached down from his galloping horse, scooped her up under his arm and rode away, along the edge of the lapping water.

Delphi bucked in his grip, hoping he would drop her; she knew that the further away she was taken, the greater the chance that she would not make it back alive. She would rather fight and die right there. She clawed at Malcolm Evolent's hand.

"Stop," he snarled. "Stay still or you'll fall and be dragged to your death under my horse's hooves."

The blood was rushing to Delphi's head. "If I'm trampled by your horse, there will be very little left of me to cut open for my autopsy!" she managed to roar, desperately trying to hold herself upright.

"Well, in that case…" said Malcolm Evolent. He pulled Delphi up and threw her in front of him on the saddle, gripping her around the waist, pressing her two arms against her body so she could not move them. She could feel the sickening heat of his breath on her scalp.

Malcolm Evolent rode harder and faster. Delphi bounced up and down with the motion of the horse. She could barely breathe at the thought that she was the Thousandth Soul, a terrible, grotesque creation, yet a prized one nevertheless. She desperately searched her memories to find proof that she wasn't, facts that she could throw like weapons at Malcolm Evolent to get him to see that he was wrong, to give him no choice but to let her go. But she could sense his excitement, his vindication, burning like a fire against her. Malcolm Evolent had finally found what had eluded him for fourteen years; he was finally regaining possession of his finest work. And, with that, the opportunity to repeat his success over and over for as long as he lived.

Delphi jumped as she felt his lips against her ear.

"Maybe you have heard things about your parents…" he said.

Delphi stopped moving.

"Maybe you heard about their talents, or about your mother's beauty, or your father's medals," said Malcolm.

Delphi stayed very still. She wanted to know. Malcolm Evolent had information she wanted and it sickened her.

"I had heard your mother, Emayo, sing, of course, everyone had," said Malcolm. "She was famous, after all. But what I didn't know was that she worked for my brother, cleaning our laboratory at night when I wasn't there. One night, I arrived back unexpectedly and stumbled upon her. I was enchanted, as everyone who met her was, but I was more enchanted by her union with Chancey the Gold. What fine breeding! And, when she became pregnant with you, well, one night, when there was no one there who could stop me, I had the chance to work some of my experimental magic on her…"

Malben's words rushed back to Delphi: "a young woman was brought to the laboratory by Benjamin Evolent to watch over me… she would take me in her arms, hold me and sing me to sleep… one day, she was gone… I heard you sing… it was so beautiful, so pure… I could no longer bear who I had become."

Delphi realised that her mother was the caring woman that Malben had spoken of. He was caged in the laboratory at the same time; he knew that the woman had been experimented on, and he knew that she had left Decresian with Chancey the Gold before Delphi was born. And in Oxlaven, when Delphi was singing Malben to sleep, he realised who she was. And he would never have betrayed the child of the woman who had brought him so much comfort in his darkest times. He didn't want to tell her, because he knew it would frighten her.

Tears welled in Delphi's eyes, tears for everyone.

Malcolm was still talking. "And months later," he said, "your mother gave birth to what she and your father told everyone was a baby boy. Shortly afterwards, I came to their home to claim him and I saw through the window your mother holding the naked child in her arms. All I saw was the child's back and six perfect gills, and I knew I had succeeded. I went to tell my brother, but when we returned, your parents were gone. Your father took the job as guide at The Falls, and the story travelled back to Decresian that your mother and her baby – a boy – had died on the journey. You can understand my confusion…"

Delphi's stomach turned. She had no interest in Malcolm Evolent or his confusion or any other hideous thought that snaked through his twisted mind.

"Did you know," said Malcolm, "that, when you were seven years old, Villius Ren found your mother? He had his reasons for wanting the Thousandth Soul. Your mother had travelled far from Dallen, far from Decresian, but he found her. She told him that she had lost her child, and he didn't believe her. He caused her great harm, Delphi. Ever since, she clings to life, confined to her bed. Did you know that that's where your father disappeared to? He climbed up on his horse, and every week he travelled hundreds of miles there and back to see your mother, to be by her side."

Delphi's heart pounded. Her mother was alive? She turned to look up at Malcolm. "Is she in Galenore?" she said. "Is that where... where is she? Where is my mother?"

"Because I don't care, I don't know," said Malcolm. "All I know is that she's in a hospital, far from here. Chancey the Gold was the only one who knew where. Your mother never woke up, Delphi. Not since the day Villius Ren came. And now that Chancey the Gold is gone, well, we'll never know where she is."

Delphi cried with a pain like no pain she had ever felt before.

As the horse galloped on, Malcolm Evolent's chest heaved against her back. A cold, dark feeling grew inside her. Up ahead, she could see the white sails of Bream's, no doubt stolen, boat.

She knew that Malcolm Evolent would use it to take her to his laboratory in The Shadowed Woods. As she pictured the mounted skeleton on Benjamin Evolent's wall, she was reminded of how it could all end.

The cold, dark feeling turned to fire. Sweat streamed down her face. She twisted in Malcolm Evolent's grip, a primal strength coursing through her body.

By the time Malcolm Evolent realised the foolishness of holding his perfect, deadly Thousandth Soul so close, Delphi's jaws had already sunk deep into his neck.

Malcolm Evolent roared in pain and bucked in the saddle, releasing his grip on Delphi. She screamed as she slipped down the side of the horse. Her feet were inches from the ground as she clawed at the damp leather. As she felt her strength drain from her, she made one last grab and caught the reins that had fallen limply from Malcolm Evolent's hands. As he fell to the sand from one side of the horse, Delphi rose from the other and was soon secured, wheeling the horse in a circle to charge to the water's edge. She jumped to the ground and fell to her knees, scrubbing at the blood on her face with icy water and shaking hands.

She cried hysterically, clawing at the scars on her back that Malcolm Evolent had called gills. She could feel them move under her fingers, and it was almost too much to bear. She had a body that she had never given any thought to before, and now it repelled her.

Delphi's sobs eventually slowed, and her breathing calmed. The sound of the waves settled around her. Then, in the distance, she heard the voice of an older man. And then another voice, one that made her heart surge. It was Oland! Delphi started to run in his direction, but faltered and quickly moved towards the rocks to hide. She pressed her back against them, and made herself as small as she could. She panicked when she saw her cape floating in the water, so close, but there was nothing she could do.

She stared out at the platinum sea, the sea that had delivered her darkest secret to her. She could still hear Oland's voice, but not his words. The older man was replying. Delphi stayed out of sight until the voices passed. She saw no other choice.

Oland Born was a saviour. And she… she was a savage. A killer. She was no different to The Craven Lodge… the very men that Oland Born had run from. The very men he despised.

55

FALL AT THE LAST

OLAND WALKED WITH PRINCE ROXLEIGH ALONG THE shores of Curfew Peak. He saw a black shape floating by the rocks at the water's edge. He ran to it. And froze. It was Delphi's cape! He stood, transfixed, as it floated up over his boots. He wanted to keep it, and yet he wanted to rip it to pieces and throw it back into the sea. Instead, he picked it up and held it to his face. All he could smell was saltwater. He fell to his knees. He buried his head in his hands, and he sobbed.

Prince Roxleigh waited for him. "Are you all right?" he said, when Oland returned.

"Yes," said Oland, clutching Delphi's cape. "Take this," he said, "and use it to hide yourself in the boat."

"Thank you," said Prince Roxleigh, walking away.

A light shone to Oland's right. He turned to see the Pyreboys were back on the shore, gathering wood for their fire.

"Oland Born," said Blaise. He stood with his hands on his hips, his legs firm on the ground. For a moment, he looked like any other boy. But his face was too pale, his eyes were too drawn, and there appeared to be so many years behind them, it was unfathomable. His face looked so familiar, now that Oland was close to it.

"Where's your friend Delphi?" said Stoker, cutting Blaise off. He glanced around the shore, and his face lit up. "Half drowned, by the looks of her."

It took moments for his words to sink in. Oland turned and saw Delphi walking towards him. He struggled to process all the details he had become so familiar with in their short months together: her choppy hair, her dark eyes, her skin, her belt and her boots and her strong, skinny arms. His hands began to shake; his heart was pounding. He was suddenly terrified to accept that Delphi could be alive, because it meant that some day he could again experience the desperate pain of losing her. But, somehow, he ran to her, because he knew… he knew that there was nothing else in the world that he wanted to do.

"Oh, Delphi," he said, throwing his arms around her. "I thought you were gone—"

"The scryer was wrong," whispered Delphi. "I didn't drown, I can swim. She was wrong, Oland. I swam to the depths of the ocean and saw the most beautiful things, the most beautiful colours and creatures and…" It was all she could say.

Oland whispered to her about Prince Roxleigh.

"We need to get back to Decresian before The Great Rains," said Oland. "We need to hurry."

The Pyreboys had lit their torches and were gathered together on the shore.

Oland turned to them. "Where's Frax? He took some things belonging to me."

Blaise frowned. "Frax was technically up for release yesterday."

"Release?" said Delphi. "Don't you need to be twenty-one? He couldn't be more than thirteen."

The Pyreboys laughed. "No," said Blaise. "He only *looks* thirteen. Which was how he managed to trick so many people before he was caught – charm them until he bade them farewell, usually with one of their possessions. There was always a little sting in the tail with Frax. Like the spark at the end of a fuse." They all laughed.

Delphi had turned white, and was trembling. Frax's words spun around in her head: "roxling witch, roxling witch, roxling witch".

She was struck with the terrible sensation that she would spend a lifetime feeling this sickened by herself.

56

SKYWARD

"I'M SORRY FRAX STOLE FROM YOU," SAID STOKER, FOCUSING more on Delphi than Oland.

"I just realised," said Delphi, "Frax used a Decresian word. He said 'roxling'. Has he spent time there?"

"Frax has spent time everywhere," said Stoker. "He goes from one place to the next, looking for favours and offering favours in return for whatever it is he wants."

Suddenly, Delphi held out her palm. "Rain!" she said.

They looked down as massive drops struck the sand around them, making marks the size of dinner plates. Oland looked up at the sky. "It's over, Delphi," he said. "It's over. It's too late."

"Too late for what?" said Stoker.

They were plunged into darkness as, yet again, the Pyreboys' flames were quenched.

"We were meant to be back in Decresian before The Great Rains," said Delphi.

"But if they are starting here," said Stoker "they will not yet have reached Decresian. There is still time."

"There is no time," said Delphi. "It will take us weeks to get back…"

"Maybe, if you were travelling by land or sea." said Stoker, "But there are other ways."

He bowed his head and, from behind him, a dark shadow slowly rose. Oland and Delphi watched as the shadow grew and blackened, and they realised that what they were looking at were wings, thick and sinewy, with pointed peaks that stretched high above the Pyreboy's head. As his wings began to spread, he rose from the ground and hovered in the sky before them.

Silently, Flint and Blaise did the same. Brennen and Tallow stood to one side.

Delphi and Oland were speechless. They watched as the winged Pyreboys ascended higher, and then dived, their bodies skimming just inches above the sand. They rose again to trace huge circles in the sky, moving with graceful force.

"Let me tell you a little secret," said Stoker, as he came to rest in front of Oland and Delphi. "Sometimes, we think that Curfew

Peak is a miserable place too. We'll take you home. Flint and I will take you home."

"Frax's story of the magic was true," said Delphi. "The magic was wings!"

Stoker nodded. "And then? Yes, the magic man caged us. For who would give wings to criminal boys? He simply wanted to see if he could."

Oland realised that it was surely an extraction, a distillation, an essence or an infusion that these boys had taken. He could tell by Delphi's expression that she had come to the same conclusion. A terrible man had experimented on criminal boys, no doubt believing if it didn't work, no one would miss them.

"How come you are free?" said Delphi.

"Only the original four of us are," said Stoker. "Me, Flint, Frax and Blaise. The magic man believes that we are loyal to him, but we're biding our time. On the other side of that mountain, there are many, many more Pyreboys who have taken his poison. It is a human aviary and it is grotesque. Cage after cramped cage, row and row of trapped boys. We were waiting for the right time to release them all, but now Frax has betrayed us he's put us all in jeopardy."

A deafening roar filled the sky.

The entire island started to tremble again, the force so strong that it knocked Oland and Delphi to the ground.

A huge crack sounded above them, and the burning limb of a tree landed at their feet. Again the mountain trembled, this time deeper and more violently. As Oland and Delphi staggered to their feet, the flames of the broken branch shone on their terrified faces.

"If you want us to help you," said Stoker, "we must leave now."

"Yes!" said Oland. "Just one more thing before we go."

He ran towards Blaise. "I think your brother is alive," whispered Oland, "I think he's in Decresian."

Blaise's eyes widened. "John?" he said.

Oland was struck by the ordinariness of his name. John... and all the sacrifices he had made.

"Yes," said Oland. "If you come to Decresian, I'll bring you to him."

Blaise's tears made pale rivulets down his dusty face.

"But first I need you to help me," said Oland.

"I will do anything in the world if it means seeing my brother again," said Blaise. "Anything in the world." He broke down.

"We're going to leave now," said Oland. "Your prisoner, Prince Roxleigh – he is a friend of your brother, John – is under cover in the boat over there. When we are out of sight, do you think you could follow us, and bring him to Derrington in Decresian? I'm not quite sure I can trust every Pyreboy, but I know I can trust you."

Blaise nodded. "I've never carried anyone before…"

"I think you've already found strength," said Oland. "And, if you are anything like your brother, you will do well."

Oland ran back to Flint, who was speaking urgently to Brennen and Tallow.

"I don't know what's happening," he was saying, "but, if this gets any worse, you need to take these keys and go… unlock the cages. If these tremors continue, the guards will flee and they won't care who gets left behind."

Brennen and Tallow began to run for the dunes.

Before Oland had a chance to react, Flint hoisted him into the air. Stoker followed, with Delphi gripped tightly to his chest. Not far behind them, Blaise rose from the shore carrying a long-dead lunatic prince.

The group was sucked up into the turbulent sky, and had soon left Curfew Peak behind them. And although they heard rumblings, and the sky flashed with light, they were unaware of what they had left behind.

Oland realised that Curfew Peak was not just a mountain, it was not just an island, it was not just a bleak remnant of Sabian. Curfew Peak was a volcano. And, for the first time in centuries, Curfew Peak erupted, spewing out its boiling red core.

57

DESCENT

THE PYREBOYS BATTLED FIERCE WINDS ON THE JOURNEY to Decresian. Flint and Stoker struggled to stay aloft, and to keep hold of their charges. But they persevered; it was after ten in the morning as they flew over the outskirts of Derrington.

"The Craven Lodge will be back at the castle, sleeping," shouted Oland over the wind.

"Where do you want us to leave you?" said Flint.

"In the village," said Oland. His plan was to go to Jerome Rynish to tell him everything that had happened.

But, as the Pyreboys began their descent, it became clear that the village was deserted. Merchants' Alley should have been coming to life, but there was not one person to be seen. The streets were eerily quiet. The village of Derrington was empty.

Oland was filled with dread.

"Where shall we go now?" said Flint.

"To Castle Derrington," said Oland.

Stoker and Flint set Oland and Delphi down on the first hill, bade them farewell and swept up into the sky on their dark wings. For a moment, they hovered together, then separated, each flying in a different direction. Oland and Delphi looked into the sky, expecting to see Blaise and Prince Roxleigh, but there was no sign of them.

"It's his first flight carrying someone," said Stoker. "He couldn't possibly be as fast as the others."

Oland and Delphi looked out over the grounds of Castle Derrington. The empty village was quickly explained. Thousands of people were milling around, setting up tents and wooden towers, unloading food supplies, tethering animals, building giant spits, raising bunting. A man walked up the hill towards them, pulling an empty cart.

"My fourth load today," he said, but with more cheer in his voice than complaint.

"What is happening here?" said Oland. "Why are all these people at the castle?"

The man looked at Oland as if he were mad.

"Why, it's the coronation," said the man. "It will be the biggest festival Decresian has ever seen! To happen tomorrow! Dignitaries from all over Envar will descend upon the castle! The king plans to—"

"The king?" said Oland, his heart pounding. "The king?"

"Well, soon to be!" said the man, with a wild smile. "King Villius!" He pointed to the castle gates where more than forty men were raising two giant wooden stakes with a banner stretched between them that read: WELCOME TO THE CASTLE OF KING VILLIUS.

"The glory! The glory!" said the man as he walked away.

Oland looked down over the crowds. There appeared to be an extraordinary energy running through them, a brightness and enthusiasm that crawled over Oland and sickened him.

"I'm so sorry, Oland," said Delphi, turning to him.

"I... I... can't understand this," said Oland. "How did this happen?"

From among the crowd, Oland saw a young, red-haired man on his knees, hammering the pegs of a tent into the ground. Beside him, Viande appeared from behind a stall. Oland had not seen him since the night of The Games. Oland watched as the red-haired man smiled warmly at Viande, and his smile was returned. Viande even patted him on the back.

"He's from the Craven Lodge," said Oland to Delphi. "And that man is one of Malachy Graham's sons! He has to be! He looks so like him. Malachy Graham died after The Games. The family despises The Craven Lodge... and here is one of them, glad to be of service to them."

"Everyone seems so happy," said Delphi.

They silently took in the terrible scene before them.

It was minutes before Oland could speak. "Now it is *my* soul that is screaming," he said.

He began to walk down the hill towards the castle.

"I need to find the Rynishes," he said. "Jerome and Arthur, the men who told me about your father, and who took me to Dallen. They're the only people I can trust." He paused. "But can I? Could they be down there with all the rest of Derrington?"

"No," said Delphi, "why would they? They could have stopped you before you ever left."

"Something could have changed in the mean time," said Oland.

Delphi tried to hold Oland back. "Don't – The Craven Lodge will find you."

"I am of no concern to Villius Ren now," said Oland. "I imagine the fact that I entered his throne room, though it incensed him, has since been forgotten. And, even if I wanted to rise up against him and end his reign, look at what you see before you: he has the loyalty of his people – that's all he needs. I have to know what happened while we were gone. How were the people of Decresian turned?"

"Going down there is a risk not worth taking," said Delphi.

Oland shook his head. "I need to find the Rynishes. I need to know if they have changed, Delphi. Because nothing is what it seems if they have."

"Does Jerome Rynish matter any more?" said Delphi. "All you need to know is that Roxleigh is a friend and an ally, and we will wait for him."

Oland kept walking. Delphi hesitated then followed him down the hill, and through the fringes of the crowd. Oland recognised many faces from Derrington village.

He stopped suddenly. "There he is!" Oland whispered to Delphi. "That's Jerome Rynish."

They started to approach him.

"Who's that walking towards him?" said Delphi. "Is that his brother embracing him?"

Oland stopped dead. "No… that's… that's Villius Ren."

Oland's heart pounded as – for a brief moment – Jerome caught his eye. A fierce pain ripped through Oland's chest. If Jerome Rynish had been broken by The Craven Lodge, there was no hope for anyone in Decresian.

But there was worse to come. Oland watched as Jerome Rynish slowly raised his arm, turned his way and, pointing his finger at him, roared his name. Before Oland could register the movement, one of Villius' henchmen was bearing down on them, knocking both him and Delphi to the ground.

58

SWEETLING

OLAND AND DELPHI STOOD AT THE CENTRE OF A long-abandoned cell in the dungeons underneath the castle arena. Their hands were shackled behind their backs and they were face to face, as far away as they could be, from its damp, rat-infested walls. In the corners, rancid pools of water had collected, their surfaces speckled with dead insects. They glanced at the door and its newly welded bolts and locks.

"They can't have just left us here," said Oland. "They'll have to come back for us. And when they do…"

"When they do," said Delphi, "I'll…"

"You'll…"

Delphi began to rotate the cuff that had been locked on to her wrist and was attached to a chain in the wall.

"I forgot," said Oland. "I forgot your… flexible bones."

Now that Delphi knew the truth about who – or *what* – she really was, her bones disgusted her. They were not bones any more, she knew. They were just cartilage. She had always thought that being flexible was an exotic gift… not an abomination.

"The Craven Lodge could just leave us here," said Delphi. "Who would care? They could leave us here to rot. They want you dead. And I'm no one to them, just a girl you met along the way." She pulled her hand free from the cuff and began to work on her left hand. "Or worse," she said, "they have discovered that I'm Chancey the Gold's daughter… and that's all the more reason for them to want me dead too."

"That won't happen," said Oland. "I won't let that happen."

Delphi pulled her left hand free. "I won't either," she said, smiling.

The door rattled, and rattled again. Delphi grabbed her chains and hid her hands behind her back. The bolts were unlocked. It was Viande who pushed his way in.

"Welcome home," he said to Oland, and laughed. Then he turned to Delphi. His face lit up. He leaned in to her, his lips nauseatingly wet, his breath rank.

"Aren't you a sweetling?" he said.

Sweetling. Oland's stomach turned. It was the same hideous way he spoke to and looked at the women who came to the castle; the women he bullied and tormented and pawed. And now it was Delphi. Oland's fists clenched, but, as he moved, the shackles took his arm only far enough to make Viande turn and laugh at him.

"But she *is* a sweetling... look at her," said Viande. "Even a boy with long blond hair can see that..." He stood back and laughed again. "Well, look at that – she's got the boy's hair, and you've got the girl's."

Delphi dropped the chains, but just as she was about to lash out, Viande grabbed her and pulled her towards him. He had hooked his arm under her chin. He started to squeeze. Delphi struggled hard against him.

"Little sweetlings don't fight back," he said. "That's not what little sweetlings do."

"You are an ignorant savage," said Oland.

Viande raised his eyebrows. "I still know when a pretty girl stands before me," he said.

Oland struggled against his chains, yanking hard at them.

"She needs a pretty dress," said Viande.

Oland looked at Delphi. She was staring at Oland, half frowning, as if she was in deep, conspiring thought.

Then, without warning, Viande threw the key to the cuffs at Oland.

"Unlock yourselves. We're all going to go for a walk, and no one is going to cause any trouble. I'm still going to hold you against me, though, if you don't mind," he said to Delphi.

Oland's stomach turned again.

All three walked to the door.

"After you," said Viande, nodding at Oland.

Oland hesitated.

"I said, 'after you'," said Viande, squeezing Delphi's throat. She made a terrible choking sound.

Oland stepped into the hallway and, in a flash, Viande threw Delphi back into the cell and locked the door.

"Sweetling," he called. "I will return for you."

He grabbed Oland by the arm. "Now," said Viande, "let's be on our way."

Oland's veins filled as they had in the arena and that same sensation rose up through his body. He didn't understand where this power was coming from, but this time he knew that he would release it without question.

Viande, oblivious to what was happening to Oland, spun towards him. He threw the key up into the air and caught it in his mouth like it was one of his Brussels sprouts, swallowing it in one go.

"Now," said Viande, "only I know where the second key is, so you better not have any plans other than to keep nicely in line with mine."

59

SLAUGHTERHOUSE

VIANDE AND OLAND WALKED BY THE CELLS WHERE only months earlier Oland had tended the starving animals. Jerome Rynish appeared from the darkness, running towards them.

"Viande, Villius wants you," he said. "You must go to him immediately."

"With the boy?" said Viande.

"Alone," said Jerome.

"Before or after I take the boy to the slaughterhouse?"

Oland froze.

"I am to take the boy," said Jerome. "According to Villius, you are to be at his side for today's coronation. It appears he has decided to have a warrior at each shoulder."

Viande's eyes lit up.

"You need to see the Tailor Rynish immediately," said Jerome. "He is preparing Villius' robes and needs to do the same for you. They're in his quarters. I am to take the boy."

Viande nodded. "I'll go at once." He strode down the hallway out of sight.

"Warrior…" said Jerome. "What a fool. And I've told each member of The Craven Lodge the same story, and each fool has believed it. Arthur will keep them contained."

"But," said Oland, "I've seen everything – I know everyone has been turned by Villius Ren. I know what's happening."

"Oland, despite your wisdom," said Jerome, "you have no idea what is really happening."

"Delphi!" said Oland. "My friend Delphi. Viande locked her in the cell. She's—"

"We've freed her," said Jerome. "She's in very safe hands."

"Who's hands?" said Oland. "Where is she?"

"She is with Prince Roxleigh," said Jerome. "He knows the castle inside out. He'll keep her safe."

Oland smiled. "Thank you Jerome."

"No," said Jerome, "Thank you for bringing Prince Roxleigh home." He laid his hands on Oland's shoulders and looked him in the eye. "It's nearly over," he said.

"What do you mean it's nearly over?" said Oland.

"Come," said Jerome, "we have been waiting for you."

"Waiting for me?" said Oland.

Jerome Rynish said not another word as he led Oland through the castle grounds and they walked up the first hill. Where earlier there was a sea of people preparing for the coronation of Villius Ren, there was now a sea of soldiers, dressed in uniforms of gold and teal – the colours of King Micah's Decresian.

Jerome turned to Oland. "Yes," said Jerome. "We have been waiting for you." Tears shone in his eyes.

"There must be a thousand men!" said Oland.

"There are two thousand," said Jerome. "Two for every one of Villius' men."

All at once, they raised their lances to Oland Born.

60

TESTAMENT

OLAND RETURNED THE SOLDIERS' SALUTE. HE SAW THAT, like the tin soldier Frax had stolen from him, some held arquebuses, the weapons that fired balls of lead.

He could barely speak. "I… I thought everyone had turned; I thought everyone had vowed their loyalty to Villius Ren."

"Oh, no," said Jerome. "All of it, the feigned loyalty, everything, is so that the people of Decresian can finally reclaim their kingdom."

"I… I have no words," said Oland.

"The livelihoods of almost everyone in Decresian were destroyed," said Jerome. "The farmers' lands were taken from them. We were all cast aside. But we wanted to fight, for ourselves, for our wives, for our children. So that is what we did. Yes, the souls screamed from midnight until daybreak every night, but those screams at least drowned out what we were doing: while The Craven Lodge were rampaging across the land, we built underground rooms where we made weapons and trained our men. We started our campaign before you ever received King Micah's letter. But, from the night you arrived at my door onward, we worked harder and faster than we ever had. And what you see before you is testament to that."

Oland thought of his life at Castle Derrington. How could he have stayed so long, passing, as he did, from one miserable experience to the next? In the time he'd been away, he had seen a world that, despite the dangers it presented, was an amazing world, and it was a free world, and it was nothing like the only world that he had known.

Jerome took out a map of the castle grounds.

"A cavalry of one thousand will charge the castle from the north," he said, "while the infantry will move to the east and west of the outer walls. Do you see those wooden towers by the castle walls? Villius Ren thinks they are platforms from which to view the festivities. But they are siege towers and they will allow us to drop bridges to the battlements. The trebuchets will launch their attacks here, at the northern corners of the castle. Our men can enter the outer ward through the breached walls.

Chancey the Gold is considering access through the moat."

"Chancey the Gold is here?" said Oland. "He's alive?"

"Yes," said Jerome. "He is." He paused. "I'm sorry we couldn't let Delphi know, Oland. But she will, soon."

Oland nodded. He pointed to the map. "The northeast tower," he said, "that's the library... and my room... None of The Craven Lodge will be there. There is no reason to attack that."

"I'll see to it that it remains untouched," said Jerome. "As we speak, Villius Ren, in his dazzling new robes, will be reading the letter that will offer him the chance to surrender."

Oland turned to him. "I know Villius," he said. "I know what he's going to do. He won't surrender. He'll find a way to stall things for nine days and nine nights... he will wait for his Fortune of Tens. And, on the tenth day, he will welcome an attack."

"Ah, he has no supplies," said Jerome. "He has no sense that this is upon him. Today, his castle was stripped of all food and water right before his eyes – after all, he was hosting an outdoor banquet. His soldiers helped a great deal."

Oland laughed.

"In fact, some of them may not be feeling too well after the food they ate," said Jerome. "Our wives made some interesting dishes." He paused. "So, Oland, Villius Ren and his army will fight today or they can starve to death."

From above came an inhuman howl. Everyone looked up as Villius Ren charged to the edge of the parapet.

"I am The Great Reign," he roared. "I am The Great Reign."

Below, from a trebuchet manned by Malachy Graham's sons, the corpse of a dead panther was launched, and sent flying over the parapets to land at Villius' feet.

He jumped over it and disappeared from view.

Within minutes, Villius Ren's patchwork army began to rush into the grounds from their garrisons. Oland Born rode his horse to the head of the cavalry. He raised his lance and charged towards them.

Everything Oland had taught himself in all his locked-away hours had come to life around him. Here he was, on a battlefield, with the cold air rushing through his lungs and the strength of a loyal army behind him.

And so, as the two groups came together, the battlefield became a fight for survival on one side, and for freedom on the other.

Oland was fuelled by the people's belief in him, by the

Rynishes', by Roxleigh's, by Delphi's. He could never have imagined how all his worlds would collide and that, if they did, how truly spectacular it would feel.

61

FALLEN

HOURS PASSED AND THE BATTLE RAGED ON. THE AIR was filled with the sound of the rocks striking the castle walls, the battering rams, the roars of soldiers, their cries of pain. Smoke wafted across the battlefield, carrying the smell of death, and sweat, and blood.

As the sun rose to its afternoon height, Oland realised that Villius Ren had not reappeared. Oland rode across the castle grounds to find Jerome Rynish. He recognised a familiar shape up ahead. It was Wickham. As he waved at Oland, Oland could see there was blood streaming down his arm. Wickham quickly clutched his side, but not fast enough so that Oland could not see the gaping wound. He cried out to Wickham, charging towards him. He jumped from his horse as Wickham collapsed to the ground.

Oland knelt at his side. "I can see now your Pyreboy origins," he said, "All that practice telling stories on the shore."

"You've been to Curfew Peak..." said Wickham. "Did you meet my brother, Mark?"

"Yes," said Oland. "He's here. He brought Prince Roxleigh and me back. He helped save Decresian."

Wickham looked down at his wound. For a moment, he closed his eyes. When he opened them, they were shining with tears.

Oland began to rip the tunic that Jerome had given him. He took Wickham's hand away from his side and pressed the bundled fabric against it. "Just a few minutes," said Oland. "Then I'll go and get him. I'll find him for you."

Wickham nodded, and his eyes started to close again.

"Don't sleep," said Oland, knowing that he had to keep Wickham conscious to give him every chance to survive. "Look at me. Tell me what happened when you left Curfew Peak." He glanced down at the makeshift bandage, already soaked with Wickham's blood.

Wickham, his breath shaking, began, faltering between his words: "The night I delivered Prince Roxleigh's message to King Micah was several nights before Villius Ren staged his attack. The night of the attack, I had already left the castle for the inn in Derrington. The young archivist was in the stables helping his father pack up a cart with their records. Villius believed that, after The Craven Lodge attacked, King Micah was dead and he had thrown him there to be taken away in a cart and burned. But, despite the arrows that Villius had twisted in his wounds, King Micah was still alive and as he lay there he discovered, under a pile of straw, a newborn baby, discarded just like him. That baby was you."

A terrible pain ripped through Oland's heart. "My parents abandoned me…" he said.

Wickham took a surprisingly fierce grip on Oland's arm.

"No, Oland," he said. "You were taken from them… they did not leave you there…"

"Who were they?" said Oland.

"I don't know," said Wickham. "I'm… sorry."

Oland wanted to scream at the dead ends he kept reaching when it came to discovering who his parents were. He felt selfish and cruel to even think of it as he crouched over the failing Wickham.

"King Micah dictated your letter to the young archivist, Tristan Ault, who tracked me down in Derrington and gave me the letter to give to you."

"By joining The Craven Lodge, you did even more than you were asked to," said Oland.

"For a good cause, Oland." His breath faltered.

Oland gripped his hand tighter. "No," he said. "No. Don't... don't. I'll go and find a doctor. I'll find Mark. You will—"

"No," said Wickham, struggling to shake his head. His lips were almost white. "Wait. I wanted to say... sorry... that for so long I could do nothing. I had my brother to think of on Curfew Peak. Prince Roxleigh, the entire kingdom, the futures of so many..." He drew in a shallow breath. "You have no idea how many times I wished I could have taken you away." His breathing grew weaker. "I don't know how, but King Micah knew that one day in the arena, as a young man, you would save another and show strength and bravery that were beyond human. On that day I was told to deliver that letter." His voice was barely a whisper. "What was confusing..." he said, his eyes closing, "was that to me... every day of your life... you showed strength and bravery that were beyond human." He managed to smile. "*The Banon Servant*... I wrote. Is inspired by you. Oland Born-Lord Banon." Wickham's eyes closed for the last time.

"No," said Oland. "No, Wickham, no. Not yet. No. I wanted time to become your friend." He started to weep. "I wanted to thank you for teaching me. I wanted to say sorry for thinking you were the same as them. I wanted… to hear more stories." He wept harder.

After a time, he placed Wickham's hands on his chest and held his own there, willing for him a safer passage than the other souls who had fallen at the hands of evil men.

62

UNDERMINED

STILL WEEPING, BUT MORE ANGERED THAN HE HAD EVER been, Oland left Wickham's side and jumped on his horse. He rode towards Jerome Rynish.

"Where is Villius Ren?" said Oland.

"Villius has barricaded himself in the great hall and has surrounded it with soldiers," said Jerome. "Luckily for us, his towers are coming down with curious ease."

"That's because it's Rigg Island stone," said Oland. "It's fragile and porous, but Villius requested it specially, for whatever reason. He will be regretting it now."

As they turned to survey the damage, a huge plume of smoke rose from inside the castle. Through the gaping hole in the castle walls, Oland could see where it came from. He stopped dead.

"You said you wouldn't touch the northeast tower!" he shouted.

"We didn't," said Jerome.

They watched as smoke billowed out from the tower's base.

"It's on fire!" shouted Oland. "The tower is on fire! My room!"

"We didn't do it," said Jerome, "I swear to you. It's King Micah's castle; it's Decresian's. We would never…"

Oland and Jerome turned to each other as they both came to the same realisation: Villius Ren had already undermined King Micah and his rule, already undermined the people of Decresian, so it could only follow that he would have no concern about undermining the castle that they all held so dear.

Oland roared and kicked his horse, sending him galloping away. Jerome Rynish rode up alongside him.

"No, Oland, no!" he shouted. "It's not safe. There's nothing we can do about that. A fire has been burning under that for quite some time now. We can't save it. We have destroyed the outer wall, we can easily—"

"We can put out the fire now," shouted Oland. "The water from the moat, we can—"

"No!" said Jerome. "Remember what we're here for, Oland. To overthrow The Craven Lodge."

"But not destroying the castle—" shouted Oland.

"There will always be casualties," said Jerome. "And, a tower is the least of them."

Oland drove his heel into his horse, and he sped ahead of Jerome. In his desperation to reach the tower, he failed to see the shape riding towards him, until a sword crashed against his chest plate, and he was thrown to the ground. The wind was knocked out of him, and his head was spinning. He staggered upright, and there, in front of him once more, was the Bastion, Villius Ren's newest recruit. He smiled a dullard smile.

"You," he said. "Dead."

Oland glanced down at the Bastion's hand and saw a sword. He hadn't expected a weapon other than the Bastion's bulk. But the Bastion moved the blade at breathtaking speed, laughing and swiping the air inches from Oland's face.

Oland pulled his sword from his scabbard. At first, he fought competently, but, with each strike that followed, he began to feel more panicked, as he feared the loss of The Holdings. A burst of rage drove him forward and he battered the Bastion's sword aside. Just as he was poised to pierce the Bastion's chest, his eyes were drawn to the flames that suddenly plumed from the northeast tower. The Bastion struck and Oland's sword flew from his grip, on to the muddy earth. As the Bastion bore down on Oland, a dark shape plunged from the sky towards them.

63

FIRE

OLAND STARED UP AT THE WINGED FORM OF BLAISE, descending in front of them. The Bastion looked like he had seen a ghost. Panicked, he struck out with his sword, slicing down Blaise's wing. Blaise cried out, but he rose into the air, plucking the Bastion from his standing, flinging him across the ground. Despite his pain, Blaise managed to dive for more victims, hauling them into the air and releasing them in a broken pile below. He had cleared a path through the battlefield for Oland and his horse.

"Thank you," said Oland.

Blaise landed. "A pleasure."

Suddenly, Blaise looked down at his wing. Blood was streaming from it. "I'm sorry," he said to Oland. "I won't be able to take you anywhere."

"You have done more then enough," said Oland. "It is with great sadness that I must tell you of your brother's passing." He led Blaise back to Wickham's side, leaving him to grieve for everything his future would not hold.

With his sights set on the castle, Oland rode towards Jerome Rynish, who was in a fierce battle with Hazenby, their swords now locked, steam rising from their bodies. Jerome's strength was holding, while Hazenby looked close to defeat. Jerome pulled his sword free, and with a swift downward movement sliced Hazenby's hamstrings and he collapsed, screaming, to the ground. Jerome staggered upright, looking up in time to see Oland pass, unscathed, through a downpour of arrows from the battlements and disappear through the breached walls of the castle. He roared out his name and quickly drew the attention of Malachy Graham's sons, who charged like a wall towards the soldiers before them, toppling them to the ground, not breaking their stride as they too ran for the castle.

Oland made his way through the eerily quiet outer ward. Villius Ren's discordant army had clearly been no match for the unity of the Decresians. Oland ran past their scattered bodies to the northwest tower. The Decresian soldiers who had felled

Villius' men were moving back and forth between the kitchens and the stables, filling every vessel they could find with water. They had laid wooden planks across the moat, and between them they carried water in a line to the burning tower. When the flames died down, Oland ran up the steps into the library. The walls were black, the air heavy with the smell of burning wood and paper and leather. He splashed through the water and the burnt-edged pages of the books that floated there. His room was still locked. The flames had not reached it. He was flooded with relief. He slumped to the floor. He was drenched, and black with soot.

Footsteps echoed up from below and a huge man appeared in front of him, bearing down on Oland, pulling him up from the ground.

"Are you Oland Born?" he shouted.

"Yes," said Oland. "Yes."

"What have you done with my daughter?" he said.

"Me?" said Oland. "Delphi? Are you... Chancey the Gold?"

Chancey the Gold's eyes were wild. "Yes," he said. "Where is she?"

"She's safe!" said Oland. "She's with Prince Roxleigh!"

Chancey the Gold glared at him. "How dare you..." he roared. "You cheeky little—"

"No, no, please, listen!" said Oland. "Prince Roxleigh is alive! He's not mad! He's looking after Delphi."

But Chancey the Gold was shaking Oland so hard, he could barely speak.

The door to The Holdings suddenly opened, and Prince Roxleigh walked out. "If I could paint a portrait of every face I see when I appear." He smiled.

Chancey stepped away from Oland when he saw Delphi behind Roxleigh.

"Father!" she cried, running into his arms.

"My beautiful Delphi," he said, embracing her, kissing her head. "Tell me you didn't swim," he said quietly. "Tell me you didn't swim."

"She did!" said Oland. "And she was—"

"Shh!" said Delphi, her head spinning towards Oland.

Chancey the Gold released Delphi and turned to Oland. "I don't know what you've done to her," he said, grabbing Oland by the arm. "But she has clearly become reckless! I've heard word of Delphi on these travels you took her on. She has done everything that she has been told not to do. Everything! She has drawn attention to herself in the worst ways imaginable—"

"And why shouldn't she draw attention to herself?" said Oland.

"She's brave and she's kind and she's—"

"I know!" said Chancey. "I know! She's my daughter! Of course I know that. But she's not safe!"

"Chancey the Gold!" shouted Delphi, her cheeks burning. "Leave him alone! Please... say no more!"

Chancey let Oland go. "I'm sorry, sir," said Oland. "I'm the one who will leave you alone. If you are worried about Delphi, she can stay here. No one knows this room exists apart from us. I will be gone." He bowed his head.

64

THE BOY WHO
NEVER WAS

OLAND RAN DOWN THE STEPS OF THE TOWER. HE could hear Prince Roxleigh call after him, but he kept running, lest he be stopped on his journey to the only place he wanted to go.

As he ran down the hallway, one of Villius' soldiers appeared in front of him. Oland reached for his sword, remembering too late that he had set it down in the library, and had forgotten to take it back up. The soldier was at least six inches taller than Oland and stones heavier. He was a grappler more than a swordsman, so he left his sword in its scabbard and threw himself at Oland, crushing his arms against his sides, squeezing his breath from his lungs.

Oland felt the strange rush through his veins that he had felt in the arena. This time, focusing on his rage at Villius Ren, and all he had done to Decresian, the sensation caused him no fear. He jerked up his arms, throwing the soldier into the air, hearing the terrible sound of the man's shoulders popping from their sockets. The soldier roared in pain and staggered backward, the colour draining from his face. Oland crouched down beside him, and gripped his limp right arm.

"Is Villius still in the great hall?" said Oland, tightening his grip. "Where is he?"

"Yes," said the soldier. Oland took his sword and left him to his pain.

Villius Ren was sitting at the head of the banqueting table, his legs spread wide, his arms hanging loose at his sides. His sword lay in front of him. He did not reach for it, he did not sit up, he did not stand. The only movement he made was to raise his eyebrows, his aim simply to mock.

Oland stood several feet from him, his stance strong and solid.

"For fourteen years, I was your slave," he said, "but my servitude has come to an end."

"An end?" said Villius. His eyes were bright with ridicule. "You're a child."

"When it suits you," said Oland. "But I'm a man when it suits you too: a farrier, a groom, a barber, a blacksmith…"

"Yet master of none…" said Villius.

"'You are an ignorant man,'" said Oland. "'You find your stale expressions in old places, carried down through generations who have never once considered them, or discarded them as threadbare. And your banquets are dull and torturous and drowning in the same talk, night after night. I would fill your glasses and your platters and guide you to your beds. So I am reminded to include in the list of my former duties… swine herder.'"

A sourness seeped into Villius' face.

Oland had been quoting Wickham's play, *The Banon Servant*, but Villius would never know.

"But what's important now," said Oland, "is not who I was, but who I never was; who, by living here, I could never be…"

Villius straightened in his seat, and sat forward. He spread his arms wide, then brought his hands together and pointed them towards Oland. "And is this it?" he said. "Is what stands before me the magnificent boy who never was?" He laughed. "Or are you a man now?"

Again, Oland quoted *The Banon Servant*. "'You are not a gatekeeper,'" he said. "'I don't seek entry into your world. So your questions and your judgement and your sense of me is not my concern.'" He paused. "'Pour your scorn into more fragile vessels: they might break.'"

They locked eyes. Villius Ren picked up his sword and, with calculated apathy, rose to his feet. He moved towards Oland.

Oland stepped forward and raised his sword. Villius' eyes widened but his focus was behind Oland. At that moment Oland felt a strong hand on his shoulder and he turned to see Prince Roxleigh. He spoke to Oland, his voice low: "You are not ready for the burden that comes with taking a man's life." Without loosening his grip, he turned Oland slowly back around to face Villius Ren. "Whoever that man may be."

Villius Ren stood before them, mesmerised by the presence he thought was dead, a man who had a genuine claim to his throne.

"Sit down, Villius," said Roxleigh, "clearly, I mean you no harm."

Villius, speechless, did what Roxleigh asked. He laid his sword on the table in front of him.

Prince Roxleigh turned to him. "Go, Oland. Leave. We will take care of this."

"No," said Oland. "No." He looked from Prince Roxleigh to Villius Ren and felt a strange energy run between them.

From down the hallway, Oland heard Delphi scream. Without thinking, he ran, following the sound. Quietly, he approached the portrait room. The smell of death seeped from the darkened room.

He could vaguely make out a lifeless form, familiar to him, slumped against the back wall. A slight figure walked towards him. At first he thought it was a soldier, and he raised his sword. Light bounced from the blade across coal-black eyes.

"Delphi!" cried Oland. "Delphi!"

He threw his arms around her. "I heard you scream," he said. "I didn't know what happened." He tried to pull away, so he could look at her.

Delphi gripped him tighter. After a moment, she spoke. "Viande is dead," she said.

65

SEPARATION

OLAND PULLED GENTLY AWAY FROM DELPHI. SHE forced a smile, but her face showed pain like it had never done before. Oland felt a powerful swell of regret – he had taken this innocent girl from her sheltered life, and introduced her to everything her loving father had wanted to shield her from. Chancey the Gold was right. Delphi was too pure for this world, too innocent to be confronted with such horror. Oland was powerless. He could return her to that world, though he knew that she was forever changed. He feared she would never again settle in the beautiful Falls; he had destroyed her world, and offered her no better world in its place.

"Are you all right?" he said. "What are you doing here?"

"I came to find you," said Delphi. Suddenly, she laid her head on his chest, and he found himself embracing her.

"It's nearly over," he said. "I can't believe it's nearly over."

"Delphi!" came a voice behind them. She jumped and pulled away from Oland.

Chancey the Gold stormed towards them and grabbed Delphi by the arm.

"I am running out of words, Delphi," he said. "I don't know what it's going to take. Do you understand that your safety will always be of more concern to me than anything else?" He turned to Oland. "You!" he said. "For the last time! Get out of my sight."

"Father!" said Delphi, her eyes lit with anger.

"Go," said Chancey to Oland. "Go."

Oland nodded. "Yes, sir." He turned to Delphi. "I'll see you later."

As Oland walked away, he heard Chancey speak to Delphi. He wasn't angry; his tones were gentle. Though it felt underhand and though he had a horror of being discovered, Oland ducked behind a pillar to listen.

"Delphi," said Chancey, "when the men from The Craven Lodge found me in Galenore and told me that they were taking me back to The Falls, I nearly lost my mind. I was convinced that they would find you. I don't think I could ever fully explain to you how powerful a fear that is. All I've ever wanted to do is protect you—"

"That's not what Malcolm Evolent told me!" said Delphi. "He said that you wanted to protect—"

"Stop!" said Chancey, holding his finger to her lips. "Stop."

Oland stood in the shadows, rigid. When had Delphi been speaking to Malcolm Evolent? And who had he said Chancey the Gold was trying to protect.

"Never, ever believe a word that comes out of Malcolm Evolent's mouth," said Chancey. "What I was trying to tell you, Delphi, is the pain I felt when I came home and you were gone. I thought my heart would break. You will not see Oland after this. I'm sorry. But you will not. We're leaving now. We're leaving Decresian, and we're not returning to Dallen. This ends here, Delphi."

Oland's heart sank. He could hear Delphi crying, and it made everything worse.

"Father, is it true what Villius Ren did to my mother?" said Delphi.

Chancey the Gold did not respond.

"Answer me!" shouted Delphi. "Is it true that Villius Ren left her for dead, but that she survived, and she's still alive – barely alive – somewhere, and that's where you go to when you leave me?"

There was a long silence.

Oland could not understand how he had heard none of this, why Delphi had kept it from him.

"It is true." said Chancey. "I love you so much, Delphi. I never wanted to break your beautiful heart with the weight of all the events of your young life."

"And you still go and visit her after all these years?" said Delphi.

"I do," said Chancey the Gold. "She is the love of my life, Delphi. She always will be."

Oland had heard enough. He ran. Time and again, throughout the course of his life, and his quest, he had been given more and more reasons to do what he was about to do. And this reason, what Villius Ren had done to Delphi and her family, rose above all others.

Villius Ren sat at the head of the table in the great hall, a golden orb of light around his head from the contrivance of his stained-glass window. Prince Roxleigh stood a distance away. Beside Roxleigh were two magistrates, along with Jerome and Arthur Rynish. In Jerome's hands were the cuffs and chains to lead Villius away.

Oland stood on a ridge outside, watching the scene through the window. He was holding an arquebus, just like the one that his newest tin soldier held. The weapon had come from Galenore. It had not been difficult to secure one from a son of Malachy Graham. Oland raised it to shoulder height.

In front of him, the golden circle of the stained-glass sun shone, even in the darkness. And at its centre was the black, perfectly framed silhouette of Villius Ren's head.

Oland gave a silent order to his army of one: *Fire.*

The sun shattered and Villius Ren was dead.

66

THE WALLED
GARDEN

HE MEN IN THE GREAT HALL RAN TO WHERE VILLIUS Ren fell, then looked out to see who had fired on him. Oland hid in the undergrowth, waiting until they left. He jumped through the broken window and went to where Villius Ren lay. He crouched down and took the ring of keys from the dead man's belt. With its ornate design and pointed tip, Oland recognised the key to the throne room. He had to know what he had disturbed that had driven Villius so insane. He grabbed a lantern from the table.

Oland entered the throne room, and was struck by the smell of decay. Slowly, the space was illuminated. It was empty except for a marble table and a single red and black rug on the floor. Oland could feel a draught, like a sliver of fresh air was trying to break through the oppressive stench. But there were no windows, no other doors.

Oland remembered Villius saying that a door in the throne room was unlocked. And Oland had known that this was not the case. He went over to the rug and kicked a corner of it back. He saw timber. He set down the lantern and slid the rest of the rug away to reveal a trapdoor. Oland grabbed the large iron handle and pulled it up. There was a small iron ladder set into the space below. He took the lantern and descended.

The tunnel smelled of damp grass and earth and traces of the stench of the throne room that reminded him of Villius Ren's breath. Oland made his way along the tunnel until he reached the end, where more iron rungs stretched up to a second timber door. Although he didn't know what lay above it, there was no alternative but to climb the ladder and open the door.

Oland emerged into what appeared to be a tower, but, when he reached the top, he realised it was a dried-out well. He was in a garden. From where he stood, and from his view of the turrets of Castle Derrington, he knew that he was still within the grounds of the castle. He was at the home of Magnus Miller. He was in the walled garden that his wife, Hester Rose, had once so faithfully tended. The garden where, for years, nine hundred and ninety-nine souls had been buried. Oland was silenced by the horror.

In the corner of the garden, under a cage of bare, overhanging branches, was a weathered stone house. Oland went around to the back door. He pulled out Villius Ren's keys and tried each one until he heard a click. He pushed the door open and was surprised to find himself inside comfortable living quarters, with tapestries and paintings on the walls, rugs on the floor, heavy drapes at the windows. He locked the door behind him, then walked down a short hallway, where he discovered a bedroom. There was a tunic and trousers laid out on the bed and, as Oland inspected them, he saw the stitching of the Tailor Rynish. The clothes were for someone smaller and slighter than Oland. There were paintings of soldiers and battles, books on all manner of subjects, a wardrobe filled with more clothes from the Tailor Rynish. Oland looked around at a bedroom the likes of which he had only dreamed of having in Castle Derrington.

He left it and walked into the living room, drawn immediately to the mahogany writing desk in the corner. There was a letter on top and a quill set down beside it. Oland recognised immediately the handwriting of Villius Ren. He picked up the letter, and, at first, got no further than the opening line.

To my beloved son, Gideon…

Villius Ren had a son. Someone had been loved by Villius Ren.

67

BELOVED

O LAND FORCED HIMSELF TO CONTINUE READING.

To my beloved son, Gideon,

These past three months I have spent in unimaginable anguish. You fled in torment, you ran, ashamed, and that I understand. I always took pains to hide my affliction from you. The night you uncovered my secret, through a simple unlocked door, I thought my world had ended.

Though I have kept you hidden, it was for your own protection. I want to tell you more about what this affliction means for you, Gideon, but I dare not write it in a letter. But, like it did me, I fear it will strike you in your nineteenth year. I first saw traces of it when you were two years old, and from then on, I did everything I could to find a cure. It was at two years old that my parents, having seen the same signs in me, gave me away. I vowed that I would never do that, that I would give you the life of love that I did not have.

I planned this coronation, thinking, foolishly, that it might draw you home. Alas, I fear you would have, by now, made yourself known. So this letter is my only hope. I have only revealed your existence to a trusted few: Wickham, Croft and Draefus, the general of my army. Croft is now dead. I am willing that Draefus will find you and deliver this to you.

I wanted everything for you that I did not have. I wanted you to read, to play, to laugh. But more than anything, I wanted you to be un-afflicted and free. I do not want my life for you. It is not a proud one.

I write this, not knowing where you are, not

knowing if it will ever reach you.

I beseech you, Gideon, to please return to your father. I vow that I will do everything in my power to cure you and, if that is not to be, we shall face our affliction together.

Your loving father,
Villius Ren

Oland could barely breathe. It was his son who Villius Ren had been looking for at Dallen Falls, not Oland. It was the absence of his son that had made him wild with grief. Oland's cheeks burned at his confusion. Villius had been forced to confide in Wickham and Croft about Gideon. And that was why Wickham had killed Croft. To get rid of the only other person who knew. That meant Wickham could use the information to his advantage.

Oland was startled by an urgent hammering at the door.

"Master," came a man's voice. "Master!" He knocked on the door, over and over. "Master Ren! It is Draefus, sir. I come with good news! I have found what you have been searching for! Open up, open up!"

Oland retreated into the corner of the room. All went quiet at the door. Suddenly, the general appeared at the opposite window. Oland ducked behind a cabinet. Draefus knocked on the window.

"Master Ren!" he said. "I know you are suffering, but please. I must take your letter immediately. Your son is in a shocking state!"

Oland stayed in hiding as Draefus walked all around the house, banging on the windows and doors. Eventually, he left. Oland stared down at the writing desk. In a gesture as involuntary as the rise and fall of his pounding chest, he picked up the letter, folded it up and slipped it into his pocket.

From outside, Oland heard a desperate scream. He ran to the window. Draefus was lying face-down in the garden with Oland's stolen knife buried in his back. Beside his body stood the newly liberated Frax, holding up a lantern, even though it was daylight. He waved it at Oland, smiling his black-tipped, tiny-toothed smile. His wings twitched.

"Your letter from King Micah was marvellous!" he shouted. "It caused Villius Ren much joy! He laughed and laughed at the idea of you doing anything of worth!"

Oland no longer cared about Villius Ren. He was dead and he could laugh no more.

"Speaking of worth," said Frax, "I got these!" He set down

the lantern and pulled a bag of gold coins from his pocket, shaking it, before putting it away again. "I saw you run across the garden!" he shouted, his tiny eyes bursting with excitement. "I came to see the screaming souls! I have found no trace of them! But I'll settle for a screaming boy!"

The sun suddenly struck a shiny trail that stretched from just in front of Frax to the house. Frax picked up the lantern and rose into the air. He laughed as he released it. As it struck the oil below the flames shot so high, he brought his knees to his chest, before soaring into the sky.

Oland ran for the back door and searched the ring of keys for the right one. After three attempts he found it, his hand shaking as he unlocked the door. As he ran from the burning house, he realised that with Croft, Wickham and now Draefus dead, he was the only one alive who knew of the existence of Gideon Ren. Oland stopped running. He took the letter from his pocket, balled it up and threw it into the flames. He waited until it turned to ash.

As Oland made his way across the grounds of Castle Derrington, one thought plagued him, and he was sick to his core.

To deprive someone of a father is unpardonable.

68

GRAVE

OLAND EMERGED THROUGH THE TRAPDOOR INTO THE throne room. He closed it gently. As he crossed the floor, he heard his name being called. He looked up to see Prince Roxleigh staring down at him from the marble table.

"Oland, you have made a grave mistake by killing Villius Ren," he said.

"I'm sorry," said Oland, "but you don't know all the things he's done."

"No," said Roxleigh. "*You* don't know all the things he's done."

"What do you mean?" said Oland.

"Fourteen years ago," said Roxleigh, "the message I sent with Wick to King Micah was not just a letter, but a box of vials: distillations, extractions, essences and infusions – the research I had carried out on Curfew Peak. They are extracts of the—"

"Traits of insects and animals," said Oland.

"How do you know?" said Roxleigh.

"Villius Ren must have found them years ago," said Oland. "He approached two doctors with something that would encourage them to carry out their experiments…"

"But my notes were destroyed," said Roxleigh.

"Are you sure of that?" said Oland.

Roxleigh considered his question. "Stanislas," he said. "He must have rescued my notes. My poor, sweet little brother, Stanislas. Wherever he hid them, Villius must have uncovered them."

Oland thought of what Malben had said. "I was told that, when Villius Ren was nineteen, he was sick, and he approached them for help…"

"Sick?" said Roxleigh. "In what way?"

"I don't know," said Oland.

"When Archivist Tristan Ault was stripping the castle of its records on the night King Micah was overthrown, he must have uncovered notes about The Great Rains, and that they would return. This was why you were told to return before The Great Rains fell. The lines in your letter: 'the mind's toil of a rightful king' was a reference to me and my work," said Roxleigh. "'A father's folly' was the tunnel my father built that failed to stop the plague; 'his son's reward' meant that is where I would find the vials. King Micah realised that, if the rains fell, the Derring Dam would be breached, and the abandoned tunnel where he had hidden the vials would be flooded, washing everything into the river, poisoning the water or, worse still, remaining intact and falling into the wrong hands.

"Today, I went to the tunnel, Oland, while you were locked in the cell with Delphi. There was nothing there, no notes, no vials, but there were signs of recent activity."

"Villius Ren," said Oland. "Frax gave him my letter from King Micah. Villius worked it out."

"And now he is dead," said Roxleigh, "and we don't know where these essences are."

"They can't be hidden too far away," said Oland, "he wouldn't have had enough time."

"But a winged Pyreboy could have carried them anywhere by now," said Roxleigh.

Oland shook his head. "I promise you, Prince Roxleigh, Villius Ren would not have trusted Frax with them. He trusted few. And most of them were dead."

"You've been gone quite some time," said Roxleigh, "how could you know what new alliances Villius Ren might have forged?"

"It wasn't Frax," said Oland. "I crossed paths with him again. He had gone to the walled garden, to visit the screaming souls."

"What screaming souls?" said Roxleigh.

Oland told Roxleigh about how the Evolents had buried the bodies of their failed experiments.

Roxleigh was horrified at the tale.

"There is something more to this," he said. "What was wrong with Villius Ren that required experimentation?"

"Benjamin Evolent said that he wanted to create amazing human beings, people with special gifts…"

"That still doesn't explain everything," said Roxleigh.

He paused for such a long time, Oland didn't know what to do. Roxleigh's gaze was troubled and distant.

"I see it now," he said finally. "I see it all." He turned to Oland, his face haunted.

"Oland, did Villius Ren disappear alone before midnight every night?"

"Yes," said Oland, wondering how he was moving from one topic to the next, and neither appeared connected. "How do you know that?"

"There are no screaming souls," said Roxleigh. "What you

heard was the sound of the wind whistling through the porous rock of Rigg Island. Villius Ren tilts the cap of the windmill every night to harness the prevailing wind."

Oland's eyes were wide. "I don't believe it! The bodies were never screaming!"

Roxleigh turned to Oland, his face white.

"Those bodies were never buried, Oland. They never made it any further than the dining table of Villius Ren."

69

POISON

OLAND WAS STUNNED BY PRINCE ROXLEIGH'S WORDS.

"But how?" he managed to say. "What makes you say that?"

"I didn't tell you the whole truth on Curfew Peak," said Roxleigh. "It wasn't just my time in the asylum that led me to believe that Rowe had been poisoned. I had witnessed something before I was ever sent away… something so shocking that… I have never before told the tale."

"Please," said Oland, "please tell me. I need to understand."

"I know," said Roxleigh. "You deserve to know. Rowe and I dined together often, taking lunch together most days. Not long after he came back from Curfew Peak, he began to miss these meals, and then he stopped altogether. One night, I walked in on him – he was eating – and… well, it was the most disturbing sight I had ever seen." Roxleigh bowed his head. "I'd rather not speak of it, Oland. Suffice to say that was my first inkling that he had in some way been poisoned on Curfew Peak. I told him to meet me the next day, but he never appeared. He was my best friend, and I never saw him again. I wanted to help him. And he was gone."

Oland's heart was pounding.

"Clearly, this affliction, this compulsion to feed on the dead," said Roxleigh, "is passed on from father to son. Villius Ren was my dearest friend Rowe's son. When I met Villius Ren earlier, there was something between us that I could not pinpoint."

The strange energy Oland had picked up on.

"But how were they afflicted?" said Oland.

Roxleigh had tears in his eyes. "My poor, dear Rowe," he said. "How he must have suffered." He wiped his eyes. "Oland, I shall tell you the whole truth about Rowe," he said. "A truth I have never told anyone, as a mark of respect to his memory."

"I will keep your secret safe," said Oland. He had enough of his own to understand.

"As you already know, Rowe slew a drogue, and a drogue is part vulture. Because the myth originated in southern Envar, we knew that this was likely to have been the Aetian Vulture; they live to be two hundred years old. So the vulture, and therefore the drogue, has the very essence of long life in its veins.

"It was only years later when I went to Curfew Peak myself that I figured this out. I knew, because of what Rowe had told me, that the seventh vertebra of a drogue is weak. I came across a dead drogue on Curfew Peak and I extracted that bone and dissected it. There are four fluid sacs – one for each animal: vulture, bull, bear and wolf. It all made sense – it's simply nature at work. If anyone is foolish enough to strike a drogue at its weakest point, this fluid is sprayed into the air. The drogue will try to live on in any way it can. In the case of Rowe, he was infected with the dominant traits of the vulture.

"So I went to Curfew Peak," said Roxleigh, "and I vowed to continue with my work. I was able to extract that essence from the drogue's spine, but I could also refine it, so it was just the essence of long life, without the rest of the vulture's traits. I tested it on myself. Clearly, as you can tell, it worked. Here I am all these years later."

"And you never found Rowe?" said Oland.

"No," said Roxleigh. "But I believe he is out there, suffering. And I hope to one day find him."

"I will help you find your distillations," said Oland.

"And I would like to also find the doctors who stole my notes," said Roxleigh. He stood up. "Now, Oland, a celebration is about to take place, so we must set aside our fears." He put his hand on Oland's back and guided him towards the door. "We shall rejoin our comrades and celebrate the liberation of Decresian," he said. "And we can celebrate the knowledge that an affliction was taken to the grave." He paused. "We are, at the very least, lucky that Villius Ren died childless."

70

AFFLICTION

Decresian had always been more than just the land and the buildings that stood on it – Decresian was its king and its people. They were so entwined and so powerful that, when one was lost, so was the other. But the kingdom was alive again. Decresians stormed the castle, throwing open the windows and doors, airing out the terrible pall left behind by The Craven Lodge.

That night, dressed in a fine uniform of teal and gold, Jerome Rynish stood in the arena's royal box, overlooking the crowd. Delphi stood next to Oland as Jerome's voice rose above all others. It was a voice transformed – by a new start and a new life. It was a voice filled with dignity and pride.

"We stand today in a restored kingdom," said Jerome. "And what we have learned through Decresian's most terrible times is to have hope. Even the darkest day is a new day. And, even on the darkest day, we can create light. Tonight," said Jerome, "we will celebrate. We come together in the settled grounds of Castle Derrington for the kingdom's first ball in fifteen long years."

The crowd cheered.

"I introduce to you a man we have heard so much about, yet, ultimately, knew so little of. A man whose vision was mistaken for madness, a man who was much loved, yet much ridiculed. I introduce to you your new king from a family with a tradition of fine and respected rulers. I introduce to you King Roxleigh."

King Roxleigh stepped forward, dressed in elaborate robes of gold and teal, made by the swift hands of the Tailor Rynish. On King Roxleigh's head, pressed down into his halo of grey hair, was a magnificent gold crown with the scrolled D of Decresian at its centre.

The cheers of the crowd were deafening. There were people who remained silent, who would need more time to be persuaded of his sanity, who would need an explanation for his curious long life, but it was too soon for the secret of the distillations, extractions and essences to be released.

"Greetings, fellow Decresians," said King Roxleigh. "I am proud to be among you; I am proud and humbled to stand before you as your king."

He held up a hand and raised his voice over the noise. "Before I speak any further, I would like to call to the royal box an extraordinary young man: brave, bold, loyal and fearless…"

Fireworks exploded in the sky. King Roxleigh scanned the crowd and found the place where, only minutes earlier, Oland Born had stood.

Outside Castle Derrington, Oland leaned against the cold stone, staring at the stars as he listened to Roxleigh's booming voice. He allowed himself to smile, but it was as far as he would go to acknowledge his achievement. To stand before Decresian was something he felt unworthy of. He turned to leave, but stopped when he heard the sound of footsteps on the grass of the battlefield. At first he thought it was Delphi. But then, in the darkness, he saw a young man walking among the dead. The moonlight struck the alarming angles of his face. He was little more than a skeleton, the effect of his terrified eyes emphasised by the dearth of flesh around their sockets. He had a similar gait to Villius Ren, and his father's same dark hair, though his was much thinner. He arrived at the body of a fallen soldier and sank to his knees. He brought his head down close to the body and, for a moment, that was how he stayed. Then he backed away, tears streaming down his face. He stood up and ran, ran from every terrible instinct that churned inside his poisoned core.

Oland did nothing more than watch him go. He was sickened by his affliction, but sickened also by his own actions, though he told himself he had done what he had to do.

He turned as he heard the sound of a horse's hooves in the mud.

"You have a troubled look," said Delphi, coming to a stop beside him, and jumping down from the horse.

"Are you ready?" said Oland.

"I am," said Delphi.

Though he didn't say it, Oland couldn't understand how she wanted to leave, after discovering that her father was still alive. If Oland had found his parents, he expected that he would stay, that it would mean more to him than any desire to move on. But he had not found them, and, though Decresian had been delivered to its rightful king, he would continue his search for Archivist Tristan Ault and the census he hoped that he had guarded.

"Are you sure, Delphi?" said Oland.

"I am," said Delphi, for, after experiencing the wider world, she could not bear to be shut away again; and this time she knew it would be as close to a prison as her loving father could make it.

Oland and Delphi walked along the edge of the moat, holding his horse's reins. As the fireworks once again lit up the sky, Oland suddenly bent double, gripping his stomach.

"What is it?" said Delphi.

Oland fell to his knees. "I… I…"

"Oland, what is it?" said Delphi. "Are you ill?"

"I just…" said Oland. "I saw… I saw…"

He had seen the strangest image – it was the scryer running free. Oland staggered to his feet, wiping sweat from his brow. Then another image struck him. The Bastions standing on the barren ground of Gort, cursing him, roaring his name into the sky. Then another image. The doctor's office at King Seward's Hospital. The bed. Malcolm Evolent, terribly wounded. Benjamin Evolent with a knife to a weeping old man's throat, as he pushed, up and down, on Malcolm's chest. The old man at the desk, his head down. The open drawer. The name, screwed back on to the plaque: Dr Farnsley Evolent.

"Oland!" said Delphi. "Oland!"

The fireworks died, and the sky went black.

Oland raised his head. "I'm all right," he said. "I'm… just… "

"Exhausted, I would imagine," said Delphi.

But Oland was more than exhausted. He had been struck by a

rush of memories: when he was a child, Villius had spilled water on the hearth in the banqueting hall and the flames had reflected on the surface; when Wickham bent with his candlestick to pick up the goblet and the flame shone on the spilled wine; on the night of The Games, in the arena, as the blood pooled at his feet and the torchlight shone on it; in the cave when the light from the camberlilies shone on the water; when the lamplights lit up the marsh; when the flames of the Pyreboys' torches struck the water… all lights on liquid surfaces. Every time, Oland had been flooded with images. They were so fleeting, so strange, that he had never quite known what they were. He had never thought to harness them, he had just pushed them away. He realised now that they were images of the future.

Oland now had the answer as to why King Micah had chosen him to restore Decresian. Like Praevisia's mother, when King Micah had looked into Oland's newborn baby eyes that night in the stables, he saw deep crystal pools, and knew that this strange boy was a scryer, that he would have foresight. And, when he saw the vision of Oland's future at The Games as it flashed across his newborn eyes, he knew he would grow into a young man of great strength and bravery.

Oland realised that, when he visited the scryer, she had

screamed at him so that he would be saved. He remembered Blaise's story: "only the scryer herself will know the Rising Scryer". She was nearing the end of her life, and she didn't want a boy of his age to suffer her fate. The scryer knew that, along with the Thousandth Soul, the Rising Scryer was the most precious commodity in Envar.

Despite the terror of his realisation, Oland managed to mount his horse and pull Delphi up behind him.

Soon, the only sound he could hear was the sound of hooves on the Derrington cobbles, and Delphi's breath in his ear. The horse galloped on, his motion solid and graceful in the worsening rain.

A bolt of lightning flashed overhead, and the puddles around them erupted with light. Oland closed his eyes. For the first time, he tried to capture what he had just seen, to harness his gift. At first, it felt like he was watching the past, but he slowly realised that, although they had common parts, it was clearly the future that was unfolding.

And then Delphi… no… not Delphi… he didn't want to know Delphi's future. He wanted the vision to end. But he had no idea how to control it.

Oland's eyes shot open. He sucked in a huge breath of air. "Delphi!" he shouted. "Delphi!"

Frantically, he reached his arm back.

"I'm still here," said Delphi, as she felt his hand against her side. She pulled herself closer, pressing herself against his back. "I'm still here."

AFTERWORD

And so, the downfall of Villius Ren was not just at the hands of one champion, but at the hands of many. The restoration of Decresian had begun, and the kingdom would go on to prosper.

Jerome Rynish was not wrong when he spoke of the archivist's oath not to burden a story with his own entanglement. There was, indeed, another line to the oath:

I am sky on sky, water on water, fire on fire, earth on earth.

Invisibility was considered elemental to the tale. But on the night I chose to become an archivist, only because it was the wish of my dying father, I knew that part of the oath was being broken: I was passing on a letter from King Micah on which the future of

Decresian depended. So I vowed only to what I could.

It gave me the freedom to swathe my fire-scarred flesh in bandages not unlike those of Malcolm Evolent in order to rescue Oland Born. When I saw his achievements in the arena, I knew how much attention he would draw and, if I took the first step of removing him from the castle, he could be safely away to embark on his quest. Although I knew nothing of Gideon Ren, nothing of his home in the walled garden, I knew of the existence of the tunnel – as a boy, it was the only way I had to sneak away from my father to study combat. I hoped to take Oland Born through the tunnel and out of Castle Derrington, but, luckily, that was not to be.

And so the Thousandth Soul and the Rising Scryer travelled onwards, each hiding a secret from the other, neither yet knowing the depth of their strength and their weakness, nor what it would mean for their future.

There are stories to be found everywhere – in eyes and in hearts and in hiding. It is for each person to choose where to look, and what to believe. In the first of *The Trials of Oland Born*, we discovered myths that were proven to be real, and realities that were proven to be myth.

In the second of *The Trials of Oland Born,* we will uncover fresh deceits. Where was the census and what would it reveal? Would the distillations, extractions, essences and infisions ever be found? And what of Gideon Ren? Would he be drawn, forever, to feed on the dead? And whose wrath did Delphi incur as Stoker carried her away from the burning Curfew Peak?

Oland and Delphi had both known such suffering by their fifteenth year, and had begun to carry in their young hearts such heavy burdens.

Perhaps time or love, like cinderberry salve, could make the scars go away.

I am Archivist Tristan Ault.
I am sky on sky, water on water, fire on fire, earth on earth.
I vow to tell the untold tales, and my master is the truth.

Acknowledgments

To my agent, Darley Anderson, and to everyone at The Darley Anderson Literary, TV and Film Agency: thank you for embracing my new, magical, still-a-little-criminal world.

To my editor, Rachel Denwood, thank you for your incisive and inspiring editing. You made this a better book.

To Samantha Swinnerton, thank you for a dazzling final act performance.

To Moira Reilly, thank you for being an instant champion of Oland Born, encouraging him beyond the first three chapters and cheering him to the end.

To Tony Purdue, thank you for everything you do.

Thank you to everyone at HarperCollins Children's Books who worked on *Curse of Kings* and helped to bring it to life.

Thank you to early readers and marvellous note-givers, Lily Morgan and Vicki LeFeuvre.

Thank you to the always-generous Dr Martyn Linnie for his entomological genius.

To my wonderful parents, thank you for introducing me to books at an early age and for your constant love and support.

If there were gold medals for siblings, they would be awarded to: Ciaran, Ronan, Lanes and Damien. The same goes for sisters-in-law Melanie and Grainne.

To Sue Booth-Forbes, dear friend and freshly minted Irish citizen, thank you for the gifts you are kind enough to share every time.

To Mary Maddison, thank you for your faith and encouragement.

Thank you, thank you, thank you to Ger, Lanes, and Majella for all the above-and-beyond-the-call-of-duty bittts that no paragraph could contain.

Thank you to composer, David Geraghty, for your inspired pieces.

To Sue Swansborough, thank you for waves, smiles, cakes, and kindnesses.

Thank you to everyone who travelled with me on this epic journey; without you, I wouldn't have made it outside the castle walls.

Special thanks to Paul Kelly, slayer of beasts, navigator of dark caves.

Lastly, but not leastly, thank you to all the wonderful children in my life. You are incredible little people. You are the reward.